Renée Ashley

# Someplace Like This

THE PERMANENT PRESS
SAG HARBOR, NY 11963

**Library of Congress Cataloging-in-Publication Data**

Ashley, Renée
Someplace Like This
p. cm.
ISBN 1-57962-090-6
1. Married women—Fiction. 2. Female Friendship—Fiction.
I. Title.

PS 3551.s387 s6 2003
813'.54—dc21

2002038188
CIP



Printed in The United States of America

THE PERMANENT PRESS
4170 Noyac Road
Sag Harbor, NY 11963

***To Jack***
***and to***
***Laura Langlie***
***with gratitude and admiration***

This novel was supported by a Fellowship from The New Jersey State Council on the Arts.

Portions of the manuscript, in earlier forms, appear in:
*Widener Review*
*Touching Fire: An Anthology*
*American Writing: A Magazine*

My appreciation to Gretchen Flock of the Massachusetts Audubon Society for her kind assistance, and to the staff of the Ringwood Public Library for their unflagging patience.

# I

## TO THE ISLAND

It has been pointed out to me that I am undefined, that I don't know what I want, and that this is my whole problem. It is entirely probable. If I knew what I wanted, I'd just go get it. But as it is, I don't know, and so here I sit on this damp stoop, outside a house we no longer own, leaving, with a husband whom, it is quite probable, I do not love, to go live in a rather isolated area, which, some time ago, gave me a great deal of pleasure.

I am too old for this.

I have always believed that with a certain age came grace and contentment. I am neither graceful nor content. I am thirty-seven and twice married. I admit only to being suspended in some sort of emotional Jell-O, confused, stymied. My thoughts about what I have taken on here leap like fish or lie as still and as numb as logs. But Evan promises me that it is exactly what we need in order to reconstruct our life together. Those are his words.

Jesus. Reconstruct.

The air, again, is white with rain. It is a scrim above the roofs; it falls with a slap to the pavement. Minutes ago, when I tried the latch on the front door, the sky glowered brown and gray and the air seemed merely mist. I should not be surprised. It has been raining on and off for days. A cycle. Drizzle, deluge, and pause. I suppose it is really the cast of the air that startles me, the rapid changes, as if some colored filter were slipped between my eyes and the world and then pulled away time and time again. It catches me off guard.

Evan tells me I worry without cause. He says that I am merely excited about this new stage in our lives, that I misinterpret excitement as concern. He could be right. And June is a good month to start, as good as any, I suppose. Even the sun begins its move now, a move away from us, solstice, and it is all motion, all slow change.

I am waiting for Evan to check the closing up of the back of the house. The new owners will come tomorrow night. Evan and I are leaving for the island, and I am not sad at this leave-taking. That part is a godsend. The house was a ghost.

Last night, in the final sweep, I found things tucked in the dark corners of cabinets, things I had forgotten we owned. Some were wedding presents from what seems like eons ago—but it was not so long ago, not really—knickknacks and china pots packed away and never missed. And then all the plants. The plants will, without a doubt, die. I have no intention of caring for them on the island where the green landscape envelops the house, but Evan can't give them away. He has become a keeper of things. Yet it is the nature of things, visible and otherwise, that I question. I wanted to explain to him about the error of carrying the old, littered life into the new, but he was too busy, too busy packing, sweeping, closing up this portion of our lives.

From the stoop, I look out. Evan has loaded the boxes, taped and bulging, that the van left behind. More odds and ends are tucked into more tight corners. All this will ride to the island, six hours on the road. I look at that hunkering station wagon and I am ready to go back, but there is no going back. I have committed myself, no pun intended, to trying. Evan virtually bursts with trying. He is some new man, some other man, vaguely familiar, but a man I do not know. His metamorphosis is fascinating, if discomfiting.

Sometime while I was gone he changed, though I do not know that my absence precipitated it. The old Evan was comfortable, and, if I did not love him, or just did not understand his love, at least he was familiar. Sometimes I catch myself looking at him now and I doubt, I seriously doubt, that it is Evan at all. It is someone else, some young stranger, a tall blonde boy desperately squeezing himself into Evan's clothes. A decoy.

I, on the other hand, seem to be eternally recognizable. This life, that life, it makes no decipherable difference. No damn difference at all.

When Evan comes around from the back, I can see that he is weary. Despite his newfound youthfulness, he has deep circles beneath his eyes, and his blonde hair, lank from the dampness, falls across his face; he walks as though his feet hurt him. He is several years younger than I, but at this moment he looks old. He can't be looking forward to the drive to the island, either, and I am certain he will be bored and restless once we are there. He swears he will not.

Evan's hand is cool on the back of my neck. He lifts my hair to give me a squeeze before he walks me to the car; he smells of lime and dust. After he shuts the door behind me, and slips halfway into the driver's seat, he keeps one foot on the street outside, his door ajar just enough for his leg, and neither of us can take our eyes from the house.

*Evan, come here! My plants, my plants will look so lovely in this room. The light from these windows .... Evan, here, look, the ficus in that corner, there by the window.*

*And his sister, Hope, saying to Evan: It's much like our parents' house, isn't it? I mean, the nature of the rooms, do you see, Evan? The stance it takes on the street?*

*And saying to me, Is this what you want?*

*And my not really hearing it.*

There is no quarreling with the fact that it is a lovely old house. The stone façade is dark and weathered, uneven, moist, seeping today in places. I can see where the ivy has left its webby prints across the stones and the rain is teasing its paths. Nothing moves, not on the steps, not at the door—only the easy flutter of the light curtain at the top floor, as if something there is waving goodbye.

I know what is on Evan's mind.

He believes in what he is doing, believes he is making the right move. It was the same when I defected, so few years after we bought this house. When my mother died. When the torpor took me again, like a dense, disabling fog. Like memory. He does not understand. He is strong and he is generous, but too afraid to know. The house is beautiful, and I am sorry for what we are doing to each other, for what we have already done. He is leaving behind this solid façade, his home. I am leaving behind a ragged streak of disorderly life laid out for a hundred years behind me.

We had no history before this house.

Evan pulls his door shut.

It is uncomfortably humid still, more so after the rain. I watch to see if I can tell when it will begin again, but I have never been a good judge of the weather. I am fooled so easily.

On the road, a hundred shades of gray: clouds, sky, highway, factories, trucks. It is flat and homely, stark, naked, and angular.

I am restless. And sweating and dusty.

Enthusiasm springs from Evan's lips like water from a fountain. As he drives, he talks nonstop, so fast, so purposefully, that his words string together like beads; it is almost impossible to tell where one ends and the next begins. It is his anesthetic, this jabber, I think. He talks like a young lover rather than a desperate, weary husband. He talks about what we have before us. "Horizons," he says, gesturing widely, outwardly with his free hand—how lucky we are to begin again, how lucky when so many of our acquaintances' marriages, our generation's marriages, have failed so miserably, so publicly, and more and more. And then he tells me again how the island has changed. His voice, accompanied by the irregular hum of the highway noise, is confident, steady. He has, he maintains, taken care of it all. He has hired a caretaker, an old man from the other side of the island, a responsible old man who, for a price, has promised to do the work.

"It'll be perfect," Evan says.

He's been sending checks regularly to this old man, and the grasses will be kept down, the rampant brush held in tow. It will be manicured and tidy. The house livable—aired, swept, dusted—just enough attention, on the inside, to let us get by for now. Breathlessly, Evan goes on about the work we can do ourselves: porches to build, rooms, another floor maybe, a new kitchen. It is anticipation milked from him by research, by a thousand magazine articles. I can almost see the pages his thoughts are torn from. "It will be fun." He intends to do a great deal of the work himself, he says, and I break into laughter because I think it is a joke. But it is not, and he is crushed at my outburst—his hurt shows, gray, in his face, and I am terribly sorry I opened my mouth. But the fact remains that Evan is no handyman; he is city to the bone. Though, even I must admit, he could still surprise me. Today after his long and early hours of tedious last-minute packing, with this awful drive, he still has energy for all this enthusiasm. Maybe I do him an injustice. The man astonishes me.

It has been more than two years since I have been to the island.

It seems decades, light years. But we do not speak of the time I was away. "We won't talk about it," he said. "Not the past." It was his New Deal speech. "We'll move forward. Start again." And I have to commend him. It may be the right thing, not to talk about that other life, or the errors made in this one. Maybe Lindhurst put him up to it. Or, perhaps, from Evan's point of view there is simply nothing to say. He never knew those people, that life. His life was separate and far away. Our life was separate and far away. He said what mattered when he brought me home: "I want you with me. I want you."

I've brought magazines and I flip through a few pages, but too mindlessly, I guess, because Evan is talking again. He gradually revs back up to his earlier pace, and I have no idea what he's talking about. His voice is parallel with the noise from the highway; they form a sort of blurred duet, singing to themselves. They don't need me. I bury my face deep in the magazine.

By the time the hum of the road returns, I am numb with sitting. The bobbing of the car, as it passes over patches where, last winter, water seeped beneath the surface, froze, expanded, blew the road apart, makes me feel as though I'm riding in a covered wagon over rough terrain. The magazine I was pretending to read is lying at my feet on the floor. Its pages flutter in the air from the vent and it sounds like the rustle of birds.

Evan must have talked himself out. He drives now, silent, one arm akimbo out the window, the wind slapping his sleeve. I think the heat has finally gotten to him, too. Sweat runs behind his ears, down the side of his neck. His yellow-white hair is flat and dull, his eyes red from road dust.

We stop several times, for coffee and soda, once to check a tire, once for gas. The gas station has an ice machine, and, while Evan is in the men's room, I drop quarters in the slot for a bag of crushed ice. If nothing else, I can hold it on my lap and keep my knees and wrists cool. But the ice begins to melt not long after we get back on the road. The bag leaks. Thin streams of icy water make crooked tracks down my legs and drip down my sneakers. Form pools at my feet. I pass my wet hands over my neck, rub my arms on the bag, and watch the dirty water, warm now, course back down my skin and spot my shirt, the seat of the car. It feels good. Evan, however, though I reach over and try to cool his head with my wet fingers, is not amused. The water on the floor begins to spread in the direction of the gas pedal, the brake. His pique shows then. His voice is raised and he wants me to throw the bag out the window. I won't. It's a stupid argument. I'm too hot, too tired to cope, and I tell him he's no fun, he's a miserable goddamn pain in the ass. I'm angrier than the situation calls for. I hold on tight to the leaky bag, hold on stubbornly as though it is saving my life.

By the time Evan pulls to the side of the road, by the time I discard the bag and shake out the mats, make a stab at sopping up some of the dark stain on the seat, we are both sorry. Sorry and feeling silly. But nobody's laughing.

I think neither of us feel as though we will ever laugh again.

*I am a kid going to camp. God, it takes forever, though it might really only be a couple of hours. There are about forty of us in the bus, screaming, singing, tucked in corners with rolled-up sleeping bags, with ratty old brown grips our mothers dug out from attics, borrowed from old aunts. We have paper bags of sandwiches, fruit, and cookies for the ride, and, already, trails of sticky juice and empty waxed cartons of dilute orange drink litter the floor. The windows won't open; the smell of tuna fish and ripe bananas in that sweltering bus is strong. It mixes with the smell of forty kids' sweat. Across from me, a girl in new, white sharkskin shorts, a striped tee, her arms bare, hairless; some boy in pressed khaki bermudas and shiny boots. They each have two dollars tucked between their fingers, money for a snack, I guess — no paper bags of fruit, no cookies. They sit there, silent and clean, sister and brother, waiting for the bus to stop, which it never does, not for food, anyway. Compared to the rest of us, they look like they are from outer space. Or Madame Tussaud's. They stare out their shared window like sedated, caged things. There is no commerce with the other children. In the rack over their heads, new luggage and brand new sleeping bags, still with the shine on the fabric. They have obviously never been to camp before.*

*I am sitting there, in that bus, my white cotton panties that my mother has sewn my name in sticking to my butt, and I think: this is supposed to be fun, why isn't this fun? I bite into a bruised peach and think: I should give a bite to the kid in the white shorts. But I don't.*

I'm supposed to be happy. Isn't getting a fresh chance supposed to be fun?

Lindhurst, the stodgy asshole, would tell me in that stunted medicinal voice of his: "Dore, you don't know what you want, you don't know who you are. You will not know until you take the time to think about it. Don't you think, maybe, it's time to think about what you want?"

God, Lindhurst! I've thought about it. I've thought and thought and thought about it. I've thought about it until I can't think about it any more. And I don't know. I just don't know.

At last we cross the bridge. The drive down the island to the tip is an hour and a half at most; our house is that far from the mainland.

The highway runs right down the center of this thin strip of land. The scrubby trees block out the view of anything that might be interesting; they also block the wind. I had forgotten. It's like driving down the neck of a bottle.

Evan drives right past the turnoff for the house.

He is going to town to pick up groceries. He looks as though he's been beaten; it must be that we're almost there. He has let down. But his will is not broken. He has regained his composure since the ice debacle, and he is more than civil, more than accommodating, he's gracious. The only certain betrayal of his weariness is in his face: I have never seen the lines at the corners of his eyes so deep, so plentiful.

I would never have recognized the town.

The main street extends much further towards the outskirts, out towards the east. That whole section is new, though the buildings have been built to blend with the older part of town.

The old feed store where we used to buy corn for the ducks has been turned into a record shop. A groan of music from inside rolls out onto the street like a tremor. The loft above, where the bales were stored, is now some sort of store as well. There's a balcony, accessible from the street by a long spiral, wooden stairway. A twisted, lacquered chair squats like a toad at the edge of the landing. A painted sign says DRIFTWOOD ROCKER, and states a price, clearly visible from where I sit. It is an odd chair, ugly, distorted, like an open mouth. And it is absurdly expensive.

Happlett's hasn't changed. I give the old general store a silent ovation. Stasis is sometimes preferable, certainly more comfortable. Evan has parked on the street, directly across from the store and in front of a restaurant. This was not here before either, though I can't remember what was. The restaurant is open to the street except for a short wood wall, maybe knee-level to the sidewalk.

Evan is smiling. We have come this far, he seems to be saying, and he bows from the waist, gesturing grandly for me to step out of the car and accompany him. He is being silly; glad to finally be here, he is giddy. His shirt rides high, stuck to his sweat. The hair on his stomach is like coiled, gold wire.

I stay put and tell him, "Be quick."

The sun beats through the car windows; it eats at my knees. It is hot here too, but at least the threat of rain is absent. It is late afternoon, and with the setting sun will come the breeze. Now that we're not moving, there is not even the warm wind to give me the illusion of coolness.

I should be able to smell the water now.

I stick my head out the window, but the rampant music from across the street is too much for me. I pull it back in. The music follows me into the car, but it's too hot to roll up the window. When we get home, already I say "home," I will walk to the beach.

A tight-lipped and heavy couple crosses the street, cuts in front of the car. Tourists. The man, as he passes by my open window, peers in, only momentarily, as someone might at a dog or a child left behind in the heat. I look back, my arm kinked out the window, my fingers draped over the rubber stripping at the edge. The woman's straw bag scrapes my elbow as she passes; she does not turn, though I know she knows I'm there, that she has touched me. I am invisible. Or she wishes I were invisible. Maybe that man, her tourist husband, has been looking at women since their vacation began. And I wonder if she really cares or whether, over the years, it has just become habit to get mad.

They enter the restaurant and settle at one of the tables just a short way back from the sidewalk. She shoves her pocketbook beneath her chair and I can see her wrap her feet around it. She is taking no chances. He reaches across the table, and I think he is going to take her hand, but, instead, he grabs the ashtray and then pulls a pack of cigarettes from his shirt pocket. He blows the smoke in her direction, then he looks my way.

I turn my head quickly, pull a magazine into my lap. I snatch my arm back in, protectively, defensively, then lift the magazine so that if he is still watching, he will see that I am not looking at them.

When I peek back in their direction, the back of a young waiter blocks my view. He is blonde and young, blonder and younger, even, than Evan, I think. His shirt, sleeves rolled up, is fitted, his body tapered; his jeans, faded, are worn, tight. His butt is high and rounded and the white strings of his apron are draped across it like thin, celebratory garlands. I am suddenly aware, very aware, of a warmth in my lap, a flush in my cheeks.

Perhaps there is some life to me yet.

The boy turns briefly and glances towards the street. I get a quick glimpse of his face, scrubbed clean, and I wonder if he is gay. So many are. Then, he is gone.

The tourists have spoken their needs to that third party and now, it seems, they will gaze out to the street until their food arrives. They do not look in my direction.

Across the street, the white half-door opens and Evan steps out, a bag in each arm and, before I know it, he is at the car door.

The smaller bag will fit in a hole behind the seat, and he sets it there with a grunt; then he moves up front. He reaches into the second bag, pulls something out, and then hands the bag to me from across the driver's seat.

"No room back there," he says.

While I settle the bag down on my lap, he hands me a can of cold soda and smiles. I take it from him and it feels good in my palm.

"Thanks."

"Welcome." The exchange is familiar and easy. And he is seated again.

I set the soda on the dash and shift the bag downwards on my legs. My eyes land inside the restaurant a last time. There is nothing of interest going on there, and Evan pulls from the curb.

There have been even more changes on the highway itself. More buildings than before, more businesses. Touristy hype spots. A huge, maybe papier mâché, animal, a giant mouse, perhaps, something grey; a thin wicker form dressed only in a tee-shirt, something emblazoned on its chest.

But the turnoff is recognizable. Along the road here, few of the homes have been altered. A fence here, a new wood or shingled house there, small changes, not many. But we have to go further back towards the shore to get to our house, which is hidden and drenched in trees and shade which lead out to the water. Suddenly I am hungry for it, for the peace that I can recall of it, and Evan is not driving nearly fast enough.

We hit the shore road and turn up, double back towards the tip again, and the old man's shack comes into view among the trees. I had forgotten about the ramshackle house and the old man who is supposed to live there, out from the sand, out in the shallow, passive waves. The shack is on a tiny island of its own, peculiar, far enough to have to row if the tide is in, but visible, clearly visible, looking as though it were easily within reach. I wonder if the old man still lives there. In all the years, I have never seen him. The story is that local boys bring him magazines, newspapers, matches, bottles of red wine that they either steal or buy with their allowance and some smooth talk from the old couple at the tiny market down off the primary road here. They bring him those things, gifts, offerings, his being a strange god, living alone there, so foreign, so different from anything they have absorbed from their parents, a novelty, a risk. I wonder how old the man is, how that shack stays upright. It's a mystery, the old man's life, and his strange house is a forever place, a myth. I will bring him cigarettes, I tell myself, and these magazines. I will buy him wine, make friends.

All myths are built on something.

## II

## THE HOUSE

The widow has been cashing the checks.

"Figured it was owed," she said, friendly, open, standing up and wiping her muddy hands on her apron, then offering something leafy, gray-green, and tough-looking to Evan with fingers still gloved in shiny black dirt. The garden had been worked. The local soil is not rich; it is sandy, dull. I watched her fingers; she wore no ring, felt at ease with the ground. "Since he's passed," she went on, "I've got to do it all myself." She looked directly at Evan when she spoke, her back, her eyes, strong, as though she could stand it, too, if Evan were suddenly to disappear.

Evan wanted to rant. He wanted to accuse the old woman, but I could see that, actually, he was afraid of her.

"I did you fine, anyway," she said loudly after us, still mopping at her hands with the lap of her apron.

Evan said slowly, "Son-of-a-bitch." She wasn't supposed to hear it.

"She signed his name," he says later, adamantly. He is incensed. I nod and say nothing. I cannot decide whose side I am on; after all, the woman is by herself. The old man died shortly after he'd made the arrangement with Evan. He'd spent only a day or so, three at the most, working on our lot—not much time to make a mark after two years' rampant growth. His wife said she'd found him in their kitchen, milk spilled near his outstretched hand, the carton empty on its side, the stove burner on low. "Couldn't sleep," she said. She did what she thought best, said she'd earned the money from those checks. Yes, she told Evan, she'd known about the instructions, but she'd worked in the house, not in the yard, since "it was people coming to live, not live-stock." She was right, of course. There was no way to tell her that we hadn't been inside the house, that at the first glimpse of the unkempt grounds Evan had flown apart, had come to her war-ready and hot.

Evan is behind the car striking out at clods of dirt, at weeds. I can see him in the rearview mirror. He runs his fingers through his sweaty hair. His shirt is spotted, clinging like plastic wrap to his chest, his back. He doesn't know where to put his frustration. He is furious, devastated, humiliated. Mostly humiliated. The ride back to the house was dead silent. Evan's hands were tight on the wheel.

I could tell him that it doesn't matter, that the yard is fine the way it is, and that we haven't even looked inside yet. I could tell him that we'll have the satisfaction, now, of feeling the changes in the palms of our own hands, cutting it down, building it up again ourselves—what he planned to do to the house, he could do to the yard. Make it all ours, like a cat pissing, marking out its territory.

When it seems that the bulk of his disappointment is spent, I get out of the car. He won't look at me; he is a child, embarrassed, tall and pink and soft. I take his hand and pull him away from the sight of the yard, down the overgrown path, towards the beach. He follows behind; he is limp. I am aching for the breeze beyond the trees. Evan is speechless, tired. We are a pair.

It is a short walk, but difficult. No one has walked this way in ages; it used to be clear. We must bend and dodge to keep from being stabbed by the thin, whippish branches, the thorny tangles; to keep our feet from getting snagged, we must step high. When we reach the sand we walk straight towards the water.

The beach is taupe-colored and firm. The salt sparkles in the late afternoon sun and our footprints, just audibly, snap into the crisp, thin surface, and then lie silent. There is no debris on the beach, no garbage. It is beautiful, orderly. A feather. A piece of shell. A small black stone.

I lead Evan right up to the water's edge where a thin skirt of froth slides forward towards our shoes. Letting go of him, I step back a few feet, squat, and fall backwards, awkwardly, onto the sand. I turn my face upwards into the cool of the salt breeze and then untie my shoes, motion to him to come along, to do the same, and, reluctantly and still without a word, he does. His feet, like white wax, look ill at ease in the sand. We take the time to roll up our jeans, leisurely, and I take his hand again and we walk the short way into the water which is shallow and turns cloudy at our steps. The sting of the hot sand, of the long day, is replaced by the cold chafe of water and sand together. It is pleasant, painful.

I am tempted to kick up some water, a bit of foam, onto Evan's pants, onto his bare arms, to draw him out of himself, to get him to laugh, but I know better. First he must work out his disappointment, then he will shore himself up. In the meantime he stands tall, still, and looks out over the surface, towards what I can't guess, while the small waves roll at his ankles.

I poke at the water with my foot, picking up small scoops of sand on my toes. I imagine that I am key to a viable cycle, throwing that sand back, knowing shades of it will wash up over and over again no matter how insistently I toss it back. It is comforting and I could go on doing it forever, enjoying the rhythm, earthy, fluid, but I can see that Evan has become restless and wants to go back to the house. He is back to business already. I should be pleased, really, that I got him to come this far. We drag our feet through the sand, bury them to dry, then brush them off again, and slip them back into our shoes.

The walk back is not much less difficult. The good breeze is blocked again as soon as we enter the grove and head back towards the house.

If I did not know the movers were coming tomorrow, I would say that we were here as we used to be, for a week, for two; these boxes and bags we have piled on the porch look impermanent at best.

Evan, I think, cannot bring himself to go into the house. After taking the second of the two grocery bags out of the car, he sets it on the steps and shakes his head. He's forgotten something in town. Gin. He sounds relieved when he tells me, as though he's found a solution to something, some problem that had been bothering him. He says he'll "run back in." He needs some time, I guess, time to gather himself back, to redouble his effort. And we both could use a drink. It is understood that he will go alone. I will take in the bags, a few of the smaller boxes we have unloaded. I, too, don't mind a little time to myself right now.

It's hard to tell, really, what bothers him most—the state of the grounds, the old woman's cashing the checks, or the sheer audacity of the old caretaker, the grim insolence of his death when he'd taken on, promised to do, the work here for us. Evan is furious with fate.

It has tricked him again; it has not delivered despite his well laid plans. He will take it out on the road for a while; then we'll sit together and have our drink. But he will never forgive the old man. He would never say that, but I know it is true.

Poor Evan, he is at such odds. I can only watch him, though; I cannot help him. I can barely help myself. All he said is true. The yard is wild, deserted-looking. But I cannot say that I am unhappy about the way it looks. It is weeds, branches, wildflowers, a crazy quilt of texture and color. Of all things, this can be dealt with, the growth. It is no major obstacle. It is raw here now. We will cultivate it, I am certain.

With Evan gone, there is time to look around. This is what I needed, time to enter slowly, to get used to it, like easing into a mountain swimming hole or the ocean in December.

The house is a salve, a balm, and its quiet fills me. I absorb it, take it in through my eyes, through my skin. The old woman has promised: the inside will be clean and ready. From the outside the house is gray and weathered, the way I remember it. It is a pleasure, the familiarity.

My God, how quiet it is here.

I don't remember this stillness. Where is the chatter? Can noise left alone too long die off? Does it burn out like a light bulb? Or is this simply a silent time of day? I cannot for the life of me remember.

But from the porch I can see the sun lowering itself, feel the air cooling. In the yard stretched out in front of me, the grass grows in comforting profusion; it grows where it did not, where it would not have dared if someone had been here to tend the grounds. It gives me a good feeling.

*Honeymoon, dusk. Cream blues, honeyed pinks, a tablet of color, dissolving, steaming above. Rustic, melancholy. Like new love.*

*"Listen," Evan whispers, then cocks his head, that head I crave, need, that face that I would like to eat, swallow whole. "The water's waiting." He grabs my hand and we run, run as fast as we can manage together, through the clean clipped flood of grass that hushes our steps, past the trees, down to the water's edge. "Listen," he says, and I listen very hard.*

Just after we were married, Evan's mother died. Much later I figured out that Evan's father had bullied, pushed, and molded her to such an extent that she had no shape left, no recognizable thing that was her own. She just turned in on herself, collapsed.

*It is our first meeting. Evan's father introduces me. "Dore," he says soberly—this is an audience—"this is my wife, Mrs. Dover, Mrs. Matthew Dover, Evan's mother." I am Dore, still. She is Mrs. Matthew. She looks like a root, borne above ground, twisted, seeking water. She is thin, wizened, old-looking for what must be her age, as though the life has been sucked out of her. I don't learn her first name, never think about it until the Will is read. Alia Dover has left the summer house to me and to Evan. It shocks Evan's father, my name in that Will. And I decide that Alia Dover has finally taken a stand. It was hers to give. She gave.*

Slivers rise up, thorns, from the wooden boards as I climb the porch stairs, finger the old handrail that leans beneath the weight of my hand. But the front door, the old wood door with the small, high window of bevelled glass, is strong, straight, the glass clean. As I enter, there is no echo despite the emptiness downstairs. I am purposefully quiet.

And I am curious.

The wallpaper has faded, but the windows are bright and gleaming; they let the sun stream in, full, intense. The musty, pungent odor of washed wood, disinfectant, rises as powerfully as would the less biting scent of cut grass. The room in its bareness is immaculate, rich with the homey smell of hard work. I can feel the weight of it in my nostrils. She has worked in here, the old widow, worked long. She was right: she did us fine.

I am drawn in. The entry is wide; the stairway is sturdy.

Upstairs, too, the floors are bare. The carpets must have mildewed, rotted, been thrown out. The wood is soft; the old woman has scrubbed up here, too, and the smell is bracing. I turn through an open doorway. Colors, the wood of the walls, have blended, become a little softer, more muted, now more the texture of barnwood, comforting, cool.

We will have this large room again, Evan and I, this one with the hearth and bay that faces the water. We will sleep here tonight; sleep well, I hope. The smaller rooms shall be made up for company, fresh and simple for friends who come to visit—a day, a week, more, to shake the city soot from their bones. That is, if Evan doesn't fell the rooms like trees, if he doesn't take them away, change things completely.

It's a foolish thought, unsettling.

Evan and I will be at home here. Again.

From this window, the water does not look as I remember. It looks deeper, wetter. Our old trail is indistinguishable from the rest of the meadow now. The edging of poppies that, all those summers, we worked so hard to keep in line has dispersed, and, widespread now, as if we were never here, orange dots the broad expanse of green.

*It's early morning; he has on that hat, that silly hat he wears only here. Stooping patiently, back bent, as though I am a child, he lets me fix a flower there, among the fishing flies, the silly flashy silver lures, none of which he knows how to use. Chapeau d'ambience, he calls it. Chapeau d'ambience. When we get to the water, the bloom is still there, stem tucked tightly beneath the hat's narrow band.*

I lean on the mantel and feel it give way—not fall, but give, tilt, as though it considered giving way and then did not. I straighten quickly, then make my way back down the stairway. This bannister, too, will have to be made steady, though today its polish alone makes it seem strong.

*Evan stands below at the dark and varnished entry. "We'll be back before dusk," he says, grabbing, with one hand, the basket of lunch things, and pushing me lightly towards the front door with the other. "We'll be starved, I promise you."*

*We are always starved.*

*Late, we come home caked with dried sand and mud, tired, pleased to be back. I crawl up the stairs and fall on to the stark white sheets of our bed while Evan showers. I am fast asleep before supper.*

The light in the kitchen is strong; the floor is uneven, still damp. It is a large room and airy; the brightness will do well in here. It's lovely. I will be happy in this kitchen. I will brew rich, black coffee, I'll have Evan buy the beans in the city; their aroma will fill the air and make this seem like home again.

I check the fixtures at the sink. Water; no rust, no surprise. The old sink has been bleached to a mottled sheen, like shell. In Evan's restoration it will be made new, chromed and sparkling, even though it is fine now, clean and workable; the floors of this room will be plastic, patterned and shiny, instead of this rough planked wood. It will be open, crisp, antiseptic. I turn from the window.

The kitchen door is latched. I flip the metal clip and cross the back porch, sidestep the short stairway and jump. I can feel the soft ground swell up around the soles of my shoes so that, for a moment, I am stuck. When I lift my foot, my shoe makes a popping noise. I walk to the wall and turn on the outside tap. This, too, is working. It is gloriously wild back here as well. There is no garden, no manicured bed of bright flowers. I am freer here than I have been anywhere in a long, long while. I rustle through the grasses, enjoying the whisper, an animal, grazing. I shift my weight and, again, feel the earth come up to meet my shoes. I enjoy the sucky noise as I pull them out, flatfooted to heighten the effect.

*The mud slithers up between my toes, a dark silk slime that makes me laugh. Sometimes I fall; sometimes Evan catches me, teases me, holds tightly beneath my arms, rings my chest, and dip and up and dip, threatening to let me drop. Smiling, he saves me, most of the time, but when he does let me slip, he is gentle, playful, and my fanny plops loudly into the shallow water.*

*"Shhhhh," he says, "don't scare the ducks." He laughs softly and pulls me out, silently, slowly. And I am very still and very quiet while I stand and let the water lap my feet.*

I am spent and I am dirty.

The ride was lengthy and tiring. I picture tonight's sleep on the bare floor. I will find a brass bed, I tell myself. And I will search out some of those old etched mirrors. They will suit this house. It will all be fine, it will work out, but now, like Evan, I am down to business. The boxes must be brought in, the groceries put away. Evan will be back soon, and I have done nothing, nothing at all that he will see.

We heap blankets on the floor, flatten them, smooth them to make a cushion, a pseudo-mattress for tonight. It is warm, comfortable. But despite the coziness and my fatigue I cannot fall asleep. Moonlight is keeping the room from darkness. All that light may be the reason I'm still awake, but I doubt it. The shadows of the trees play unevenly with that strange light, making patterns on the ceiling. It's fascinating. Mesmerizing. Kaleidoscopic.

I consider getting up, getting something to eat, to drink, and then I remember the old caretaker, the milk at his fingertips, the burner on low, and I decide quickly that I'll stay put. But I am restless.

Evan is sleeping soundly. It's all I can do to keep from surreptitiously giving him a kick, waking him up to keep me company, but there is a sturdiness in his sleep, a hum to it. It is not a snore. It is more like a purring: smooth, solid. It is the sound that tells me all is well with him.

And I am too aware of my own body. I am antsy. I can feel the flesh surround my bones. I am getting flabby, my ass, my thighs. I know it. I'm getting soft, getting old. I am going to have to do something about it soon or it'll get away from me.

I move away from Evan and throw the blankets off. Naked and on my back, with effort, I lift and spread my legs, an enormous V, reaching, up, up, stretch, God almighty, up and out; I press my legs wide, far apart, until I can feel the strain in my crotch, deep in my inner thigh, until I can feel it pull all the way back down to behind my knee, then I slowly bring them back together. Tighten my behind, let go. It's all I can do to keep from laughing out loud. The picture I make must be a scream, but the tension, the pulling, feels good. It's better than lying still, and I focus on the exercise, learned somewhere, Jesus, who knows where. If I do this much more, walking will be tough tomorrow. I should do it every night, but of course I won't. But right now, stark naked and exposing it all, hollow and opening up to the ceiling, to the moonlight, all of it, open like a well, I stretch, pull till the skin between my legs burns with it, then release. Tighten, Christ it hurts, feels good. I do it until I can think of nothing else, nothing but the physical sensation, the tension, the relaxation. Beside me, Evan sleeps like a child. He sounds like a puppy sleeping, dreaming. My bouncing around beside him doesn't seem to disturb him at all. What a day he has had.

I do it until I cannot do it anymore, till the knots at my hip joints tighten and twist, a dutch rub deep inside my buttocks, killing. The pain gives me a sense of pleasure, affirmation. I am alive, I feel. Kindled with that knowledge, I turn to Evan.

Thinking to wake him gently, excited by the physical tension in my own hot crotch, I reach for him. He murmurs and turns towards me, but he does not waken. I touch the hair on his head, fine, clean now, his face. He is warm, pleasantly soft; the skin of his cheek is wrinkled, an echo of the crumpled pillowslip beneath his head. I press myself against him, feel the pressure of his cock against me, feel him stiffen, grow, even in his sleep. I back off, reach for him with my hand and with this he wakens and draws me towards him hard and I think I will smother against him, wrapped, lost, and he whispers his love and his eagerness and he is a boy, a child, and he is kind and strong, and when he enters me the two of us are happy, happy and hungry for what will come next.

## III

## PLANS

Morning is like New Year's.

Bright sunlight is rimmed in resolutions. Evan is a pal; very early he is out. He has dressed in his shabbiest clothes, and, with a kiss and the proverbial promise, he has left the house to me and gone out to conquer the grounds.

He has rummaged through the shed. Clippers, trowels, aerator, a spade, scattered across the porch, on the stairs. The lawnmower stands upright at the foot of the path like a general. It is all I can do to keep from poking my head out the door to tell him that the ground is too wet, too soft, to go to battle so early today. But the spade lies on the grass, already a dead soldier.

Evan is the driving force behind the winning of this particular war. Though he says it is his sense of aesthetics that forces him to crusade against the rampant green, to trim it back, to cut it down, I know better. He, quite literally, wants to get a grip on this place, to demonstrate, for himself, that the matter is in hand. I can see it on him; he wears his need like a medal. He wants to run the dirt through his hands, he wants to finger the roots of the weeds he pulls, to experience their tenacity first-hand, and to fight back; he wants to see the shiny black bugs scurry back down beneath the soil. He is intuitive sometimes, Evan is. Like a woman, but not articulate. This is a front on which he is certain to win.

He is up to his elbows in soil, grass clippings, limbs and leaves, the bodies of the dead. But I think I have found the slip-up in what I see: though he is certainly doing battle, he is awkwardly split. There is no doubt he wants to dominate the wildness that has chagrinned him, no doubt about that at all. But what Evan wants this morning is not war, but concord. He wants to have already won. He wants some sign that all is right in this world, or, if it is not, that gravity will pull it all quickly into place. What he really wants is to be the old woman, the caretaker's widow. He wants to know he is right; he wants to be so sure of it that it is no longer an issue. He's hoping this land will tell him so. That much is clear.

The warm house to myself, I hunker in. I take a lesson from Evan. If I'm going to do this thing, I'm going to do it right. I rub my eyes in an effort to banish the urge to return to the furry nest of blankets. I shower and dress, old clothes, clean and fresh. I am a TV commercial's dream of homeyness: dungarees that make my stomach look flat, my hips wide and fecund, Evan's old shirt, tails knotted at my waist, sleeves rolled up perfectly to the elbow, tennies with a hole in the toe. I tie my hair back with a bandanna and stare at my reflection in the window. The waist, the nip of flesh that peeks between shirt and waistband, is a bit thick, and the thighs look bloated, but other than that I am perfect. Perfect.

I settle in on the floor, coffee in hand, legs spread like a child and flat in front of me so that the stretchings of last night stretch again and the muscles there give just the faintest of complaints. I slap the pad of paper onto the floor between my legs, lean forward with the pen in my hand. It's down to business.

I begin making lists. I love lists. I get a real lift from legitimately scratching something off a list. It's part of my Lindhurst legacy, too, maybe. He taught me that if something can be seen it can be dealt with, at least put into perspective. I'll grant him that usually it's true. It's the invisible, the unnameable stuff that gets you.

This is my favorite stage, this planning stage. I get charged up. The first thing on the list is to attack those thighs. There's just a light whispering, a nagging little ache, a nudge like a conscience, though God knows it's not as bad as it might have been. But I am alert now to the danger that lurks in the upper regions of my legs. The list:

I. Trim thighs

It's a good start. It's not like I can just take a knife and carve off the excess, though it would certainly be easier. I'll have to work on it. How to get at the thighs:

A. diet

I'll give up solid food. I am feeling thin just thinking about it. I have seen it on TV, read about it in magazines. Models do it all the time. I can do it. Today the movers will arrive and with them will come the blender. Hallelujah. My salvation. I'll also have to shop, stock up. Now I will need another list, a grocery list. I set the first list, the "DO" list aside, and off comes another sheet. Zip.

The Happlett's list:

1. protein powder
2. yogurt
3. orange juice
4. fruit

I've got it all figured out: throw it in the blender with some ice. Turn the bugger on. Start with strawberries, next day switch to banana, etc. Next, drop in a peach. Ice. Variety is the key. If you don't get bored, you can supposedly go on forever. I figure two meals a day. These thick-trunked thighs should look like mere seedlings in no time. I'll take vitamins. I should take vitamins. What the hell.

OK, so, maybe just one liquid meal instead of two. Surge forward in moderation. I am better at lists than at diets.

I consciously refrain from putting "exercise" on the "DO" list. I have been through this before. I will not exercise regularly; there's no point in torturing myself. I am honest. I am building something here on the island. Character. Insight. Besides, exercise will come more naturally here: walking, working in the yard, swimming. It cannot be like the Lindhurst time, not so sedentary, not so ponderous, so still. Besides, when the TV is connected, I will do thigh exercises while I watch old *Quincys*. This is the country, the island, and I am not so old. These things are all on my side.

OK, so the thighs are taken care of.

I'm thinking about the evenings.

I'm going to need to take the stress off this newness, off the regimen. Evan will be gone before too many more weeks, five days at a time. A little something before the fire in the evenings, I think. A reward. A toddy, so to speak. Another piece of paper. A list for the liquor store:

1. Amaretto
2. Bailey's
3. Cinzano

Straight to the thighs without a doubt, but I'll walk it off—I'll walk to the liquor store, work off the booze. After all, I'm going to need something. I'm going to need my strength.

For the new me.

I am going to hover about this house like a bee over clover, like

Betty Crocker over her test kitchen. I will be the archetypal homemaker. I will try, anyway. Switch pages, here we go. Back to the "DO" list:

II. Learn To Make Jam

Rapture. The kind with the little berry seeds left in, thick and sticky, patined with the gloss of sugar, gooey, the kind whose seeds stick, stubbornly like little nettles, in between your teeth. I can feel the diet resolve fading already, receding like ebb. The feeling of jam takes precedence: I puff up with pleasure. This is the clincher, I think, the epitome of the new me. Evan will beam. He will be certain I am well and happy. Adjusted. I will change the name on the mailbox to Smucker or Welch: I can see it all now. There should be enough berries out there, in our yard alone, to jam the world. It would be a sin to waste them, a crime against nature. Of course, I've never made jam before, but God knows I'm going to have the time to experiment now, and it'll make the house smell good. It should anyway. I've always been a sucker for houses with something on the stove.

I have this old memory of being in some aunt's house. I'm not even certain she was an aunt and if she was I haven't the foggiest notion of whose side of the family she belonged to or where she lived. I don't even know how old I was. In the memory, though, like in some dreams, she is known; it is just in the remembering that she is not in the least familiar. But I was a small kid and she was making something, quince jam or apple jelly, rhubarb something maybe. It was sticky and tarty. It boiled like lava, blopping, thick and noisy. I remember being tempted to dip my finger in the pot because of the glistening sugars. I wanted to wear it like a jewel. And I remember the steam in the kitchen and my hair drooping in limp sweaty strands across my forehead. And I remember that the tang seemed to absorb the air, make it soft and palpable, like the musky scent of sex does when it takes over, and that the hot clip in my nostrils was something with a hell of a bite to it. I remember the sensations as clearly as if I were there now. I remember wanting to stay in that kitchen, perched on the edge of the rickety wooden kitchen chair, elbows heavily parallel on the thick pockmarked wooden table, chin lumped in my hands. I remember the woman, round and dark-haired, aproned and curt, looking like a cutout from a farmwife's magazine. I remember her telling me matter-of-factly, "You don't smell it when you've been breathing it for hours on end. You don't smell anything good at all." I remember her saying she was sick to death of it after a morning's work and that she had to go on anyway and that it was hard work, certainly not child's play. She said that, too. I wish I could remember who she was. I do remember, though, clicking my child's tongue silently, head down, and, even then, thinking that she wasn't much of a romantic. But the smell was narcotic, a fantastic ether. And I wanted to help, I remember this clearly too, but she told me I'd get burned. "You'll get yourself burned," she kept repeating, wiping her sweating hands across her forehead and onto her apron. "Burned." As though "burned" were synonymous with "damned." And she'd turn her back on me and fuss with her pots, her jars, and all I'd see would be her rotund, solid-as-a-brick posterior lolling from side to side and the steam rising up around her as she worked.

But I'll have to hang curtains in the kitchen first. Ambience. So:

III. Hang Kitchen Curtains

(*buy* kitchen curtains)

If I'm going for homey, I want the picture complete. The picture is not complete without curtains. No one makes jam in a curtainless kitchen. Go all the way. I will also learn to make bread.

IV. Make Bread

I have a food processor that came with dough hooks. They're still in their little plastic pouches, pristine, virgin. I've never even read the instructions. I will wear an apron and wipe my hands on it. I'll tie my hair back in a bun.

I will organize my leisure time to avoid sloth. I'll have to keep busy once Evan begins commuting. Nearly whole weeks to myself. This was the plan, the deal. After our initial weeks here, Evan is to flow back into the stream of the real world. He will stay in the city. The apartment is there for him to use. His father left it to him, a pied à terre, male legacy. Perfectly Matthew Dover, really. Stocks and shares to the daughter. The apartment to the son. It had been Matthew's home base after Alia died, his secret before she did, I think. A legacy of space and secrets. Evan will phone me every night. He will come here, home, for the weekends. Evan has decided that this will give me the time I need, the time I should have to recover whatever portions of myself I've lost. Or misplaced. Time to regenerate. Rekindle. Or Evan's word: reconstruct. Good Lord.

When he first called, when they called him, and he tried to gather me back home, I said over and over, adamantly, that too many pieces were missing. "Missing," I kept repeating. At the time I knew what I meant. I have no doubts that Evan coupled with the grand poobah Lindhurst to lay this plan out for me, this time to consider, to think it all over. No doubt he decided that I must be trusted by myself. That I must trust myself. This is their leverage over me. No matter. I know I'm not crazy. Not really crazy. Not crazy crazy. I know I am confused, riddled with something I can't name. I will stay busy. I will broaden myself, as they say. I will become more interesting, more interested. I will develop a curiosity about my surroundings, take the pressure off, the focus off, myself. I will:

V. Read Books
VI. Read An Occasional Newspaper
VII. Take Walks
VIII. Get To Know The Island

Under "Get To Know The Island" I have the book Evan bought me. It's around somewhere; perhaps in the boxes the movers have. No. No, it's not. I saw Evan fiddling with it last night; it must have been in the car. He had it in the living room, looking something up, I think, as a prelude to this morning's outdoor delirium. I will locate it soon enough. Evan must see that I am trying. I will read books in the evenings and on the weekends I will share what I have learned with Evan. But I must plan now for my time alone. Structure. Articulation. It is always the key.

The bird book is where I thought it was, open on the window seat. The cover has been torn, a large white bird's head separated from its body. I flip through, the book on one knee, the pad on the other. Now I am a juggler.

I will investigate (I am adamant; I write in black ink):

A. The Book
1. seaweed
2. eelgrass
3. marshgrass
4. scallop shells
5. horseshoe crabs
6. sea turtles
7. seals
8. cormorants
9. juncos

Not a bad start. I replace "9. juncos," a sad sounding sort of name, with "9. grackles." Spunky, the word "grackles." Juncos, according to the caption, will not show up until October. Grackles in August. I should be ready for grackles by August. I have the rest of June and all of July to bone up. This could get to be fun. There's a list of birds here as long as my arm, and color illustrations. Maybe I'll turn into a real bird person and Evan and I will spend our vacations in exotic places with binoculars strung around our necks like primitives' amulets, looking for the rare avi-something-or-other, or the almost-never-seen thingy bird. Maybe we'll learn to communicate in bird talk, maybe we'll dispense with English altogether and grow feathers, oily and slick, to help us shed what comes at us from the outside. I have heard of people getting really caught up in birds. It could happen. Mostly retired couples with knobby knees poking out from beneath their bermuda shorts, I think, and odd-looking single men in safari hats and khaki. That's OK. I'm retired in a way. What the hell:

B. Buy Field Glasses

All the way. I'm going all the way:

C. Buy Bermuda Shorts

Evan will like this. Conspicuous consumption with direction, involvement. No anomie, me. If I tell him I'm going to get the glasses he will make a detailed survey. He will look them up in *Consumer's Reports* and weigh the pros and cons of each make, of every model, of weight and magnification. He will shop around in the city, this price here, a better one there. He does not do this because he is poor. Evan is not poor. He does it because it is the thing to do. It feels good. He would never feel right about his purchase if he had not made it by the rules.

I will buy the glasses without telling Evan first. I'll call it a surprise.

So now I am moving. Before we slept last night, Evan crooned to me, "Dore, you'll get in the swing. You'll love it. You'll see . . . ." His voice was like white noise, but he spoke earnestly.

OK, I'm in the swing.

Just after noon, when Evan strides through the door from his yard patrol, I stuff my lists between the pages of the torn-asunder-bird-head book and slam it shut.

That part's done with. I have made my plans.

When I meet Evan at the entryway with a kiss, he shines. I take his free arm and tuck it securely under my own, press it to my side. He smells of green. I lead him to the kitchen.

Lunch is an absolute bonanza. A pig-out. Evan is grubby and ecstatic from his yard campaign and he has brought in a small bucket of spoils, early berries, tumbled together. He picked randomly, he tells me, these here, some others over there, a few of some of these, ah, whatever was ripe, and those, those over there. We mix them with baskets of berries from Happlett's. What we have before us is a total imbroglio of blue-reds and black-purples; it is a jumble, a fructose nirvana. The fruit is tart, bursting; it stains the cream purple, and our teeth. The early hot spells have paid off. Berries and cream and sugar until we can't swallow another spoonful. The baskets are empty. Evan's lips are stained deep blue. With his blonde hair, he looks like a ghoul, or Andy Warhol, and I am still picking little seeds out of my teeth with my nail when we decide we are not really finished. Evan has a cache of goodies in the fridge. Thick, heavy bread, honey mustard, thin slices of turkey and of beef, tomatoes, lettuce, and chips, wonderful, salty, greasy potato chips. God. We are in heaven.

And we are wiping our mouths on our hands and rinsing our hands beneath the rush of the water in the sink when the movers arrive. Their timing is good.

The van, enormous, weighty, digs canals in the yard where Evan has mowed. It looks to me as though the truck is sinking. The men are only a little worried about it, more that their truck will founder, more that they will miss their dinners or their wives or their lovers, I think, than for any concern for the ground beneath their wheels. They are hulky, wide men, and they make Evan look airy and odd with his slighter build and purple lips. When he offers to help them, the head man, blue shirt embroidered "Buck" over the pocket, looks amused, blatantly so, as though the offer comes from a sick child, spindly and awkward.

"It's what we get paid for," he says, though not too unkindly. He looks as though he is going to pat Evan on the head and scoot him off the perimeters of the action, but he does not. I am glad. So Evan directs, then. This here, that there, the boxes of books downstairs, the red wing chair, "watch the upholstery on the door jamb," near the fireplace in the living room.

I slip into the kitchen, nonchalant, invisible, and slowly begin to make myself at home, to poke and to straighten up after the lunch blitz. The sink may never be white again and the thought oddly pleases me. Of the two of us, I would be the only one to learn to love it with blue stains, patches like dark clouds.

I catch a glimpse of the men only now and then when one of them backs through the swinging door to set a box marked KITCHEN on the floor, but soon arrives, ah, the kitchen table, the chairs, more boxes, the butcher's block, the baker's rack, boxes and boxes of dishes and platters and bowls. The kitchen looks like a flea market stall and I am alone. But I can hear the rest of them, heavy steps in, lighter ones out, and by the time the truck is empty they are calling Evan by his first name and slapping him on the back and I am weary, leaden-lidded and sore from my center out and not sure, not at all sure, why.

And it is hours, hours, and beers all around, then the men gone, the grass pressed down into the mud again, no dinners missed, no wives, no lovers, as far as we can tell, and the daylight is faded and we are too tired to eat, though surprisingly enough it is time again, and we build a fire in the front room from damp wood and cardboard boxes. We sleep in front of the flame which goes cold long, long before morning.

## IV

## A CERTAIN CREATION

Time brushes past us with the indifference of a crowd. With it, it takes two of the houseplants, spider and pothos, that have been sequestered out on the back porch. My feeling is that these were the first of many to go. I think they'll all simply give up trying to be heard over the noise of our settling in. Unceremoniously, I throw the remains of these first two over the railing and carry the pots out to Evan's shed. I tell Evan, "Well, the first two have croaked." Evan calls me an incurable romantic.

We have settled in like burrowers, as though nothing were as important as being at home. For days I gripped my boxing knife purposefully and, with care, with aplomb, cut away from myself, cut through the tape of each and every carton. I put away the contents of every last box; I know where virtually everything *else* we own is to be found. Something's missing and it's not with the books, not with the linens. It's nowhere. I'll be damned if there's one here. It's a little hard to believe we don't own one. Everybody owns a *Bible.*

I do, though, come across two different translations of the *I Ching* and a moldy first edition of *The Carpetbaggers* that must have lain wet from some beach trip or other from heaven knows what year. I have discovered a collection of erotic short stories that I didn't even know we owned, and found, as well, the complete works, as of two years ago, of Stephen King which I did know we owned because I bought them. But I cannot find a Bible. I have looked everywhere. And it's bugging the hell out of me. So once again, with this normal and relatively meaningless quandry, it's as though nothing at all has really changed around me except the setting. Once again, there is something I can't put my finger on.

I wanted to take a look at the creation, or Creation, as The Writer might have put it. Creation. The first one. Not the myriad subsequent, lesser ones. Evan conjured up the picture for me late in the day, innocently and indirectly, of course. I could tell something was brewing because all the while he built the evening fire—a trickle of flame, mood not heat—he had that look of wanting to say something. I waited while he settled into his chair, leaned his head back into the corner of the wing, and then, again, while he sank down, sighed deeply, clasped his hands over his breast, flexed his arms outward, and contentedly cracked his knuckles. His smile was beatific. Full of himself, of us, he pointed out that we will have been here seven days. Seven Days.

At that instant, I saw the manicured hand of God drop meaningfully from the heavens and, with arrogance, with élan, zap into existence the newly cleared parking space, the walking path, the hedgerow; I saw sparks fly as He zapped up the piles of fresh and folded linens and plugged in the bedside clock so that the digital numerals would blaze with orange light. Then the vision was over.

It is not as if we've done nothing here ourselves.

It was Evan and me. And a few moving men. And the widow who cleaned. No mystery there, no magic. The vision was a Disney classic, dredged up from an animated upbringing. We get the credit this time.

Evan has accomplished, we have accomplished, something substantial here. He spoke as though our burrowing in were something remarkable, a real coup, and, I guess in a manner of speaking it is. A certain creation of a particular environment from another. A carving out, a filling up. Perhaps it is a pattern of creations, a cycle of sevens, because, in the past six days, Evan and I have succeeded in transforming, in re-creating, the house and grounds. I like it, oddly enough, this change. Though I'm not sure I'm comfortable with my liking it yet. But that is how it stands.

Today we can rest.

It gives me goosebumps.

What Evan has done in the yard, I would have thought impossible for him. It is perfect. It is subtle. It is exquisitely real and right. Somehow, Evan has managed to leave a liveable wildness. Certain that he was going to strip the entire area, dominate it, make it his, I braced myself for the shock. But he has not done that; I misjudged him once again, in degree. The yard still belongs to the woods that surround it. The blend is immaculate, no dividing line, no artifice.

He has simply tamed, somewhat, in our small area, its green exuberance; he has given us room to walk, to wander, without the distress of entanglement, of discomfort. He has carved us a soft nest in the woods, and the house sits, inviting and warm, near its center like the safe, protective shell of an egg.

The concentrated effort clearly suited both Evan and this place. It is still a country house on country grounds and Evan has not, even once, cursed the old man for dying and leaving him the task. I am certain, in fact, that Evan is grateful. He was hungry for the oblivion of involvement. Now he has tasted it and it pleases me to have witnessed the process. I could not have done better—nor as well. And now he stands on the porch like a kindly overseer and regards his domain. It is a pleasure to watch him nod his head in silent agreement with the grasses that bend so lightly and easily in the afternoon breeze. "Yes," he seems to be saying, "we have managed, we have managed quite well."

The house itself, in this short time, has warmed up, lost its damp feeling. The pungent antiseptic smell that welcomed us has been replaced now by the more restful aromas of woodsmoke, bacon, and coffee.

The interior has filled out nicely. I say that not only because the inside after the widow was my work, but because after being here an entire week, the house is used to having us here. It has opened up to us. It is liveable, kind, and comfortable. I could love this house again.

I have seen to it that the cupboards are no longer empty and that curtains hang in the kitchen, cheap and smelling faintly of Happlett's storeroom, but clean and crisp, their folds still standing out like the edges of envelopes, pressed in from being so long in their box. Pots and kettles are shined; they hang perfectly from cast iron hooks I screwed into the beam which abuts the outside wall. They give me pleasure, those heavy, bright pots suspended there.

In the kitchen, again, is the old pine table, the table that has been in this house for as long as I can remember, for as long as Evan can remember. At first, we stuck it out on the porch along with the plants to get it out of sight and out of mind, but the glass and chrome of our city table was alien and garish in the rustic, old-fashioned kitchen. We switched them, moved the glass table to the porch and put the remaining, death-defying plants on top of it. It is bound to catch dirt, and it will probably rust from the dampness out there, and all that is OK. It is more than OK. The pine table belongs inside where its shiny fresh surface will catch the sun from the window above the sink. Evan was accommodating. He stripped the peeling varnish from the old table, stripped it bare; he coated it in clean, smooth, white enamel, thick and opaque, and it stands now like a proud old woman, knotted but upright, in the middle of the room, taking the limelight, directing us around itself as though it and it alone has a right to the center of the room.

I am in love with the table and its new place in my clean new life. It is as if the table and I are in cahoots: I have shoved a matchbook under its leg to keep it from wobbling.

## V

## TIME, FOR INSTANCE

When we get bored, we make love.

I am learning his body again, and my own. Both are hungry, reaching like the open mouths of baby birds, and blind. We make love everywhere. There is nothing else to do.

It's an amazing thing, boredom. It creeps up on you, like needing a haircut or going gray; except with boredom you don't know it's got you until it's too late and then it snowballs, grows way out of proportion. Suddenly you find you're lost to it and you don't even know what it is that's got you. Well, not for a while, at least. But after that, nothing sounds good, not even the good stuff.

It's just that the work part is done now and Evan and I are cloistered here. Sometimes it feels more like we're entombed. It's claustrophobic; we are underemployed and we have become incurious. We try to keep busy, but time hangs on us, loose and sagging like the skin of an old, old woman and we are left to fight the tedium with our bodies. I read his; he reads mine. We study each curve, each mound of muscle and flesh. We go at it as though we will be tested later on what we discover. We would both pass the test. But the boredom is dark. Like bruises.

What has happened to me is ironic. Time, who was supposed to be my friend here, supposed to be on my side, has absconded with my instruction sheet for settling in. It has jilted me terribly, time has. I am quite aware that I am being childish, petulant. I know it and can do nothing. I know, too, that I should, instead, be grateful, eager to pull it all in, to welcome it as fate, luck, destiny, anything—my good luck in having found the right thing for me to be. But each time I mentally throw my arms up in the air and let my frustration fly, I hear that old catty voice that chides, *Who the hell ever said anything would be fair?* And that's the shitty part.

It's the perfection. The hell of the routine, that is, the dearth of any effort. It is clockwork nonpareil. I mean, who'd have thought anything would be too right? And the wrongest right is this: I am so domestic I stink of it. Evan breathes it in; I choke on it. All the old patterns, the fantasy thoroughnesses, came back so easily, too easily. My goddamn bread rose on the first try. I wanted the satisfaction of working hard; I craved it. I wanted to really sweat with the effort of becoming, to focus on the altering. But I don't. Like magic, everything is taken care of. It occurs through me, but brainlessly, as though I were programmed for it, built expressly for this purpose, precise, efficient, mechanical.

For a few moments, maybe a few minutes, I escape. Maybe I'll be perched on a rock, digging the heel of my shoe into the lichen that grows there, or poking at the moss on some stump under trees that have managed to keep standing, or I'll be walking barefoot along that thin crisp strip of sand that has baked like a wafer where the sea has been pulled away from it, and I'll be fine, peaceful, borne off somewhere private and warm, nowhere at all. Then all I have to do is simply turn in the direction of the house and wap! it happens: a click, a snapping into place like someone shoving a cassette in, and then, whoosh!, the tape begins to reel through: I must pick up eggs, butter, Baggies. Spinach noodles. Some Cheetos. Defrost the chicken. I must pick up my corduroy jacket at the cleaners, Evan's shirts at the laundry, must go to the post office and buy stamps to mail the bills. There is no turning it off. It runs on like that, out of control, too fast, too perfectly. Even the jam, though a little thin on the first try, was not bad, not bad at all.

Some balm, time. It was supposed to give me that space to ease back in, evolve, adapt, and, instead, at breakneck speed, I have been catapulted back in time.

Christ, I've turned into a goddamned Betty Crocker clone.

Evan has that bewildered, psychologically dishevelled look; he looks as though he's the only one feeling the weight of it all, as if he has stepped down and there was no step. He watches my blind performance in awe while he wrestles with his own adjustments, but it is the blind watching the blind. The unfairness of it is this: where Evan worked so diligently, so steadily, he who thought it would all be so easy, so natural, once we were in this place, I have skated through. It's all backwards. It is as though the shoes I've stepped into fit too well, too well for shoes that have not been worn, broken in. It just seems that they should pinch, even if it's just a little, somewhere.

Lindhurst would eat this up. The whole matter brings to the surface little spurts of rage that I cannot direct, escaping steam. But perhaps the anger is saving me from something else, maybe something worse.

*I sit down on the chair directly across from the large, immaculate desk. The name plaque, brash gilt on deep, rich walnut, says Dr. Harper Lindhurst. It reads like an assault.*

*He offers me coffee, tea, prolonging the discomfort, the hollow space in my stomach, in front of my eyes. When I decline, he goes to a bar, almost invisible and to the rear of the room. He offers me a drink. No thank you.*

*When he has finished his calculated preliminary putterings, he settles down on his own side of his desk and he leans back, weaving his fingers together as though he is already considering what I have yet to say, and he smiles.*

*"Well, Mrs. Dover, Dore, may I call you Dore? Why, Dore, do you believe you are here? Tell me. Why are you here?" His hands, still intertwined, are held aloft, above his chest, and he has leaned back even further.*

*Angry and embarrassed, I know he knows. He has my file. He thinks I am a fool, simple-minded. Nuts. I clutch at the arms of my chair; I am trying not to leap up and kill him. He does not miss this. I would like to put his walnut-based spindle through his heart.*

*"Good, Dore," he says melodiously, easily.*

*I hate him.*

*"Be angry," he continues. "You have every right to be angry."*

Though we may contemplate delight, we have found, both Evan and I in our efforts, that it is not some fruit that can be cultivated, not forced like hothouse tomatoes or melons or sweet winter strawberries. That, or Evan and I are no true gardeners. Delight, as it is, must just come. And spontaneity is slippery, tough to get a foothold on. We are studied. We are trying. It is not the same thing. It's that step down again.

It goes like this:

The crisp new, old white table is set for lunch. I have gone out of my way to make it nice. The tablecloth is new, red and white checked, real cotton, though, not oilcloth, not plastic, a tablecloth like in the movies. A bulbous water-green bottle of wine stands center stage next to the crabapple I have cut from the yard and arranged in the shallow, footed bowl, hand-painted and ornate, that Evan's mother gave us early in the first year of our marriage. The bowl clashes with the tablecloth, a minor aesthetic faux pas, but it is my concession to our history. If I think of it that way, I can make it work. White luncheon plates at each end of the table are flanked by spotless flatware chosen by Evan for its durability, its design. Evan is seated; he has his elbows on the table and his chin in his hands. The skin around his eyes, his forehead, is bunched up, furrowed, like those silly Chinese dogs. Evan is thinking.

With a pancake turner, I am scooping warm crab puffs onto Evan's plate. They bounce like the little thuddy rubber balls that come with kids' jacks. Onesies, twosies. Evan pours the wine.

He makes a small noise of appreciation as the last crab puff flops dully onto his plate and then he moves his chair in, closer to the table. He is tanned and sunburned both; he is the color of fresh salmon steak, a steak topped with a sauce of blonde hair. He clashes with the tablecloth, too.

Suddenly I am alive with it: I find myself shaking the spatula in the air as though it were a finger. "Evan," I say heatedly, but not hysterically, not yet, "we are not spontaneous. Why? WHY?" It is a serious question. I am not certain whether I have stamped my foot or not.

Evan laughs.

"I'm serious." I set the spatula down on the table; the grease runs down the flat blade and onto the cloth. The stain spreads across the fabric like a shadow. "Let's do something spontaneous," I tell him. I am petulant. At the time, I do not remember it is an old line.

Evan, though, perhaps just a bit wary of this new mood of mine, snorts as though something has lodged itself in his sinuses. He is working hard at not laughing, and I don't get the joke. He puts his hand up to his mouth as if to wipe crumbs from beneath his nose and he inhales, he breathes in so deeply that I think he will suck the air from the room. Then he lowers his hand, and when he does I can see that he is smiling. His lips are stretched wide, a rubber band that will snap.

"OK," he says tightly. I can tell he is humoring me. I can also see now that he is nearly holding his breath. "OK," he says again, easier this time, exhaling. He looks at me helplessly.

"Planning spontaneity," he says, getting a grip on himself, "is funny. Inherently. I can't help it." He lets go; he breathes like a bellows. "It's impossible," he continues. "See?" He is desperate.

And of course when he says that I see it and of course it is. But that doesn't make the feeling go away.

OK. I am the fool, the brunt of my own old joke. It's OK and it's impossible, and in our both seeing it we are *really* together for the first time in days and days, months probably, and, even at the moment, I realize that to have this one instant of understanding again, I would grant Evan any three wishes, any three wishes at all. And I would live up to them.

It is a relief and we both fly apart. My laughter joins his and we are hilarious together. We can't stop. Tears rise and spill. They run down my cheek and leap onto my shirtfront. Evan's face is nearly in his plate, he is so bent over with it.

It is a good, spontaneous laugh, a laugh like an orgasm, building, erupting, and bursting like party favors or fireworks, and then over. What follows is an absurd silence, the absence of everything but the exhaustion, a depletion that sinks like cold air to the bottom of our mirth. Then, the final arm across the gut from the ache of it all, the drying of the tears. The thinking of how to manage it again. Just for one more moment.

We spend the evening in town and have dinner at the open-air restaurant. The night is full of tourists; what the hell. We're tourists ourselves, it seems. Our waiter is tall and dark and distinctly effeminate. The blond boy who caught my attention when we first arrived on the island seems to be off. That or he has gone. It is not uncommon here. They come and go quickly, often invisibly.

We walk along the street of shops and galleries and it is fun, fun like we're young and it's the first time we're on our own, like we are friends, like we are new, that kind of fun. We talk about it later: the restaurant was cool, fresh; the food was rich, and we drank too much wine.

Evan and I have made contact. The rest of our waking night is warm with affection. We make love and it is a ride on the waves of the sea.

And then I am alone again and Evan is sleeping a child's sleep upstairs, tucked in, too warm under the comforter we have gotten on the mainland, surrounded by the glassy brass of the bed I have chosen by myself.

I literally follow the thread of moon outside, and in moments find myself pounding my fists against the narrow porch step. I am pounding so hard that my arms burn with it and the soft bunching up of the flesh at the bottom of my rigid, rock-round hands is stinging as if I have been bitten by a thousand insects, tiny threats that were invisible in the darkness.

Only when I am too tired to pound any longer do I begin to see the humor in it. But even then the humor is minimal. What the hell is it I want? Christ almighty, would someone please tell me? Why isn't it working, why isn't its working good? Is this what we were after? This stillness? Food, sex, and sleep? I am afraid we will be asphyxiated somewhere in between.

Evan has set up a new picnic table and two new benches; he has also wired-brushed and restained the old ones that sit back behind the pitch pines at the edge of the yard. They look good and Evan is proud of his efforts. He is working up to a celebration. Two, in fact.

Hope is coming on the fourth. Our first infusion from the outside, and a healthy one at that.

She will arrive like a circus, I am sure. Her husband, Finch, will lead the troop. He will drive up to our front yard and scan the possibilities; then he will pull forward so that when Hope and the kids tumble from the car, they will land directly in front of the porch steps and they will climb and roll into the house like human bowling balls. I will have to put everything fragile up to keep Hope from spending all her time in high voice. The kids are curious; perhaps no more curious than any other children of their age, but these are not any other children. Hope will, I'm sure, brief them before their appearance: "Try not to break, Lieblings. Don't touch. Please do not worry your Aunt Dore. Be *good*." And that will be that. Finch will, from time to time, shout warnings or imperatives. He will look up from whatever he is doing and without even really seeing them, he will know what they are doing wrong. They will hear him or not, as they please at the time. It will be a charitable time, a familial time, visiting Uncle Evan and Aunt Dore. Evan will bask in their compliments. He will tug at the children's hair, roll them in the grass, and stuff blossoms and weeds in their belts and pockets, check behind their ears. He will make certain that Finch sees every improvement on the grounds. I will, in turn, direct Hope around the house, pointing, discussing the fine points of establishing life on the island, here in this house, so far from them, from just about everything.

I am looking forward to their visit. I am beginning to believe that we will make it, Evan and I. Sometimes I believe it. We have been cut off for what seems like so long. The reunion will do us all good. Hope has always been my friend.

"It is absolutely idyllic," I hear him tell his sister when he calls her from the pay phone on the main road. "It is the best move we could have made. We can't wait to see you. We'll be looking for you about ten."

Next, he calls the telephone company and arranges to have a phone installed at the house. Things, now, are beginning to show some life again and we will merge with at least one small part of the world that we both know is out there.

There is that to celebrate. And this other: tomorrow is our anniversary. Tomorrow we have been married at least one thousand years.

## VI

## ANNIVERSARY

I have dreamt of Lise and I awaken alone.

I stumble to the kitchen where the aroma of coffee beckons, and I sit and hold my head in my hands. I wish for oblivion but, instead, Evan bursts in, a crazed and noisy parade of one.

The clatter is phenomenal: his boots on the wooden stairs, the complaint of the screen door—"Inner Sanctum," Evan laughs, his arms stuffed awkwardly with brown paper bags—and he is setting his bulk of purchases down on the uneven floor with a muffled thud, grinning, arms angled sharply at his sides, enormous, poised, ready to soar.

"And we're off . . . !" His arms zoom out to the right, towards the door, a leave-taking dance of sorts, frantic in a way, possessed. His eyes are eager, green like the moist mosses that cover the large shaded stones at the edge of the smaller bodies of water. He rubs his hands together in a show of enthusiasm; the sound of their meeting is loud to my ears, and not uncomforting. "Zest" is the word that comes to mind. Evan is full of "zest" today, lately. I raise my eyes, curious, and watch him.

"Boat's all ready. Lunch is set. Here we go . . ." Zoom. His last three words are given a heartier sendoff than the others, "Here we go"—perhaps the "we" even more so than the rest. Or do I imagine this? Jogging, bouncing, he can't stand still. He stumbles against one of the bags in his energetic shuffle; it topples. Two apples and some grapes, a small jar of mustard roll across the floor. He is nervous, of course he is nervous. He has wagered so much on this new start, this reconstruction. He believes in it; he has to believe in it. "A picnic!" he says lightly, hopefully, a tenuous reminder that I have promised to cooperate, that I have given my word to accompany him on this particular day. "A perfect morning."

I watch him closely. He is perceptibly slowing, uncoiling in the face of my non-responses. He is wary; he is stubborn and cautious. His hands are now nearly motionless at his sides. In thought? Atrophy? Despair? They look heavy, but, no, no, they are alive again and they flit about at his sides like crazed rodents.

He is determinedly, doggedly cheerful. It exhausts me.

Another start: he takes a deep breath. "Drove to Happlett's, wine and cheese, brie, cheddar, you know . . . ."

I do not satisfy him with the words he wants to hear; I find that I cannot raise my eyes, cannot look at him this time. I want to tell him: Not yet, not yet. I want to say: I don't know that I can do this. I can hear myself, but my lips won't move: Lise, Evan, I dreamt of Lise.

And he continues. He shakes the brie in the air. "Same stuff you liked so much before. Remember," he says, "two years ago?" A break in his dance. He has made a tactical error. He screws up his face, unconsciously emphasizing his miscalculation, his mathematical blow-out. That is the time we do not mention. We were not here two years ago, nor last year. Those were the summers we did not come, could not be here together. I do not let on. Then his dance continues, he has missed only a beat and has caught himself. There is more to think about. He is wily: the cheddar is for him. I do not eat it. It is his demonstration of his separateness from me, of the differences and the space between us. It is his concession, a subtle act, to let me know he understands. It is a curious gesture, cheese.

*I am wearing the lavender dress I wore three months before to Hope's anniversary party. Now she and Riva are chanting like Druids, over and over, "Something old and something new, something borrowed, something blue," over and over as though they are searching for some missing element in the rhyme. Their voices blend together like liquids.*

*The bouquet Hope hands me is tied with crisp white ribbons.*

*"This takes care of 'new' and 'blue'," she tells me.*

*"Ribbons and rose," Riva shouts from across the room, in case I didn't get it.*

*"What about 'old' and 'borrowed'?" Hope is thorough. Her eyes are bright. She has become a friend in these last months. The*

*bouquet is from her greenhouse, the enormous bauble in the wide, flat yard outside this glassed-in room. A single blue china-like tea rose surrounded by a meadow of anemone, nigella, forget-me-not, purples and blues, stark points of white, richer than any night sky.*

*"God bless the greenhouse," says Hope.*

*"God bless the sister-in-law-to-be," I tell her, holding the flowers up like a torch, the Statue of Liberty in second-wedding drag. "Incredible."*

*Riva takes the bouquet from me and walks it over to the table, and then she is back and tugging on my arm. "Borrowed," she says, and she wrestles her gold bracelet over my hand and onto my wrist. It is a mighty tight squeeze and we are nearly convulsive with laughter.*

*"Perfect," says Hope.*

*"Old," I say, pointing, "is the pin." I poke my finger at the stick pin on the shoulder of my dress. "My mother said it's older than God. She bought it with her very first paycheck. Or my father gave it to her. Either one. She's told me both," I say, and look at Riva who is dancing her nervous hop and nodding knowingly because she remembers my mother so well. Truth, even way back then, was a nebulous commodity.*

Evan stands over the grocery bags and waits for me to speak. Then, out of the blue, noncommittally: "Kittens," he says offhandedly. "They've got kittens again." He is still standing, wriggling, by the fallen bag. A grape wobbles precariously near the edge of his thick-soled boot. I wait for the misstep, for the sticky-sweet smell of grape to rise with the heat and to take me with it. I cross my legs, lean forward on the table. It creaks. "The Happletts," he says, "every summer, it seems." His caution, his carefully calculated timing permits him only the slightest of breaths here and I wonder how he'll get his air. "Shall I bring one back?" He shifts his weight, misses the grape, and watches me intently, waiting to, wanting to weigh my response. He breathes deeply. I am fascinated. "An orange one?"

I have lost track. An orange what? What was it?

Jesus. A kitten.

Happlett's. Evan's effort to bring us together here in this new, this old place. Evan's effort. A kitten. No, I do not want it, do not want something small to care for. I am no mother cat. I am too busy licking my own wounds, Evan, can't you see? I want to say: How blind. . . ? Evan, I need more time. . . . But I say nothing, nothing at all. I do not want to waste the words. And I do not want an orange kitten.

I ignore his overture and return to the lesser problem of the picnic. To please him, and in spite of my dream, I say: "Let's go." But my words are somehow not clear, my meaning, my sound, and the unfamiliar voice falls cold through the warm morning air. I look at Evan to see if he has heard. I am not certain whether I have spoken or simply imagined that I have. As I push back my chair, the wooden leg scrapes meanly at the old plank floor, a fingernail on a chalkboard.

Evan is breathless again. The wood-on-wood wail, anticipated pleasure, fear, I cannot tell. His normally staccato words blend into an even, hurried drawl: "Dore, c'mon." His arm is bobbing, his hand dangling, a fish on a hook. "Dore," he says more slowly, directing me like traffic, though not impatiently, not unkindly. He is beckoning: "Let's get some sunshine. What's happened? Let's get some sun. It'll help."

But he's late, too late. I have stopped listening and I am out of reach, and out of control. "Some sunshine" sounds foreign, babbly, child's talk, Lise's talk, and I cock my head towards him. I drift, light, daydream not memory.

*"Tell me about the sense of cleanliness you had," Lindhurst would say.*

*I would elucidate for him. "Not cleanliness. Just empty. When I went there I could be anyone I wanted. I didn't have to be that other woman. I was nobody's wife. Nobody's mother. I'd moved as far away from that other woman as I could. A continent of distance. I was living on my savings, on the money from the house. On the hope of not remembering. I was starting fresh. I could hide or lie about whatever I wanted. I could make people think I was anyone."*

*"Who did you want to be?" His voice would have that innocent, speculative ring.*

*I would not answer him. "I was empty," I would tell him. "She was there and she was missing too."*

*"Blank? Like a slate?"*

*"No. Not blank. Empty. Hollow. Hollow and filled inside and*

*out with what happened. Not blank at all. Littered, littered with what I knew, with what I felt."*

*"With guilt?"*

*"Yes, of course guilt."*

*"And what about Peter?"*

*"Peter?"*

*"Was he guilty?"*

*"No. It wasn't the same for Peter."*

*"And were you littered with Peter, too? The reason for your being with him was gone. Lise was gone."*

*"Yes. I was littered with Peter. He was detritus. I would look at him and I couldn't imagine why I'd ever been with him. Except for after Lise. I didn't know who the man was."*

*"And did you finally let go of Peter?"*

*"No. Not let go. He drifted out like the tide. I never really had Peter at all. He was there for Lise. Lise had him, not me."*

*"Did you try to get him to come back? Did you try to bring that tide back in?"*

*"Why would I? Why would I do that? That life we'd built was based on Lise. When she died, what did I need Peter for? To remind me?"*

*"What would he have reminded you of, Dore?"*

*"That it was all gone. Don't you see? The meaning was all gone. Like we were living on a house made on stilts and suddenly the house disappeared. We were left standing on air, nothing supported us."*

*"And did you fall?"*

*"Like a couple of rocks."*

*"And did the fall hurt?"*

*"Don't be an ass. Of course it hurt."*

*"What hurt most? Lise's death? Peter's disappearance? Or the invalidation of all those years?"*

*"Lise."*

*"Are you sure?"*

*Too far. Lindhurst would always go too far. "What are you trying to say?"*

*He would be baiting me, saying nothing, waiting . . .*

*"You're a fool," I would say. "Lise died. That was the worst."*

The face and the words are baffling. Perhaps I am confused by the music coming from the water. From our boat? From kids' voices. A radio. I can hear it clearly from here, playing something old, Big Band, Shaw or Goodman, I never know the difference, but it is something from much earlier than now, something solid, and it is right for this place. Today, here, doesn't matter, not really. All the days are the same. How long have we been here? Certainly not long yet. Or forever. How many days? Weeks? Right now, I cannot even begin to guess. This place is timeless. Evan is a magician, a fool, though I do not believe he recognizes this. Time to celebrate my return, our being together again, my insinuated recovery, our anniversary, our anniversary. We have come here because it is far from the city, from the friends who mean well enough, who believe they have only our well-being in mind. Here we no longer need to explain, have no means to explain. We have come here because it is far from everything else, because it is a good place, because, no doubt, the doctor said to Evan, "It will do her good." Evan is naive. Before this time, we have never been unhappy in this place.

And so, to please Evan, I nod. Yes, we will go.

But the telling still eats at me, a morning's, a week's concern, a lifetime's. I am shamed by my own silent whining, my childish, powerful complaint, though it is sincere. But perhaps, when we have stopped somewhere green and light and the wine is poured and the brie is spreading on its paper plate in the sun. Wait until, maybe, he says something first. Then tell him: I have dreamt of Lise, Evan. I have dreamt of Lise.

The cup is cold in my hand. I imagine the coffee in my mouth, though fresh, to be bitter. I stretch lazily, falsely, long pale arms reaching upwards, out, grasping for time. I yawn, my mouth open, wide, baring teeth, unbecoming. I am awakening, or slipping back, I cannot tell. He is waiting for me to stand. It is an effort to let go of the cup.

On my feet and moving towards the door, I murmur as I pass, as if to no one in particular, not the words I mean to say, not "I have dreamt of Lise," but "Happy Anniversary, Evan." And I am relieved, at last, to know that I have said something, anything at all.

Evan's words float softly to my back, the only part of me visible to him, for I am gone. They may have been "I love you."

The rowboat is battered and weary-looking, scarred from years of violent weathers and disuse. It wobbles, unsteady and unsure, as I step into its center. Evan is holding my hand, bracing my arm at the elbow as I settle, slowly, to one end of the boat. As he steps in, the little vessel does not lurch, does not pull away from his step. I do not know whether it is my own weight that has stabilized it or whether the small boat is simply more secure beneath the sure and certain footfall of Evan. I brush at the folds of my summer skirt and promise myself that I will not think about it.

Evan rows with the firm assurance of a man who has grown well and long in the country. But he is a city man. That we should be here, in this spot, away from the city, the crush, with no real plans, is strange, incongruous. When I met him he was busy, busy and charming. He charmed me. Liked me. It took me by surprise—that someone could like me. That he could. And when he persisted, when he really wooed me and loved me, how could I not return that love? But now, I am afraid for him, for me, though he swears this new solitude will renew him, give him time as well. "The new us," he will say if I ask him why we are here. "A new leaf, another chance."

He does not see how it can be too late.

When I mention his rowing, he says, How could he not know how to row? He has spent a lifetime of summers at this house. He glides, like a part of the water, an extension, a well-engineered machine; the oars turn and pull beneath the surface and the muscles in his arms harden and swell. His awkwardness gone, his smooth body drags me from my reverie, makes me draw my fingertips back from the cool tongue of the water at the rowboat's edge and reach out to touch his bare arm where it invites me. I close my eyes. As my blind fingers reach the skin where the vein swells with his effort, Evan smiles and leans to kiss me lightly on the wrist.

A fish, something small and glittering, leaps high to the left of our boat by the rocks, leaps and smacks the surface with a flashing sound, the sound of cold water and flesh meeting. The ripples do not seem to touch us.

## VII

## SQUIRRELS

The cr-r-rack! is like a sonic boom and then suddenly there is the lunatic chirruping of a thousand birds.

Evan and I bolt from the house as though it has been fire-bombed, more outright spasm than plan or curiosity. The afghan that snugged our knees, our hips, is thrown aside as though it had burst into flames; even the door that blocks our way out seems to just blow away, a gaping, sucking exit. And suddenly we find ourselves standing outside, barefoot in the half-dark, half-dressed, confused as hell, and we are squinting in the direction of the noise, but we can see nothing unusual at all.

We keep moving forward until we see what it is: a limb broken free from the oak. It lies in the grass like the rotting hull of some low skiff or dory, partially obstructed by the grass that pokes up around it, by its own chameleon coloring in these woods, in this evening light. It is almost impossible to imagine that it has settled so quickly into this stillness and invisibility after the ruckus it made.

The adrenalin had prepared us for something more exciting than a fallen limb.

We both stand there, limp with anticlimax. Then, while I shrug my shoulders, Evan inspects the woodfall. He pokes at it, and suddenly he becomes, by at least an order of magnitude, more interesting than the source of the seeming explosion. He is electric. He bends and ducks; his arms twitch, flap, and gyrate in turn, as though he does not know whether to fly or tread water. He jiggles as though he is being manipulated by some manic puppeteer, my husband at the end of his string, a marionette. And with a shout he becomes a shallow-breathing maniac, bellowing, "JEE-SUS H. CHRIST! I THOUGHT IT WAS THE GODDAMN END OF THE WORLD!"

It is perfect and it is all I can do to keep myself from throwing myself down into the grass and laughing myself sick. It is very funny. Evan at loose ends. He is so appealing this way, natural, vulnerable. He would be stunned to know that I prefer him when he is vulnerable. If I were to tell him how attractive he is right now, he would be certain I was making fun of him. I make a promise to myself, solemn as hell, not to taunt him with this later.

His face is red, redder, red as a farmer's. His voice is uninhibited, riddled with more vitality than I've heard since my return. Dynamite. No conscious effort, no restraint. From where I stand, it feels as though someone has opened the window in a stuffy room. I breathe it in. I can't get enough.

Pointing down now, Evan examines the branch. It is large, rotted at the crotch where it broke away, hollowed. The roar of frantic birds has ceased. Not a bird to be seen, in fact. No bodies, no spectators, not visible anyway. I get the creepy feeling I'm being watched. Once the idea sets in I can't shake it off. I am certain that I can feel them, great numbers of them, hundreds, maybe thousands—the numbers grow as the conviction does—and they are watching, watching with hard little bird eyes, opaque eyes, eyes like BB's, while we gravity-burdened humans with our unfocused, whitey orbs bumble in our own stir down here. It's an ambush, a ploy. Suddenly I am that woman in that movie, the Hitchcock movie, *The Birds*. Yes, I am that woman and Evan is that man, that man, what was his name? The gooseflesh on my arms is proof.

I wait, stark still, for the attack, but nothing happens. The silence falls on me like slow rain, and it soaks me through.

Then it begins slowly.

From the far side of the limb winds a thin, wavering thread of sound, a weak note, and what sounds like another, another or the same one but stronger, more resonant, like two strands now, and then in only moments it swells into a seeming chorus of mewling, shaky yawpings that blend inside my ears into a sickening stricken note, a cry that pulls me apart from the inside out.

Shit. Something is dying.

The recognition makes my stomach lurch and it slams back down. My throat will explode. It is all from that sound, that horrible crying. I close my eyes, shake my head to clear my ears of it. Instead, I see little stars, little rods, like neon insects flying around in front of my eyes. Jesus. No way will I look, or help, or try. Whatever cries like that, so shallowly and thin, is hurt, hurting. There will be nothing to do. I am not fool enough to believe that we can save some small thing that is crushed, birds, maybe eggs and birds, mashed in the fall.

I totter back and decide that it is enough that I remain upright. Helplessness is a vacuum. I will not be sucked into this sort of pain. They are small and wild, I am sure; they have parents, kin; it is not our concern. And to be snatched from our own cozy, evening perch for this, this is not fair, not right to pull us from a full day's beach meanderings, shell games, seaweed fights, a fast bite to eat and a slow hour of making love, not fair to drag us out and to make us witness a feeble life and a small death. How can we make love after this?

I wait for Evan so we can go back into the house together, but he is intent now, and, despite the coolness of the evening, despite the breeze that has somehow made its way past our ring of trees and into the clearing, I am hot, hot with the little neon stars that orbit in front of my eyes, with the spots, with the helplessness, hot with Evan's nervous abandon, hot in my own skin like a potato baking. Sweat breaks out around my eyes, across the bridge of my nose. Perspiration runs between my breasts and down onto my belly. I make an effort to breathe more deeply; I reach for my composure, strain to be rational. We are not doctors, not veterinarians, not even faith healers. We can do nothing. Let's go.

I lift the hem of my flimsy nightie as though it is some precious gown to be saved from the night ground instead of the thin, raggy, over-washed cotton it is. I hold it up and turn away. I am going back into the house, leaving Evan here, two shades paler now, bending closer to the hole in the wood. I will wait in the house, wipe up the drinks we spilled in running out here while he does whatever he has to do to make himself easy again. If there is mercy killing to be done, then Evan will have to do it. I am not up to this. I do not even want to know.

I manage three paces towards the house before I step on a sliver of stone that lodges itself with a single sickening thrust into the ball of my left foot. It feels like an ice pick. While I am bending, foot in hand, to pull the shard out, to see how badly I am bleeding, there is a moment in which the silence seems complete once again, when the mewling seems far, far off and Evan seems to have evaporated into the evening. Perhaps whatever it is has died, or in dying is so weak that it can no longer complain.

"Shit!" Evan breaks the pall.

His voice is hollow, cavernous; it draws itself out, comment, awe, not summons. I think he does not even know that I have fled the scene, that I have been hurt in doing so. I spin around at his cry. He is crouched lower now, on his hands and knees, neck bent, head tipped and bobbing like a curious dog inspecting the scent at a hollow log too narrow for him to enter.

"Oh, shi-i-i-t." It is a moan. He is twisting his neck, pushing closer to the opening with his face, prodding with his free hand, the one that does not hold him up off the ground.

"Holy goddamn SHIT!"

The chip of stone pulls out of the bottom of my foot easily. It did not enter as deeply as I had thought. I toss it back into the grass, press my thumb to the cut to check for blood—there is none—and I step high and carefully on my way back to see what he's got. Now I am the one doing the marionette impression. Pulled to and fro, I am self-conscious. I do not want to seem weak or indecisive in front of Evan. But I am being too hard on myself. Evan doesn't even see. He is so lost in what he has discovered that he is oblivious.

I hoist the strap of my nightgown as I step over the branch and settle my eyes on what has him so rapt. I bend down low next to Evan, on my hands and knees, forgetting the nightgown, shoulder to the ground; the strap falls again, and I push my face forward. I am feeling a part of Evan's intrigue now, though I expect nothing but a toppled nest of birds, broken eggs, scrawny, open mouths, perhaps some blood, some small bird-bodies. I knew I felt bird eyes, their parents and cousins in the trees, watching, waiting. These are their battered young ones, ones that could not fly in time.

But they are not birds. "Evan! What *are* they?"

I have frightened them again by my yelling. At the sound of my voice the chirping begins low again and rolls up, louder—but, God, they *sound* like birds! Their seeming single cry crescendos before it cracks and sputters into independent brittly yawks—thin, wiry, hungry, curious squawkings. They look like thumbs. They are pinky, hairless, like minuscule pigs; they are squirming like fat insects, homely-cute-disgusting. The hole is literally crawling with them; they are falling out of some sort of soft mound.

Evan is counting. I stand and brush off my elbows.

"Six . . . seven," he says smugly. All traces of the maniac are erased now. "And they're all wriggling," he says. "They're all alive."

He is pleased, as triumphant, as proud-sounding, as though he himself has had a hand in their surviving the fall, as pleased as though he has done something virtuous, something generous in finding them. Or perhaps this is not the case at all. Perhaps he is simply delighted. Sometimes I do not read him well. Perhaps the unexpectedness of their fall has brought him back to life after our late afternoon sinking-down.

His eyes are on me, expectant. I can see that he is waiting for me to share his enchantment. Sometimes I think I don't know this man who seems to take it all in. "Evan, what the hell *are* they?"

He looks at me unbelievingly. His eyebrows, white-yellow like today's noon sun, are raised, arching, round and full trajectories, cow-jumped-over-the-moon sort of eyebrows. He is startled for a moment, I think, because I do not know. He figured I was with him, understood, was as thrilled as he was. He thought, assumed, that I knew because he knew. I can see that much in his face.

And that seems rather a lot to ask of a person.

When my failure to respond points out to him that he is alone in his glory, his eyes lose their light. But then I can see a small glow spread. He has found an opportunity to lead me, a common interest, he hopes. His eyes come to life again as though I have flipped the switch that completes the circuit behind them. A smile rolls over his face, fluid, smooth, full.

"SQUIRRELS!" It is the equivalent of "Eureka!" And he goes on: "We have to move them." I can almost literally hear the wheels turning in his head. "Something'll get them out here."

"Evan. . . ." I want to tell him about futility. I want to talk to him as though he is a child, hold him close and explain that no one person can do all things, be all things.

"Get me a box, Dore. Get me something to put them in. A small box." He bends down to the log again. Behind him the light is fading. He reaches in, but I stop his arm before it enters the hole.

"The parents won't come back if you touch them." I state this as fact. I do not know that it is true, not for certain, but it seems that I have heard it. People often do more harm than good. I've heard that, too.

Evan has pulled his arm back. A thought flickers for just the smallest of moments and then he has decided. "No option," he says flatly, certain. While he speaks I pull at my nightie, lift it off the inside of my thigh where it is sticking to the moist skin. The moment I let it go, it falls back and sticks again. He sees me. He has withdrawn his arm and now he shrugs. "If we leave them," he says, "they'll be eaten alive." He is speaking literally. "Cats. Coons. Who the hell knows what else." He is building up to rail against fate, the workings of the cosmos, the local food chain. "We have to move them."

He is right, of course. I put myself in the squirrels' place. I squirm with them, wriggle with them, one in a pile of fat, stubby worms the size of Vienna sausages. I would not want to die out here, would not want to be that small, that blind and unprotected.

He wins. I know he is right. But damn him for it.

I am drafted into his Save-the-Squirrels Army and I have been more pleased about things. I do not want this grief, but it looks as though it is going to be mine nevertheless. My alternative is to brush Evan off, to tell him that if he wants to play good Samaritan to dead squirrels, then he can do it alone. I could save myself. I could walk back into the house. He would manage. He would not tell me that I am cruel or unfeeling; he would not tell me that I think of no one but myself. And because he will not say those things, I will have to help.

"I'll get a box."

Evan scoops out the hole. It is a nest made of leaves and grass, hair, fur, small, pliable things. A piece of red string stands out bright against the earthy colors of the twigs and leaves and needles. The nest looks filthy and is probably lousy.

I run towards the house.

Evan meets me on the porch, the nest cupped in his hands. I set down the tissue box, bits of blanket and sheeting, and Evan gently transfers the babies into the box and tosses the remains of their original nest over the side of the railing into the yard.

It takes only an hour before the new bed is crawling with fleas. The tiniest fleas I have ever seen. The babies seem unaware, but they must be in agony.

A new tissue box, dumping the pile of tissue onto the table and dashing out to the porch with scissors, more blanket, more sheet. A new bed. Evan picks each squirrel up as gently as he would try to catch a dandelion fairy in the breeze. They are squalling like any seven normal hungry babies. There is nothing else we can do tonight. Tomorrow we will figure out how to feed them. We are tired and feeling inept. We are weighed down by a long day, by gin, by the horrible cyclic question of responsibility. We stare into the semi-dark. In the dimness, the mother squirrel passes by.

Evan is the first to go into the house and the screen door taps closed behind him. He has taken the babies to the kitchen for the night.

I watch the squirrel from the railing because she has slowed and is looking towards the porch. "We didn't know what else to do," I tell her.

And I follow Evan to bed.

"It came to me in my sleep," he says proudly. He is standing over me while I come to. I stretch and begin to pay attention. He has a small brown bag in his hand. At nine this morning, Evan was at the door of the 5 & 10 forty miles from here. He has a plan.

While I move towards the bathroom, Evan is at the dresser, pulling the scissors from the drawer, ripping open the brown bag. I pause to see what he has.

Half a dozen doll bottles tumble out of the bag onto the dresser top, those milky white plastic baby bottles with the pastel nipples. Evan is cutting off the tips.

"This is the answer!" he says. "I can't believe I didn't think of it last night." He is shaking his head, smiling about what a numbskull he has been. I try to guess what time he had to have gotten up to accomplish this feat, or if it was the outcome, not of will, but merely of circumstance, and, instead, his brainstorm was a by-product of an inability to sleep.

"Didn't you sleep?" I am feeling guilty. I slept long and hard.

"Off and on," he says, but he is no longer thinking about such things. He is on to feeding the squirrels.

Downstairs, Evan fills the bottles with milk he had set out before he left.

The squirrels are sleeping, but at the sound of our footsteps the wailing begins.

Evan holds the first squirrel between his thumb and index finger and guides the nipple into its toothless, pink mouth. The milk dribbles across the little nubby face, down its neck onto Evan's arm and onto his shirtsleeve. He picks up another bottle and tries again. Same thing. He seems to decide that particular squirrel is defective. He places it gently back into the box and lifts another from the nest of blankets. Drop by drop. He waits until its mouth is open and then squeezes the bottle. Drop. But by then the mouth has closed again and the milk is on its journey towards Evan's sleeve. Some has gotten into this one, he is certain, he says. He is triumphant.

"They'll live," he declares. It is as though he's the doctor and the squirrels are a dozen of the world's most hopeless jungle fever patients. Each in turn is, drop by drop, showered by and infused with milk. What seems to be an increase of cooperation on the squirrels' part is actually evidence of the honing of Evan's skill. Gradually, as each baby is placed back in the tissue box, somewhat sated, or merely exhausted from the ordeal, they go to sleep. They nuzzle into each other, tie themselves into little squirrel-knots, and are silent. The process takes an hour and a half. Evan is exhausted.

In the kitchen we have our coffee and nearly swallow whole the half-dozen sweet rolls that Evan picked up on his way back from the 5 & 10. We eat quickly and unappreciatively. Then, we too are ready for a nap. We drag ourselves into the living room and huddle on the sofa. We are asleep within moments.

In almost no time, we are awakened by the clamor.

We run out to the porch where we have put the babies for air, certain that some carnivore has gotten them. But there is nothing there but the babies themselves, squiggling about in the box and screaming their high-pitched scream. They are only babies. They are helpless. It is feeding time again.

We take turns, Evan and I. Squirrel duty. They have established a four-hour schedule. Their body clocks. Our body clocks dictate at least eight, but it does not matter what our own bodies tell us. The squirrels will die if we do not feed them. We are obliged. We've started this thing and we can't stop now.

The squirrels are sick.

By evening they are bloated, bellies like balloons, but hard, ready to burst. They are no longer shitting; the nest is almost clean. They are plugged up, they are screaming, and they will die. It is all we can think of.

By one o'clock, the most docile of the babies is dead. We are devastated. We have failed. We are incompetent. How could we have presumed to take responsibility for such small, such fragile lives?

Evan calls the vet. The man is kind and patient over the phone, but he makes no secret of the fact that we are not likely to succeed in saving the babies.

While Evan talks, I watch the mother squirrel pacing the yard, a good distance from the porch. She sits on her hind legs and looks towards the house. Even in the dark, the teats on her white belly are plainly visible. I can see her with my eyes closed. How can we not keep trying? I have never felt so helpless. I cannot look at the mother squirrel.

Dr. Micherson suggests that we give the squirrels goat's milk, that perhaps the cow's milk is what is causing the plugging problem. Or maybe baby formula. They need enemas, he tells Evan. *Enemas!* To clear their anal passages, relieve the pressure, to give them a "clean" start. Evan remembers to tell me about the pun, though he swears the vet was not being insensitive, swears he didn't even realize he'd made the joke.

How the hell do you give an enema to a squirrel the size of your thumb? Jesus Christ. The man is trying to make fools of us.

So fools we will be.

Warm soapy water. Evan digs the eyedropper out of the medicine cabinet. He boils it, but it is too big. Much too large, maybe two or three times too large. This is impossible.

I am ready to give up, but Evan is on the phone again. When he comes back into the room, he has the car keys in his hand. "I'll be back as soon as I can," he says on his way out the door.

"Where. . . ?" But the sound of the car door replaces his response.

In less than an hour he is back, carrying a plastic bottle with an arched needle-nose on it. Looks a lot like a disposable douche bottle to me. But this tip is the tiniest imaginable. A chemlab bottle, he tells me. From the vet. "He wishes us well."

Evan cleans the bottle and fills it with warm, soapy water.

And it works!

Evan holds the babies firmly, lays their bulk against his palm, steadies their heads, their wiggly necks, between his fingers and he inserts the tip of the bottle. A slip would be a hideous disaster. He gives just the tiniest of squeezes and then pulls the bottle away, massages the tummy—and it does work! It really works!

Six times he goes through this process. Evan's face carries the weight of the world, of war, of life and death. The smallness of these lives is no measure. They are lives. Evan is wonderful.

We change their bedding and fall into our own and we all sleep, sleep like wasted children.

Each day is full.

We change their bedding with each feeding, split feeding shifts, though Evan, certainly better at it than I am, is more willing to make the night treks, more willing to force himself awake, to handle them gently and lovingly despite weariness and exasperation.

The squirrels get used to the routine, used to us, and feeding time gets progressively more clamorous. Now, no four hours pass without the sound of that same thousand birds rattling through this house. We respond like fire fighters to the sound of their alarm. We are needed, pushed to capacity, running on whatever extra comes with a situation such as this.

Evan finds the second fatality two days later. I find him carrying the tiny body out to the backyard in the palm of his hand. He is carrying it as carefully as he would were it still alive. He is burying it in the back where he hopes the mother squirrel will not find it. He would like to cry, but he will not. He is apologetic.

"We lost one," he says.

I mean to tell him that it's not one, it's two now, but I don't have the heart. Evan is in mourning. It is sad to see. I am bilious with grief as I watch his back.

The next day is cooler and we move the tissue box to the top of a metal pail that has been turned over a light for warmth. The whole set-up is in the garage. We are cautious, wary now, and at every feeding we are braced for more deaths. The squirrels, though, are lively, eager eaters. Their swallowing action is good now and their tiny tummies fill and bulge healthily after each feeding. When they are through, they curl up and try to sleep in our palms. They complain bitterly when we set them back in their box. They are seeking the warmth of our bodies, or perhaps just the contact. They nose, now, between our fingers each time we pick them up. Evan says they are instinctively looking for nipples, nudging, scooching forward, low, eager, their warm, soft little bellies smoothing against our palms. They are developing personalities.

By the weekend, one baby is left.

Perhaps it is just his age—he is older, he has had time to develop—but this one has real character, a distinct personality. He is growing hair, a sort of mouse gray-brown. He is beginning to look more like a fuzzy creature, now, than an immature alien. It has been three weeks since the limb fell. He just may live.

"Don't get your heart set on it," Evan tells me. "Please, Dore. Don't bank on it."

We name him Banker and we give him a party. We bring his box into the front room. We light a fire. Evan cracks open a bottle of champagne and we snuggle close, with the box on the table, in full view. We toast him, "To Banker!," and he is sleeping when we go to move him, so we leave him until his next feeding.

He is adorable, curled up tightly like the smallest of cinnamon rolls. We have accomplished something, Evan and I. We have saved Banker. He is robust and spunky. Banker is bound to make it.

This night, when we turn out the porch light, the mother squirrel is nowhere to be seen.

# VIII

## FOURTH OF JULY: HOPE

The jay here and the jay there seem to be communicating. Their voices are as rough as sand and stone gravel; their sentiments are gargled. Their knees, twig-like and backwards, flex and bob, and their blue rock bodies buoy like fat kelp polyps in the tides. I am fascinated by their babble, lured by their confidence. Their song is a code that excludes me, teases me. Sometimes I truly believe I am on my way to deciphering it. But jays and codes will have to wait. Right now, other things call. The jays will be there. They always are. Squawking their secrets into the air.

For now, I expect Hope and Finch and the rest to take the place of bawdy jays.

I am wrong again.

They arrive at ten, but my smug blueprint for their arrival has missed the mark. I should not be so surprised, but that goes without saying. This, too, goes without saying: there are some conditions in life that work as the constants, the predictables, the givens that allow a person such as myself to slip into a sense of comforting security in a world of discomfiting flux, a sense of safety, false or not. Sometimes, times like this one, I feel as though I've walked into a kaleidoscope, the end where the tiny fragments of colored glass shift and remake themselves, re-design their position in the overall angular scheme of things there. Sometimes, sometimes I think I will never learn.

We rose late, Evan and I, and skittered our way around this house like insects, each with our own priority, our own direction. Then, finally, it seemed, I wiped the last of the toast crumbs from the drainboards, reset the matchbook under the leg of the table, set out the plastic glasses for the kids, cracked open the ice trays, refilled them to overflowing, and dug the cookies out from the back of the topmost cupboard where I had hidden them from myself. Then Evan fed Banker and exiled himself to the yard to swipe off the picnic tables, sweep off the benches, set right the exterior host-and-hostessing grounds. He is still out there setting things right when they turn our bend.

From the corner of the porch where I am munching coconut cookies, I see their wagon turn its blind face towards the house; its blunt beige nose points in our direction like a homely, hesitant animal. I stand and brush the crumbs from my lap, but the car stops abruptly at the edge of our property. Inside the car, a flurry of mime-like activity is visible, silent heads lip-syncing, arms rising and falling, bodies twisting and turning like fish in the sun. The gasp of the parking brake is the only sound I hear.

Hope glances for a moment in the direction of the house, but it is a gratuitous motion and she does not seem to see me. She is in the driver's seat. I have never seen her drive the family before, and, in the face of this, my own invisibility is a strange sensation and it begins to embarrass me. So when she turns back to the hubbub in the car, I slip inside the house. I pour out the coffee I made only a quarter hour ago, and I make fresh. I wash my hands.

Something is up. They're having a pow-wow out there.

When the coffeepot is plugged in and chugging again, I peek out the window. It is a case of *What is wrong with this picture?*

I count heads.

Wrong number.

Finch is not in the car.

I hurriedly scan the meadow around where they are parked, but he is not there, or not in sight. I cannot believe he didn't come. He would not not come. We have something in common, Finch and I, and we both recognize it though we are unable to lay our communal finger on what it is. There is an affinity. Finch would be here, Finch is one of the givens. Finch with Hope. Both. Together. It is impossible that he would not come, that they might have come without him.

I step out onto the porch and start towards them. They are scrambling from the car by the time I am at the foot of the stairs and before I am even halfway there I can see that the smallest of the three children is whimpery. Robin, the youngest, is wiping his nose on the arm of his shirt. Anna, who is twelve now, and who has obviously tried to cut her own hair again, has streaks on her face where the tears have washed away the road dust. She looks up, sees me coming, and jabs at her face with her forearm, trying to erase the evidence. She is conscious of the self she presents, trying her own patience, I think, like us, in trying to make it better. She will not want to be caught crying. Twelve is a miserable, rotten age.

Hope's hair is caught at the nape in a straw-colored ponytail; moist twine-like strands cling to her jaw, familiar thin ropes of hempy hair stuck to her sweaty skin. She looks so much like her brother. But she looks like hell today. I have never seen Hope look like hell before. It is the first time that I have glimpsed that the family, that anything at all, may be too much for her.

Doug is still in the backseat of the station wagon, rigid and motionless. I worry that he has been forced to come against his will, wonder if he is angry. He is at that age now, other friends, other duties. Relatives and outings like this one a pain in his ass. I am sorry if he has been coerced. He is so still back there that I would almost believe that he is asleep, almost, except that now he is waving half-heartedly, smiling as though he is being pinched.

Hope throws her arms around my neck. She is hot and welcome. "I've missed you," she says breathily in my ear. She smells of sweat and slightly of despair. "Oh, Dore," she sighs as she wraps her arms around my shoulders and presses her cheek to mine, " . . . what a ride." To me, it sounds more like "what a life," and her breath is long and heavy on the side of my neck.

"It must have been," I tell her, warmly, I hope, but my arms careen from my sides and my voice becomes too insistent. "Where's Finch?" I don't give her a chance to tell me. "Why the hell did you park out here?" I'm rolling now, a ball of curiosity, of concern. "What's the matter with Doug?" Then, before she can respond, Evan's voice bursts from the front of the house: "HOPE!" He is striding out towards us, lanky and hot, mopping his face with his hands, then wiping his hands on his pants. He has been setting the old stone ducks aright at the back of the house. I can see the flakes of white paint on his pants, on his forehead. "Where's Finch?" he says, craning his neck, looking for him, as he grabs Hope's shoulders and gives her a squeeze. "You lose that guy again, Hope?"

Hope laughs, finally. She reaches up and playfully swats Evan on the side of the head with the palm of her hand. Evan's reaction is that of a child; he would like to wrestle her to the ground.

"He's in the car, nitwit brother. Give me a chance." She shakes her head and smiles crookedly. "Lately he sleeps like the dead," she says. "He's, let's say, difficult to wake up." She is still laughing as though laughing explains it.

Evan laughs, too. "Willful bastard," he says.

"We were going to put the screws to him out here," she says, "before we got to the house. Dore caught us." Hope talks as though this is normal procedure, as though Evan and I have simply forgotten the routine. Yet, no one is moving towards the car and Evan's face is taking on a peculiar glaze. He looks at Hope and then over at the station wagon as though he thinks she may be lying.

"In the backseat," Hope tells him while she inspects the sweaty palm of her own left hand. "He fell asleep sitting up. Then he fell over on Doug. Doug's afraid to move. Smart kid." She turns the hand palm out and wipes at her brow with its back. The perspiration leaves a turgid coating, like oil, on her hand. She looks at it, then dismisses it as though it will take care of itself. Only then does she look towards the car. Doug, still sitting there, is not looking back. Robin is wandering, bored already, beginning to stray towards the beach grove. His small hands are jammed into his pockets and he has managed already to shed a single shoe.

"Robert!" Hope's head swings around and her hands fly to her hips, large bony, winged things perched there. Then, suddenly, she is no longer looking at him. "Come back, now," she says. I have never heard Robin called Robert before, though that is his name. He has always been Robin. Hope's Robin. Finch's Robin. "Come here," she says to him and draws him firmly to her side, holding his hand now as if all her control rests in that one grip.

It is too intense for me.

I interrupt her grasp, scoop Robin up, and let him straddle my hip. "Hi, Gooseberry," I say to him and nuzzle his grimy cheek. "Your dad take a nap on you guys?" He looks down at the front of his overalls, gazes there as though something secret and precarious rests in the chest pockets. He says "Hi" solemnly while his finger corkscrews in his nose—it is obviously all he has to say for now—and then deftly the finger in question slides towards my blouse. I catch his hand and hold it. "OK, Kiddo," I tell him. "OK."

Anna appears before me with a gesture that says she will help me with Robin, that says she is used to helping with Robin. "Anna!" I chirp, and pass Robin, instead, to his mother again. He squirms like larva in her arms and she lets him slide to the ground where he wriggles at her feet. "You've grown!" I say to Anna and she smiles at the inanity, forgiving, tolerant of my unfortunate adulthood, and the tear tracks that divide both cheeks kink like bends in twin roads, and she holds back for a moment and then hops up to give me a short, quick hug. She is heavy, but knobby. "Heavy bones, kid," I tell her, groaning happily under her weight, giving her a loud, smacking kiss on the end of her grubby nose.

"Hi!" she says directly into my face. It is as though no time at all has passed, no gap of two years, and this sort of horsing around is commonplace. "Did you make deviled eggs?" she asks. Priorities. I let her slip to the ground.

"Eggs? Oh, God, I forgot the eggs!" I try my best to look abashed. I let my eyes wander everywhere but in her direction. "I'm sorry," I say to her and, in mock shame, focus on the grass underneath my shoes. "Will you eat carrot sticks instead?"

She is not sure whether or not I am kidding. She is waiting for me to give myself away.

"Or how about lettuce leaves? Will you eat lettuce leaves?" She is getting anxious. "Yes, of course, deviled eggs," I say, letting her off the hook. "An extra dozen with your name on it."

The relief in her young face is palpable. Anna takes after Finch. I have to laugh. She is transparent. She will bloat on deviled eggs and she will go out of her way to fart loud, sulphurous farts to make her proper mother absolutely nuts. Everyone will try not to laugh, then tell her to behave. It is not all hell being twelve; there are some compensations. She will sneak eggs while her mother isn't looking and I will sneak cookies but Anna will catch me. I will refill the egg dish on the sly; we will be a conspiracy and smile knowingly. Anna is an ally at twelve, precocious and sometimes petulant, but always trying to please when it doesn't immediately interfere with acting her age.

She is in rapture about the eggs.

"Thanks!" she says, gay now, and, as if all is well in the world, is off, bending low, seeking the tiny yellow wildflowers that crouch low in the meadow.

"Oh-h-h, Lord Almighty." The car springs to life, it seems, and we all look up. "Ouch."

"Shit." The groans come from the car. "Damn." Finch is upright now and he is rubbing his eyes.

"The dead arises." Hope's voice is pleasantly sarcastic. Her own face is a palette of relief.

Doug, no longer pinned down in the back of the car, bounds out. He is much taller than the car is high. The rear door closes with a snug, loud whomp.

Evan, who is getting nervous, sees his opportunity and loses no time. He is fast on his feet; he opens the driver's door quickly and slips in. He greets the groggy Finch over his shoulder while he turns the key and lets off the brake. I hear a jovial "Hey . . . Sleeping Beauty . . ." but that is all. The car is rolling.

Wordlessly, the rest of us roll into action too.

Hope walks on towards the house behind the car; she follows in the tracks left in its wake. Robin drags like dead weight from one hand—his wayward shoe has somehow found its way to her other—and Anna follows squaw-like behind her mother, her eyes to the meadow floor still searching for the butter-beauties.

From nowhere, Doug touches my arm. "Aunt Dore, it's good to see you." And I think he means it. He leans in closer while his arm slips around my shoulders. He is taller than I am. Then, so much like his mother, he mentions the unmentionable: "I'm glad you're back, Dore. I missed you," he says quietly, confidentially, keeping an eye on the others ahead all the time. He has the voice of an angel, I think.

We walk arm-in-arm behind the rest and say nothing more. He is big now, seventeen, grown-up, but I know he does not want to hear that; still, we both know I'm thinking it. He does not know what else I am thinking, though. He does not know the extent of his kindness, those few words; he does not know that this going against the "house rules," his acknowledging that I've been gone, is the fairest thing he could have done, the most grown-up thing any of them could have done. Hope's words were good, but Doug's risk was greater. He is young. He is the wisest of all. And so, instead of speaking, we trade glances and laugh, each for different reasons, and he escorts me to the house. It will take an hour, I figure, an hour and a couple of sneaked beers, for him to warm up to the gathering after whatever went on in the car, after a two-year gap in our partying, in our knowing each other. An hour, I think, and then he will be OK again. Just one of the men. We pass right by the car, and, from the first porch step, I turn and put my hands on his wise shoulders. I tell him, "Thank you, Doug," and I press my cheek to his. It is a man's face, scratchy and cool. And quietly, "I missed you, too," I say.

"Oh-h-h-h, Lord. Mother-of-mercy, I'm sorry." Finch is wholly embarrassed when he stumbles, still foggy, out the car door. He drags his hands down his face, pulling the flesh out of shape like raw dough. "Goddamn it. Goddamn it to hell." He shakes his head and looks at us through bleary eyes. He seems naked. "Slept like you can't believe," he says. Then, thinking we must be waiting for some explanation, he says lamely, "Musta been more tired than I thought."

I squeeze Doug's shoulder and then dash over to Finch. I take his hand and kiss his enormous, tough knuckles. His hugh palm cradles the whole side of my head in response. "A beer, Sir?" I say. I curtsey. "Cold. Wake you right up, Rip Van Winkle."

His eyes rest on my face while he says, "Sounds good," and he tells me I have lost weight. I puff up and pretend to kick him in the shin. "Fat chance," I snipe. "Reverse Psychology Attempt No. 1 Fails in the Face of Cellulite." I say it as though I am reading a headline and I pat my upper thighs. "God." Then I put on my pout and try to keep it there, but I am a lousy actress. I am buoyant with relief. Finch is here.

"FINCH!" Evan has already zipped into the kitchen and returned with two beers. "Are you OK? For Christ's sake, we thought the family had come without you!" He is kidding, but not kidding, and Finch's face goes as gray as rain.

"Of course I'm here," he says defensively; then he shrugs it off, laughs. His voice grows. "You can't have a party without me!" He walks to the porch and stands by Hope, who patiently holds out a wet washrag. He takes it from her and swabs up and down at his face with the energy of a thirsty man at a hand pump. I can see that the pick-me-up is doing some good, that he is regaining his color, his strength, and his humor. He looks up, towards Evan, from the blossom of washcloth around his chin. "OK, pal," he says menacingly, “where’s the *cold* beer?”

We are back on the right foot. Things should go smoothly from here.

Evan hands Finch a can. Finch turns the can on end and presses the round top into the middle of his forehead. When he pulls the can away it leaves behind a grotesque red ring deep on his skin; on the edge of the ring is a mangle of welt from the pop-top. It looks like a navel. He grins like the lovable goof he is. Then he pops the top.

It is all so mutable, so quick.

When we are inside, slipped out of our shoes, second cup of coffee in hand, gooey with Danish, and yapping for real, it is as though nothing at all has changed. In less than an hour, eleven o’clock, the men will drift to the living room, pulled by the mysterious magnetic force of the television. Evan would not miss the parade. Finch would not miss watching with Evan. They will piss and moan dramatically at every noise they hear, at every slight interruption that draws their attention from the abysmal conglomeration of historical trivia, tinny high school and military bands, crepe paper floats, Minnie Mouse, Mickey Mouse, rock groups, Miss Fourth of July. Much more important than any tangible thing here in this house will be the stately horses, the patriotic trappings, the Grand Marshal, the thirteen cannon of the airwaves. The program will last nearly four hours. Hope and I will bait them only once or twice; then we will let them be. But we will make periodic offerings, as though to angry gods, from an arm’s length. Scraps of fruit, vegetables, dip, chips, deviled eggs, beer. They will accept these pseudo-sacrifices as their due; they will be happy as the proverbial clams. Hope and I will wander, in between times, drink gin, and sit out in the yard, watch the children, talk, I hope. This is the comfortable familiarity of tradition and the day would be sad without it.

So much and so little changes, really.

I suppose it was predictable that already Robin, with his poor clipped baby’s wings, would have stumbled into the library table in the process of carrying a platter of crackers to the men. He has bruised his forehead severely. The blue V-shaped indentation is already swelling and it is easy to see that the mark will spread quickly across his head. We pressed iced rags to his face and crooned to him to be more careful and that it would be all right. Last time we were together like this it was Anna, some minor catastrophe, mini-calamity, another table leg or a broken glass. Hope is efficient, always, sympathetic, rational. She is so used to this. I keep forgetting how they are always hurting themselves, always falling and taking furniture with them, taking my breath with them. I am the maniac who leaps to my feet wailing, certain that, each time, they are mortally wounded. At one time I was as immune to this reflex as Hope is now. My immunity was lost with Lise. The knack will not come back.

Cookies and soda and the promise of more are good for getting the kids over their initial bruises and skepticisms. They are like the religious faithful now, utterly convinced that all is well, all is taken care of. Whatever happened in the car has passed, whatever trepidations they experienced about coming here have evaporated. They are sure now that their father will not eat them without provocation, that their mother will not bind them to a tree if they do not toe the mark. They have seen for themselves that Aunt Dore-Who-Went-Away-But-Who-Is-Back does not look much different from before and will not fly for no reason into crazy pieces like feathers into the wind. They expected to be able to see, I think, what ailed me, what kept me away, what made me different from what I used to be. I believe they are not really disappointed, that I am familiar and that this is easy. I watch them and try to imagine what they think of our coming here to stay—that we have somehow mystically arranged to have vacation all year long, or that we are fugitives from the law, or that we have not paid our bills, or our taxes, or our dues, or that I am just as crazy as a loon, their disturbed aunt in the island tower, and not fit for living anywhere else. They are old enough for conjecture now. Who knows what children think when something familiar proves false.

Over the fresh redwood boards of Evan's table, we talk about our lives. It is not deep talk. We drink gin and bitter tonic and I tell Hope about the terrors of the wobbly thighs. I tell her about the rapidly abandoned fiasco of the liquid diet. She laughs and dittos my concern, both about thighs and diet foods made with powdered protein. It is difficult for me to conceive, Hope with jiggly thighs, but she swears it is her curse as well, and I believe her. Nature can be a fickle, inconsistent thing, I tell Hope, but she corrects me and says that it is time and age and gravity which cause the damage. "That's the curse," she says laughing. "Time, age, and gravity. The other Trinity." We exchange exercise routines. Hers, without a doubt, is the more strenuous, and she does, in fact, do it. She does not drink Amaretto or Bailey's while she works at it. Her sins, she explains, are sequential, not simultaneous. I understand, and the picture she makes sends us into spasms of womanish giggling. It is magic for the two of us to be together again and we laugh until our throats are dry and our cheeks ache. We discuss our men. Our men, we say, are good men despite their faults. But what are their faults? Poor things, we say, and laugh some more. Our men are strong and kind, yes kind, we are lucky in that, yet they do not always know what it is we want or need. They do not know, in the final clause, what to do for us. This is wrong, we confide, wrong. We were told, or at least led to believe, that the men would know everything, could fix anything. That is the myth we lived by. It does not matter that we do not know what to do for ourselves. So, we empathize with them, but we do not fully forgive them, not really. We talk in broad terms: yes, we try, no, nothing is perfect, yes, we know we are not perfect either, not by a long shot, oh no, and it becomes a hilarious litany, echo-ridden, silly, and fun. We decide we must have been twins, separated at birth, psychic doubles, each with half a brain, that we have the same core, the same slight wedge of difficulty, of discomfort, of discontent. Then we decide, no, no, we are just women, just women, but we are laughing, laughing and filling our glasses and slicing more lime to the tune of our confessions. And then Hope says, "I have found what I want. For now." The words linger there between us, and I wonder about Hope's new look, about how much her new carelessness, this new shabbiness of hers, has to do with this newly disclosed or newfound contentment, how much of it is hand-in-hand, how much incidental. And I wonder if, perhaps, Hope is unhappier than most and she is not telling me, or if she is depressed or ill or crazy, too, but it is all foolishness. Hope is glowing beneath the loose ends. She is telling me the truth.

The current shifts. Hope chatters about the house, how it has changed, how it is warmer now, more inviting, how Evan and I seem to have come together and how happy she is for that meeting of people she loves, how this was the best possible course Evan and I could have run, so wise, she says, so straight, how well we have done, and, by the way, how do I really like it out here, so far from the city? So far from the center of everyone else's insane whorls?

It is very strange, but it is the first time I have had to think about it in those terms. I tell her, but it is news to me as well. "I haven't thought about the city at all." And then I have to think: How long is it we've been here? It is a real question. And I return to the conversation: "I guess I've been too busy to think about it. Too busy or too bored." We laugh again because it seems such a flippant, unreal answer. Then I think about what she has seen, and it is true, Hope is right, the house is a nest now, a lovely hole in the wall of the forest, a niche bounded by the water, and Evan and I have been curled into one another, we're closer, we live like people sleeping spoon-style. I realize that we have tuned the house to our needs, our tastes. We have stocked and favored, and I recognize now—hindsight is such a clearer thing—that we have enjoyed ourselves. And that it seems, truly, as though we have been here for years, forever, that we have been comfortable, busy, and relatively content, no more baffled than the rest of the world, I think, no more crazy. And I wonder if Evan sees it this way. He has not said. But his suits are clean and his shoes polished and tomorrow—tomorrow!—he begins his commute. He will swim back upstream, back to the city. I will not see him again until late Friday night, four days this week instead of five. I think of all that time, all the weeks like this to come, of all the chores and assignments I have given myself, all the things to do to fill that time, and I wonder how long we will live this way, apart and together, a yo-yo of a marriage, a yo-yo, and of whose making? And though the answer supposedly lies with me, I have no clue, except that now, at least, I wonder.

Hope asks, "What will you do with all that time? Won't you be bored?" She is serious now, concerned. Her hand covers mine. "Won't you be lonely?"

I say, "No." And I have to breathe deeply to clear my head, and I say, "I'm going to be fine."

And she begins to speak, then stops.

"I know that's true," she finally says. "I know it." And then, "We're all going to be just fine."

By mid-afternoon the children are rampant with boredom. I don't know what to do for them, but feel that I am responsible for their happiness today. I do not want them to remember this visit as god-awful. I put on my clown face and roll Robin onto the ground. Anna watches from the sidelines, aloof. She does not want to admit that she is still child enough to want to tumble in the grass. She is watching, but she is hungry for the play. I try to coax her in, but it only makes her pull back more.

"Ignore her." It is Hope's advice, and it sounds cruel, but I do it.

In a very few minutes, Anna has joined the free-for-all on the grass and we are roughhousing like three kids, one too large, too clumsy to be completely carefree. I am trying not to hurt them, not to throw my considerable, relatively speaking, weight against them when I pin them to the ground. Trying not to break their arms and legs. I am making every effort to see them, to be careful. And it becomes impossible not to think of Lise, of how she would play with them, be with me, impossible that I should even think of not thinking about Lise: how her hair, her thin child's hair, would fall in her eyes, hide her features, how the four of us, anonymous in a tangle, would tumble like this, like stones in a river, and we would scream childish screams, high-pitched and long, like banshees, and we would do it over, and then over again, and then, inevitably, the edge would wear off and the kids would tire of this adult version of play. They would wander off to find rocks and feathers in the forest, together. They would strip sour grass and honeysuckle and suck the cords like hungry raccoons sucking eggs, eagerly, purposefully. Both girls would be proud of wet sneakers, mosquito bites, cuts and scrapes from brambles and shells; they would collect treasures. They would band together, the two girls, and they would exclude baby Robin because he *is* a baby, because he is a boy; they would make him angry, make him cry, and Hope and I would console him, mollify him, and then he would sleep the sleep of the disappointed, and by the time he woke the girls would be bored enough to accept him again, to play with him, play responsibly, play lovingly. Then not too long from then he would be the one to take only so much, only so much of girlish, silly company.

It is impossible not to think about what it would be like, about all of them together, but it is the right thing to do, not to mention it. There is memory for me, but even that fades, wavers, sometimes, and postulation takes its place. It has been a lifetime long. I am the only one here who knew her; all the others, they know *of* her. That is not the same. If I were to talk about her, they would be concerned, worried for me that I would fall obsessive and depressed, and so for them I will not mention it. I will keep my mouth shut and roll in the grass.

*Lise is crawling in the grass behind the red metal swing set at the park. Other children walk around her, small thing, seemingly not seeing her, not watching for small fingers beneath their summer sandals, under their bare feet, yet no one hurts her, no one touches her. It is as if those other children are the seeing blind, have radar for their own kind. It is amazing to watch.*

*Later, in the sandbox, the small hand raises its tiny fistful of grains to the lips. From the bench, I can see the small mouth open. Running forward to stop her, I step on the tiny hand of another child in the grass whose mother has turned away in deep conversation. I grab Lise and shake her hand empty, wipe her mouth, kiss her cheek and tell her, "No, Lise, no! Don't eat it!" And by this time the wail from the background is a high pitch and the mother of the child is holding it up, kissing, not knowing what is wrong and the child is too young to tell her. I am sure that she is not seriously hurt, just frightened perhaps, inconvenienced. But I see now, understand the blindness of adults. It is a literal blindness. Sight is only for your own, selective, restrictive sight. But Lise has not eaten sand and the other mother thinks her child merely bored or sleepy. The small girl is thrown up over her mother's shoulder and they walk away. As they disappear, that child's face bobs, looking my way. The child is not blaming me. She is glad to be gone from where people do not see her, glad to be in her mother's arms, warm, safe, seen.*

And at last Anna and Robin and I are too tired to go on. They have lost interest in tussling and I haven't got the wind to continue anyway. I had forgotten how much work this sort of play is. Hope, in the meantime, has combed her hair, fixed her face and two more drinks. No glass has ever looked so good.

"How hot is it?" I ask her, reaching for the glass with one hand and pushing my hair back from my face with the other. I can smell myself.

"Too damn hot," she tells me, smiling. "I don't know."

"It's got to be ninety." I sit on the bench beside her. My rough-and-tumble seems to have subdued her as well, despite her refreshed appearance. "God . . . . I'd forgotten what it's like . . . ," I moan.

Hope is serious. "I don't think you ever forget," she tells me.

I would answer her, but for her tone. The hollowness in her voice tells me that the horseplay here has come to an end.

We sit silently over our drinks. I cannot tell what Hope is thinking, but she is pensive, staring down into the frosted glass as though into some deep, clear pool. And I wonder what she sees in there.

"CHOW!" It is Finch's call.

The two of them, Evan and Finch, are striding towards the table, platters of ground beef in hand, bags of buns, a tray of mustard, ketchup, onion, pickles, lettuce, tomato. The two of them have emerged, renewed, from their TV trance and are ready to join the world again. They are funny together, funny friends.

"A person could die of thirst," Evan says, looking around him. "Finch? Something to drink?"

Finch is sculpting burger patties. He looks up. "I left a beer on the table in front of the TV," and then he's back, intense at molding.

"Hope?" Evan asks.

"I'm ginned out," she says, shaking her head, and then, when the new thought hits her, "Cinzano and soda, I think, Evan. With a twist." She is watching Finch at the grill. "Thanks."

Evan looks my way, but I shake my head.

"OK, then," he says, "I'm gone." Behind him he leaves a trail of sound, a martial hum, something he no doubt heard on TV.

I follow, a tagger-along.

I pass him by in the kitchen where he is busy bartending and poke my head into the living room, looking for the kids. Only Doug is there, slouching in the chair in front of the TV screen. He seems to be listening intently to something about patriotism. A fat man on the screen, wearing a three-piece suit and sporting a mini-flag as his boutonniere, is waving his arms, gesticulating like a madman. Doug's eyes are riveted to the screen even though I know he's heard me behind him.

"Doug? Can I get you anything?"

He doesn't turn around. "No, thanks," and he holds up what is probably Finch's abandoned beer can. "Thanks anyway," he says to the TV.

"We'll be eating soon," I tell him. "Get hungry."

I rejoin Evan in the kitchen and ask him, "Did something happen with Doug?"

"When?" He's surprised.

"During the parade? Did something happen?"

Evan looks bewildered. "He didn't watch the parade," he says. "I thought he was with you."

I begin to sense more than I really want to know. I snort a dull "huh," as if I must have been mistaken, and I let it go. Evan obviously has no idea of what I'm talking about, has begun to hum his tune again, and I am certain that the matter is out of his head before I have finished speaking.

We go back out, drinks in hand. A new beer for Finch, Hope's Cinzano, Evan's gin.

And outside again, instead of joining the adults, I go in search of the two smaller kids, to see what's up with them, to gather the clan for the meal. I follow the drift of childlike voices.

I find Robin lovingly petting the stone ducks. Anna lies on her back on the bench behind him; she has her eyes covered with her arm, engrossed in telling Robin a story about a goose family and its adventures on migration. She seems to be a master of her subject, and Robin interrupts her only to ask questions about geese in general, not the geese in her story. They are so rapt, both of them, that neither hears me come up.

"Do geese really do that?" Robin asks.

"Of course they do," Anna tells him adamantly.

"Food!" I shout and startle them both.

Anna jumps as though she has been caught in some indecent act. ". . . and they all lived happily ever after," she says suddenly, perfunctorily cutting the story off as though it were an aborted mission. She stands and straightens her shorts and the skimpy top which have twisted around her awkward young body, and she makes headway towards the others. "I'm hungry," she says, and nearly runs me over.

Robin is left sitting in the close-cut grass, staring at the stone mama duck. When I sweep him up in my arms, he says, "That was a stupid end." I nod. I have nothing to say, no excuses for the nature of geese or of little girls. We are both suddenly sullen, as though we have been fantastically, blatantly cheated. Robin looks as though he will cry, and I brush the hair from his eyes. To him it must seem a terrible muddle.

"What's the matter, Robinbird?" I ask. "Bored?"

He does not know how to answer me. He has been briefed, I am sure, on what he can and cannot say. Even at this age, he is trying to weigh his answer. I feel sorry for him.

"It's OK, Robin. I'm bored, too." I give him a light kiss on the forehead, and feel I've got to make up for this bleak conversation.

"Did Evan tell you about the squirrels?" I ask.

He shakes his head "No" and looks me right in the eye, cautious, as though I might tell a squirrel story on the order of Anna's goose story, might cut him off, leave him unsatisfied.

In the meantime, Anna has come back for us. She pulls in closer at the mention of the squirrels. If I am going to tell a story, well, she is bored enough to want to hear it too.

"What squirrels?" she asks.

And I tell them. I tell them that only one has survived.

"Where is it?" Anna believes she has found the antidote to this afternoon's tedium.

Robin's eyes widen.

"In the garage," I tell them, but I wonder if I am doing the right thing. "He's very small and he's been sick," I tell them again. "We can go see him, if you like, but we can't bother him for long. We can't touch him. OK?"

The two heads are nodding continuously, silently, bobbing like heads on springs.

"OK," I say. "Let's go see him."

"What's his name?" Robin is excited.

"Name? His name's Banker."

"Why? What's Banker?" His young mind, his questions.

"It's just his name, that's all. Don't you like it?"

Robin bobs his head again, quick short strokes, a small bird pecking at the ground for worms.

Anna is walking ahead of us, faster, towards the garage. I catch up and open the door. The bucket and the unplugged light are clearly visible in the center of the floor.

Anna dives for the box.

"ANNA! DON'T YOU DARE!"

I fly forward and pull her back from the box as though it is her life that is in danger, not Banker's.

My heart is beating up behind my eyes. I force myself calm. "Please, Anna," I say softly, reasonably, too slowly. "Don't lunge at him. Don't frighten him. We can't be rough with him. He's been through a lot." I explain again about the feedings and about how we have been keeping him warm at night. I know to them it sounds like a needless, stupid adult lecture, but it seems like the thing to do.

Robin, frightened by my outburst, is still standing at the entrance to the garage. He probably thinks I've exploded into the crazies again. I don't want him to be afraid of me.

"Come, Robin," I say softly, and I beckon gently with my hand. "Come see Banker."

And we huddle over the box.

They are calm now, quiet and concentrating. They are utterly fascinated by poor Banker, curled, like a fetus or a cat, into the corner of the box, around a shred of blanket. I watch them as they watch him. Anna is penitent, her hands at her sides; Robin is, I am almost certain, holding his breath, and I draw their promises from them once again and leave them alone with him so that they can share their small folks' secrets, so that they can feel trusted, responsible, redeemed.

"Three minutes," I tell them. "Come out for dinner in three minutes." I leave knowing that, if I am lucky, they will be out in ten. I go into the house, fix myself a stiff gin, and join the adults, rejoin the world that I am supposed to understand.

The sun sets late, and the darkness, like mist, seems to rise from the earth, milky and opaque; it envelops the house from the ground up. We are exhausted and raucous at the ceremony of leave-taking. Hope is effusive, Finch is the card. Evan, I think, is drunker than I'd figured. He is kissing everyone he can get his hands on—Hope, Finch, the kids, each, one by one, and Hope again, and again. The jays, never far from our view, chatter their way into the banter, the promises, the goodbyes, the good intentions. And I am thinking even while it is happening that the jays are wily. They are present for more than their evening pickings; they are there to see them go, to watch because there is something of note going on. And I am with them: I know, too, that something important is happening, something that I should take note of, though I can't name it, couldn't define it if I had to. I have known since they arrived, known throughout each step of this long up-and-down day. There is no mistaking signs such as today's, no misunderstanding. As their car pulls away and the bright red eyes of their taillights withdraw from our yard, Evan's fragile demeanor cinches the certainty. It is not paranoia; it is fact.

When we go back in, we sink deep into the sofa. We are wildly tired, spent. Evan looks as though he has been on trial, looks as though he has been acquitted, acquitted but in a procedure that has left him with a sense of the possibility of guilt. And I wonder what it is Evan might have done in this instance, what it is he could be guilty of.

We are both bone dry and anxious.

Two drinks: a gin and tonic for Evan, Amaretto and cream for me. And we begin to talk. We talk tentatively at first, as many silences as there are words. Then the momentum builds, builds more in Evan than in me, and the words take precedence, they tumble, break out on him like a rash, the truth—Hope, Hope is leaving, she is leaving Finch and the children, leaving the house, the family, she has another life, she is happy, not sad, and nothing, nothing will ever be the same again—and we are both left vacant and nearly inside-out, and there is nothing left to say to fill the space that crouches inside us both like a hunger.

And the questions turn about and make themselves my own: What the hell can have happened to the certainties? Are there no sure things? What the goddamn fuck is all this about? The recognition looms as hard and as ungiving as concrete. There is no escaping it. Not at all. The only sure thing now seems to be the unraveling, the not-knowing. The accident of any particular lifetime. What the hell is all that for? How does one outwit it? Outrun it?

And suddenly it is too real, the fact that Evan must leave tomorrow, must return to the city, even for the short while of the week. There is no escaping that. As much as both Evan and I would like to let it ride, as much as we would rather simply go hide ourselves beneath the comfort of sleep, feed him later, any other time, Banker must be fed once more before we can go to bed, must be tended to so that at least for him life will be safe and reliable. Although he is bone-weary and sad, Evan is good enough to take on the task while I pull myself together, while I go upstairs, turn down the bed, and wash up, compose myself for sleep.

I am toweling my face dry, scrubbing at my scratchy eyes, when I hear his footsteps on the staircase. The sound is hollow. When he enters the room, his face is stricken, sickly. I turn to him, thinking that he has been injured somehow, or that he has suddenly fallen desperately, seriously ill. And then I know. He doesn't have to tell me.

Evan and I bend into one another, huddle as though we are frightened, children who are afraid of the dark. We are tangled into each other and we move towards the bed as one. We crawl onto the blankets and we cry.

Banker is dead.

## IX

## SOME DISTANCE

For Hope, July 5th is Independence Day.

It is my first thought, too early in the morning.

Then, gradually, as I lie there, the thought is displaced by the silence. Stone silence. There has never been such a stillness, and it makes me feel very small, shrunken and dry, in a house made for bigger, juicier things. I curl up tighter, slip down further. I pull the blankets up over my head and I go back to sleep.

Morning begins at noon.

I am hungover, physically, emotionally. My blood reverberates in my veins like some tight, hymen-like membrane, tympany, each breath I take, each hair that falls limply around my face. Evan did not wake me when he left. I heard nothing. Not the airport taxi, not the door. Without thinking, I reach to his side of the bed.

The scorched smell of coffee forces me onto my feet. It is like the smell of burning tires. I blunder sleepily down the stairs, towards the kitchen, and, yes, Evan has left the pot on for me — good Lord, how long has it been on? I pull the plug and try to get my bearings. I pour the coffee into the sink and rinse the dregs from the pot. Evan left at five. The coffee has been on seven hours. I open the window above the sink and hope the smell will go away. I put on another pot. Eight cups. I am going to drink them all.

While I wait, I pour myself a glass of grapefruit juice. The first sip is worse than swallowing moonshine. Instantly my sinuses are flooded with the same sharp, flaming sensation. I cough again, twice, to clear the passage. I wipe my eyes and take another sip. It is bracing.

I am coming to.

In the living room, I throw back the curtains and find that at least some of the drumming that has been going on in my ears is real. I can hear the steady tattoo of rain beating on the grass outside, hear it tapping the leaves on its way down. I cross the room slowly, flick on the radio, and twiddle the dial until I come across a voice that is neither whining nor howling. An indifferent voice. The storm hit south, this voice says; what we are experiencing is just the northern tip of something much larger. Our area, the voice assures me, will get no worse; the storm will pass us by completely by late this afternoon. And I wonder if Evan flew through the storm; I wonder what it's like in the city where he is now. Surely he has remembered galoshes, umbrella, or there will be some in his father's apartment. When he calls, I will ask him. I must remember to ask him what he was doing at this moment, at 12:25 p.m. I must remember to tell him I was thinking about him. I turn away from the radio and back to the empty room, and it is like staring at a face devoid of features. I am struck dumb. I will be alone in this house until Friday night. Four days, four if you don't count the full morning and more that I've already slept away. All that time and space, mine. And I can do whatever I want.

With my coffee, I sit, and the stillness and the expectation wrap around me like fog. There is no gnashing of mower blades, no clank and thrash of hoe and rake, no voices, no footsteps. No promise of them. Even the birds seem to be napping. There is only the thrum of the rain and that is steady enough to be no noise at all. The walls themselves seem to pulse larger with the silence; every concrete thing within my line of vision seems dwarfed by it, everything but the empty spaces in between which are now somehow cavernous and looming. I am thinking: I can do whatever I like. But the thought does not alleviate the silence.

And I can do whatever I damn well like. It's a gift. A gift. My gesture is emphatic; I spill my coffee. It runs across my knuckles, onto my wrist, into the lap of my robe. I lick the skin at the base of my thumb, then across the knuckles and the rest of my hand, and then I drink.

I can hear myself swallow.

Hope confided in her brother. Evan told me the two of them talked after we ate, sometime after the air had hung heavy with inactivity and we had all become restless. It was while we walked on the beach, Evan and Hope far ahead, Finch and I lagging behind, keeping our attention on the younger two who were, in turn, boisterous camels, mysterious Arabs, and giant radioactive crabs. We kept busy, kept one ear open, one eye wide for Doug who had jogged far ahead of us all, who turned back only once for a quick glance, as though he were checking on a companion who had fallen behind. It was then they talked, while Finch and I kept things ordinary, kept the kids in tow, kept our thoughts to ourselves.

Hope is leaving Finch.

She has found work in the city; she will share a small one-bedroom apartment with a friend, a man friend. She will see the children every other weekend. She is glad she married Finch, glad she bore the children. They are all her friends. Now it is time for her, time before it is too late. Mostly, she told Evan, it is the act of leaving that will be difficult. Her degree has come in handy after all. All those Tuesday and Thursday nights away from home have paid off in kind—a life away from home. She will not make much money. Enough to live. She will give Finch nothing for the kids because she will need all she makes to carry her end of the new arrangement. She loves them, loves them all, but she cannot, will no longer live with them. She leaves today. Has probably already left.

I can see what Hope has done: she has combined restlessness with direction. It is a prudent combination. Restlessness alone, though the risks are far fewer, is really nothing but crazy, empty air.

Hope said to me, "I think I have found what I want. For now." It is a realistic foothold. I know why she didn't tell me more: she wanted it to be enough. At least for now. And I am happy for her, sorry for her, because change is seldom as easy as it is desirable. I make a promise to myself to call her in a week when she is settled, to tell her that I love her, to tell her that I think she has done the right thing in following her instincts, in following through, though I am disappointed she did not tell me about this man. I am curious about the man. And when I call, I will never mention Finch.

But poor goddamn Finch.

It was so stupid of me.

The incident in the car was only the smallest tip. Finch and Doug going at it, long, flailing, meaningless; then Finch passing out, gratefully, in all likelihood, sheer exhaustion, sheer escape. All that effort to keep things normal. The enormous strain, that last day together, a public day. A stab at it, before it wasn't any more. Then Doug blowing their cover, needing a reason to go wild, looking for a fight. Yes, he told them, he understands his mother's situation—that's what he called it, her "situation"; what he doesn't understand is his father's passivity in the face of it. Part adult, part kid stomping his foot while he still had the chance, before they got away from him, before it was all changed and hard. Letting them know he doesn't like this, not at all. Everybody in on it: the little ones crying, Hope driving, thinking—what? Finch in the back, exhausted, slightly drunk, trying to reason with Doug: It is done.

And Finch was right. It was done, theory as good as practice. They will all miss her desperately for a while; she will leave an enormous hole in their lives, the kind of hole that fills only gradually, sometimes never. But she said they will miss her until they learn to cook for themselves, until they throw the bleach in the dark load a few times, until they get the hang of it. Evan said she explained this as though it were out of her control. Some sadness, some amusement. It is what will happen. They will grow into it. A sad shrug.

The imagining of the sounds and voices is so real to me, the reasoning so right, and I am so a part of it, that I shrug Hope's shrug. The tightness that has crept across my shoulders and through the core of my neck is a reminder that there is more to this than Hope. I cannot live Hope's change for her; she would not let me. I've got my own row to hoe, as they say. Lordy. I shrug again, my own this time, a slight, nearly committal shrug, and I swing myself up and out of the chair.

Too much thinking.

What I need to do for myself is get out of this house. A shower and a late lunch in town. Get the goddamn show on the road.

I can do whatever I want.

Amazingly enough, the voice was right. The rain has passed. The sun is out, and I find a place to park on the main street even though tourist season is at its peak, a season, in some eyes, not unlike hunting season, and, I'd say, if someone were to shoot potluck down this open street, it'd be a fine bagful indeed. Actually, the tourists keep the town. Winter here is a boarded-up thing, a few diehards, fishermen and the tougher locals, mostly the poorer, or the odd ones with a reason to live away from the mainstream. No, no; no reason to slight the tourists. Every one and his brother is here, right now, today.

I merge with a group of what looks like retirees, old men and women, lots of grey hair, pastel polyesters, hairless old men's legs. They get off the bus at the corner and swarm like randy bees onto the sidewalk, calling to one another, poking, pointing, hooting it up, grabbing hands, and all, each one, giving instructions—"Come here," "Go there," "Follow me." They have voices like geese. The bus driver, a man in his early thirties, pulls away from the curb, a look of immeasurable relief in his tired eyes. He has brought them . . . how far? No matter. I let them carry me with them along the storefronts. I am invisible amidst them and I peer into windows, step up and over thresholds, finger goods, spend money. I am in a buying mood. I buy things they buy: postcards, pens, and things I believe I want: a cheap waterproof watch, some rubber sandals, bermuda shorts.

When I reach the far end of the tourist walk, I am confronted by silent, blank-faced dwellings and a nearly barren beachfront. No action there. I'd rather be with the old folks. I cross the street and let myself be swept back in the opposite direction. As I drift, I buy fresh seeded bread, marmalade, spiced meat, a small box of fudge, and a hot dog which I eat as I go and which must be made of air because it does nothing at all to assuage my hunger.

Dozens of noisy steps later, I lick the last bit of mustard from beneath my nose and toss the waxed paper wrapper in the bin at the edge of the curb. I am in front of the old feed store, and it seems to sing a different song today, quieter, kinder. Either the music has been turned down or it is lost in the garbled "ohh"s, "ahhh"s, and "Hey! Charlie, look over here"s of the tourist glob. I am still famished, distractedly so, but I am not through buying yet, and the need to spend is even stronger than the hunger. Though the record store is bearable today, there is nothing there that tempts me. My last resort, I go upstairs to the woodworker's shop, the loft above. I need just a few more minutes, a little while longer, then I'll go to lunch.

Where I expect to find dust and disappointment, I am swept up in movement and the smell of linseed and lemon. I am surrounded by mirrors, all sorts of old mirrors, new mirrors, bevelled, etched, cut, and carved. They are everywhere, hung and propped all around the edges of the large loft room which, itself, is overstuffed with furniture, crazy furniture, oiled and buffed, enveloped in upholstery of fabrics thick and sham, soft and real. It is like being in Wonderland. All around me is a tangle of movement, chair after astonishing chair, cubby-holed rootwood desk after Victorian loveseat, black lacquered table after serpentine burl, all recorded in the mirrors, all sent back, repeated in mirror beyond mirror, well on into a seeming infinity of mirrors and chairs and loveseats, as though it were all swirling around me, taking me with it, and I am so dizzy from surprise that I back out onto the porch again to catch my breath.

I fall gratefully into a chair.

It is the chair I spotted from the car the day we arrived, and the rapport, this time, is instant. It is as though it has been waiting for me. Its arms are the smoothest things I have ever touched, and it cradles me, rolls beneath my weight, smooth, soporific. I lean back into it and close my eyes; the sounds from the street below drift up around me like pale smoke. I am suspended there, in this savior chair.

The strident voice of a woman tourist rising to the top of the stairway slices through to the bone. "What on earth is this world coming to?" she cries. Her head is shaking disapproval and, though she is winded from the climb, she has the energy to jab her finger at the air right where my hand is resting. I open my eyes. Her face is a mass of matte peach, her hair nearly purple. "Who would pay money like that for such gaudy crap?" she shrieks.

I don't want to rise, but I know I must. I'm as much on display as the chair. I stand and move over, beside the woman. She looks directly at me.

"The world is *nuts*," she says, and turns to join her friends inside.

I approach the chair again, touch the swirl of wood at its back. She is right. It is a monster of a chair, a strange dream. It is excruciatingly expensive. It is in the absolute height of bad taste.

I buy it.

And I buy the old etched mirror, the one that reflects a thousand rocking chairs, the one in the undulating frame, tendrils, sea waves, nymphs. I buy them both for the bedroom, because they are fluid, because they are moving, because, alone and together, they give me strength.

They are perfect, I say, handing my check over to the grizzly salesman, and he nods as though he has known that all the time. His son, he says, is loading the truck right now. He will deliver them today. With that, and his smile, I am satisfied.

And, as though I have made room for it, my hunger turns me end for end, a voracious wave of happy emptiness. It is all I can think about.

When I enter the restaurant, I am beyond ravenous.

I do not wait to be seated.

I pick a menu from the top of the stack on the bar, and make myself comfortable at a table near the street. Only one other table is occupied, a strange young man with a very little girl in a dull green dress and yellow knee socks. I cannot tell if she is his or not, sister, daughter, or what, but they are eating their meal quietly, their faces turned away from the street. They speak periodically, but softly, so I cannot hear what they say. They are a strange couple; for young people, they seem very old.

The menu is extraordinarily heavy in my hands. I tell myself I am getting weak from hunger, that I may not be able to hold it upright until I can make up my mind. Then I laugh at my own joke. Wasting away, ho-ho. A mere shadow. . . .

I pour down the list of entrees: everything looks good. I pick breadsticks from the basket at the center of the table and run my eyes up and down the page while I chew.

I want it all.

Each time I make up my mind, something else catches my eye. I settle on spinach salad and the scampi. Extra garlic; I'm feeling rash. And white wine. But then the Lobster Newburg whispers in my ear and I am uncertain again. It is such a commitment; I do not want to make a mistake. I am back with the scampi and taking one last look at the list when my eye catches a flash of movement at my elbow.

I am so startled, I cry out.

The menu flies shut of its own volition. It lands in the breadsticks. My hands jet to my throat as if they can keep my heart from jumping out of my mouth. I feel apoplectic.

The boy laughs out loud, but it is an apologetic laugh.

"I'm so sorry," he says earnestly, amused. He is the same boy I saw wait on that tourist couple all those weeks ago. His blond hair catches the light from the street; he is tan, and his eyes are very clear and wide. "I didn't mean to frighten you." He pauses and looks at me with concern. His hand goes to the back of my chair. Some of the laugh has gone out of his face. "Are you all right?"

My own eyes must be as large as doughnuts; my hands are still at my throat. I would like to act normal, as if he hadn't caught me off guard at all, but no sound is forthcoming when I try to speak. In my head I am screaming: *Where the hell did he come from?* I lower my hands, clear my head, and try to speak again.

"JESUS CHRIST, YOU SCARED ME!" I blow it out as though all my wind is invested in the statement. I didn't even know I was going to say it. It is not an accusation. It is an observation. I am horrified.

I start to laugh myself, now.

"I'm sorry," he says again, and smiles tentatively. He swipes his palms against his jeans at the hip. I have made him nervous. His face is rosy with goodwill, and I can tell that his instinct is to touch me, to assure me, or, in lieu of that, to slap me on the back as though I were choking or hold me down as if I might otherwise levitate and fly away. "Can I get you a glass of water?"

I laugh out loud again; this time my laugh is more like a dry croak, and suddenly I feel the flush rise: the breadstick I had stuck in my mouth while I was looking at the menu is nowhere. Nowhere. I reach up automatically and brush around my mouth for crumbs. I lower my face, run my tongue over my teeth, and check my lap. I say as nonchalantly as I can, "Yes. Water, please. That would be . . . nice." While he is away from the table, I scan the area around me for the missing breadstick. I believe it has wholly disappeared when I spot it about five feet away, under another table, halfway between me and the odd couple. It is half-chewed and wet at the end like a discarded cigar.

I pretend it isn't there.

The waiter comes back with the water and I sip it while he watches.

"Thank you," I tell him in my best lady-in-a-restaurant-alone manner. I have regained control. I pick up the menu again and open it. He takes his cue and begins reciting the day's specials. I fend him off: "Oh, Lord, don't confuse me, just don't confuse me," I tell him. "Give me the scampi. The scampi. Extra garlic. Spinach salad." I look up at him. "Before I change my mind again." We both break into smiles as broad as our faces.

"Something from the bar?" It is a prescription, not a question.

I wonder how long this exchange is going to go on. "White wine," I tell him. The poor kid wants to keep me sedated. He thinks I'm a wing-ding who's going to act up in his restaurant. I wonder if he thinks I'm a tourist. "Half a carafe," I say modestly.

"Good," he says. Then he is gone.

I watch him go.

I figure twenty-four, twenty-five at the most. The behind, and something about the shoulders, the rolled-up white sleeves, the posture. The tight little ass. Good ass. Covered in worn denim, as tight and as smooth as fine upholstered furniture. Yes. Uh-huh. And I am grinning like an idiot again, and even more important than his fine behind is the fact that he is bringing me food. I grab another breadstick, glance to the floor where the other one lies gathering dust, and I bite. Scampi. This is going to be good.

I settle down. Dry breadsticks and water are dulling my tastebuds, but not my hunger. Wine and garlic will make them come alive. I'll think about something else, about the chair, the wonderful, atrocious chair, and the mirror that will reflect it. I know exactly where they will go. They are perfect. Perfect.

I don't let him take me by surprise this time. I see him coming. I watch his approach, carafe and glass wrapped in the fingers of one hand, my salad in the other. His balance is good.

"Wine," he says regally, setting it down in front of me and pouring. "And salad." I get the distinct feeling he knows I'd like to just push my face down into the bowl, feedbag-like, and eat. I also get the feeling he's waiting for it to happen, that it's all he can do to keep from saying "Go for it!"

I sip the wine.

"Good?" he asks.

I nod vigorously, part of me wishing he'd go away so I could eat, part of me wishing he'd join me. "Good," I say.

"Good," he says again. It is a comedy of "goods." My intuition tells me he is not this lingering with everyone, and I am pleased. "If you need anything . . . " and he pauses as though he is trying to make a decision and then says, "wave your napkin." And he's gone again.

The salad and the wine only serve to whet my appetite, and

when he brings out the steaming scampi and takes the salad plate, I am back at the breadsticks. The restaurant is beginning to fill up. There is only this boy and one other on duty. Time for banter is shorter now.

"Scampi," he says. The plate is writhing in its own heat under my gaze.

"Extra garlic?" This is important.

"Megatons," he replies seriously.

I want to say: it's a good thing I'm sleeping alone tonight. But I don't.

The shrimp is fine, but there isn't enough of it. I eat with relish, but when I am finished I am only slightly less hungry than when I came in. I figure I must be getting drunk. I am watching the empty dish; I can almost see the aroma of garlic and butter rising. If I were home, I'd lick the plate.

I'm still watching the dish when he returns.

"Ah," he says and whisks the plate away from me. "Dessert? Cheesecake? Chocolate layer? Sherbet?"

I shake my head and smile. I would like to eat them all, and could, but for some reason I won't eat any, not here, not in front of this boy.

"Just the check, I think," I say to him, and hope the remorse in my voice isn't as obvious as it seems to me. I'll pick up dessert at Happlett's, I tell myself, and sit in front of the TV and eat until I blow up.

He is busy now. He gives me the check and he is off.

"Come Again," says the back of the check. He has signed his name below, "Lew."

He is in the back and out of sight when I leave.

I see the flames from the road, and I am certain the old man's house is burning.

I wheel sharply right, throw it into Park, and dash through the nearest clearing in the trees, through the seagrass, and across the pock-marked ground to the sand. I am outraged, breathless, terrified: *It can't burn down now.* I keep thinking it over and over: *It can't burn down now* as I run. *It can't burn, can't burn, can't burn.*

I stop short.

The source of the flames is a feverish late-day bonfire. And, as though they have just entered the picture, the gaggle of teenagers comes into view, the coolers of beer, the sandy blankets. I can't believe it when I stop long enough to hear the thunderous beat from the boom box, the mixed voices, the empathetic cheers from the periphery where a portion of the group is playing volleyball, boys against the girls, their net high and taut across the sky, their laughter childlike, their mannerisms and dress deliberately, markedly sexy. Almost all are turned towards me expectantly, as though they think I am someone's mother who must have been running towards them, for them. I stop, dig my shoes into the sand, and look around me. Far to my left, the old man's house sits solidly in the water, still, silent, not burning. And by the time I face the partyers again, they have lost interest in me and have turned back to their camaraderie.

I am too roused to go straight home.

I walk down the beach to the rocks where I can sit and watch. I choose a perch in the full sun, no block for the wind that sweeps in off the water. I sit and watch the old man's house. My vantage point is good: I can see the front and the full length of one side. Not much will get past me. I pull my shoes off and bury my toes in the dry sand. I lean back on the palms of my hands, and I watch.

The only thing moving out there is the water. The breeze whips up little waves that shallowly batter the edges of the sand around the shack. I sit for what seems a long time; the watch I just bought is in the car, useless, and I have no perception at all of how much or how little time passes. Nothing changes. There is no sign of the old man, no children caravaning up the beach towards his house, no offerings, no gifts visible at his scanty doorstep, no old god to open the door and collect his due.

I have a plan.

I walk back up the beach determinedly, past the teenagers and their fire. I am part of the scenery for them now; they barely see me. I cross the street to the car and open the trunk. I riffle through my purchases, take the watch and the fudge and push them down low, safe, into one pocket. I rush because the carton of ice cream I stashed in the front seat is looking suspiciously soft. I tuck a paper bag into the other pocket, and head back, cutting through the trees farther down the road, avoiding the fire, the revelers, making my way back down to the beach, opposite the shack, where I quickly pull off my shoes, roll up my pants, and walk into the water.

Up close, the shack looks different. It is weathered, yes, but not nearly so ramshackle as the view from far back led me to believe. Its very concreteness is unexpected. It is a real structure on a real spit, not a figment, not a wish, but someone's home. I pull the watch and the candy from my pocket, roll them in the brown paper bag, and leave the package wedged in the corner of the door's sill where the wind will not be able to dislodge it. I do not linger, but turn and wade back out immediately, and only once do I turn to see that the package is still there.

I move around the house like a clapper in a bell, rebounding from one point to another, hearing the echo of my own noise in the hollow of my home. A single bird serenades me. The call is erratic and gruff, a bleat like the youngest of calves or lambs, like an abrasive sigh. He is invisible to me out there, and important, and I remind myself that I should place a feeder in the pine.

At the kitchen table, the last of a long, dry series of chocolate chip cookies finds its way to my mouth. I chew and picture the source of the call: some stout jay off to the blind side of the house, tilting his blue crest as if to catch the wind, winking his black pea eye. I have no doubt that I see it as it is. I lift my hand once more, open my mouth and feel my tongue slide out in expectation . . . but the last bite of cookie is already gone. My fingers pressed together holding their invisible treat look silly even to me. I lean my face on my empty palm and think: I give up. I give up reminding myself that fourteen ounces of dry cookie will swell tenfold with the addition of liquid. I acknowledge that I am thirsty beyond reason, and I rise to put on coffee.

While I run the water, the bird calls again, but this time he is cut off mid-cry, his voice replaced by the scramble of wing on air. No matter how I stretch and turn, I can see nothing from the window over the sink, so I rush to the living room where I lift the curtain and gaze out. There on the sandy ground before the big oak is a shiny black oilslick of a bird, bigger than a jay, sleeker. He seems to sense me at the window; he shakes himself, preens as though he knows he is being observed, slowly, vainly, and then he turns towards the house and throws his guttural complaint at me as though it were a hardball pitch, and then he is up and off, his yellow eye as cold as a glass bead, and he is gone towards the water. I hear myself shout after him, “NO! Don’t go!” and then, “Oh, you son-of-a-bitch. Come back . . . ,” but the bird is already gone and he wasn’t listening anyway. I drop the curtain and head upstairs to the tune of a resounding “Shit.”

Dusk turns to dark while I am in the shower. When I emerge, fresh and dripping, somewhat renewed though tired, I am ready for the night and what it has in store for me. When I am dried, I collapse into the chair, which is curled like a new smile in the corner next to the bed. Across from me, the mirror reflects the view from the window, and there the moon, like a copper boat, is suspended.

This secondhand view is spectacular.

I dash down the stairs and yank a tray from the bottom of the pantry. I pile it up: large clear glass bowl, spoon, napkin. Then to the freezer: the pint of chocolate-chocolate chip, two frozen mint patties, half a dozen frozen Oreos. I smack the mint patties, still in their wrappers, hard on the tile, splintering them into a zillion uneven shards, jimmies and chunks, and I toss them back on the tray and run like the devil.

The balancing act on the way back upstairs is a feat worthy of an acrobat, but I am stunning in the role. I am crazed: don’t want to miss the moon, can’t wait to get to the ice cream, am dying to be settled in the chair and smug by the time Evan calls. I figure I have thirty minutes.

But the moon has already changed.

When I throw myself through the bedroom doorway, I see that the slice of moon is still pinioned against the black sky, but that it has gone paler now, more yellow than red.

I bend carefully into the chair, tray teetering on my lap, and I prop my feet up on the bed in front of me. I watch the sky in the mirror change. And I build a chocolate monolith. True architecture. Chocolate-chocolate chip, a sprinkle of mint, large and small, a crumbled oreo, then ice cream again, thin layers like ribbons: ice cream, mint, cookie, again, a veritable high-rise. And cardboard tub and wrappers cast aside, it is even more delicious than it looks, and I am utterly lost to it, to the mingled flavors of chocolate and chocolate, to the sweetness, and to the sky in the mirror, and the bottom of the bowl rises up to greet me amazingly quickly, too quickly, though it may not have been quickly at all, really, and, though the moon is pale white now, white as bleached bones, Evan still has not called.

I stand and, in doing so, find that my center of gravity has shifted from all that ice cream. I try not to think, not to ponder my thighs or my behind or the fact that Evan has left an enormous space behind him and that if I keep up this eating I'll be well on my way to filling it up on my own.

I take the debris downstairs, set it in the sink in a pile, tray and all, and decide how to fill the time. I dig through the packages that I threw on the kitchen table when I got home. I paw past the sandals, sniff the bread, and then find what I am looking for: the postcards, the pen. I will write to Hope. I will do it now—something constructive, something good—while I have the time, before I forget or let it go, while I wait for Evan. The postcards are wonderful: fishing boats at sunrise, fishing boats at sunset, seagulls looking bored on a pier, a scuttle crab, a whale rising, all of which could have been taken anywhere at all. I choose the last in the pile: the falling sun, the glassy beach, small long-legged birds like pickets at the edge where the water turns to sand. This is the card I'll send to Hope.

Upstairs, and back in the chair, I begin:

*Dear Hope,*

That is as far as I get. Every phrase I think of, every thing I want to say sounds trite and foolish, false: Hope, you are my friend; Hope, you have found what you want; Hope, I am glad, do well, be happy, call when you can; Hope, I love you. And I keep in mind that her new man will see it, that he might very well be the one who collects the mail in this new relationship—I am not so naive, I know no man, no woman, even, is beyond reading a postcard from the mail. I try to keep in mind that he will try to interpret it, that he does not know me, that I do not know that he knows of me, do not know what he knows at all. And I am shaking my head, eliminating each line as it comes, when the telephone rings.

It scares me half to death.

I catch my breath and try to slip all the facts back into place. I take my time, then reach for the telephone, try to give it all of my attention, and remember that I will tell him about the chair, about the mirror. I will tell him about sitting on the beach looking for the old man. I will tell him I thought of him. Twelve twenty-five. I will not tell him about the chocolate-chocolate chip.

We talk like lovers on the phone: he loves me, he misses me, how am I doing in the house alone? Do I need anything? Am I warm? too warm? Did I eat? He tells me his day was routine despite his prolonged absence, that his father's apartment has the closed, musty smell of rooms in storage, that he craved my French toast but settled for Adolofo's take-out pizza rather than fuss for himself. And I am hmmm-ing and yes-ing and I tell him how large the house seems without him, how quiet it is. I tell him the invitation to Riva's wedding finally arrived and that in one month she will marry an invisible man named Geoffrey, and we will party like rabid skunks. Thank God, I say, if she is happy. Thank God, I hope he is good. I tell him about the bird that flew off, the one with the yellow eyes, how he got away from me, and we laugh about that, and during the conversation I crawl from the chair onto the bed and I see that from where I lie, looking directly out the window, the moon is not visible at all. We talk as though the distance between us is something new. We talk as though it is much, much more, and much different, from the distance between us that I have enforced for so long without really knowing, until now, that I was doing it. I let him have the last word, the last "I love you," and though we will speak again tomorrow, I know that I miss Evan and, for the first time, I see that we have become friends since my return and that I value that friendship. And that now my friend has gone away. We say goodnight, "I love you"s still hanging in the air.

I bury my face in the pillowcase on his side of the bed, and it smells like Evan. I wrap the smell of him around me and it is only minutes before I drift into sleep with the lights on, brighter than the afternoon's sun, upstairs and down, but just before I slip away from that last infinitesimal foothold on consciousness, I realize that I do not have Hope's address, and I am dully confused because, for some reason, it does not upset me as I think it should, and then I lose my grip and sleep slides over me like a breeze.

I dream that I am back at the old man's house, watching from the beach, and that I have been there for nearly forever, have been sitting with nothing happening, and then I have to blink to be sure I see it, but I am nearly certain that the door to the shack out there in the water begins to open.

## X

## PALEONTOLOGIST

When I was a kid I always said, when anybody asked, that I wanted to be a paleontologist, though I don't think that was ever what I really wanted to be. I think it was just that 1) not many kids knew what a paleontologist was, so I thought it made me sound smart to want to be one; 2) it impressed my teachers—people who, at the time, I believed it was crucial to impress; 3) I knew it had something to do with dinosaurs and I also knew that all the dinosaurs were dead, so, if it accidentally came true, I'd be working with something that couldn't hurt me; and 4) I could spell it. Nobody else in my class could.

I remember Donna Ames wanted to be a doctor. She was always, for her age, our age, an intense girl, but she wanted this really bad even for her. She wanted the skill to heal. She did not only want to comfort; she wanted to fix. And when, on "Career Day," parents came into our class in the morning to talk about their jobs, and Linda Schwab's mother suggested that Donna might want to become a nurse instead because it was mostly men who were doctors, Donna looked Mrs. Schwab right in her heavily mascaraed eyes, eyes that stood out like plums beneath her white cap, rose from her seat without saying a word, whispered something to Mrs. Spencer, our teacher, and left the classroom. She didn't come back that day.

Donna knew what she wanted.

I remember she saved her milk money in a big pickle jar with the label soaked off (her mother had cut a slot in the lid), and when the jar was full, she and her mom would sit together on her bed and roll the nickels in those paper sleeves you get from the bank. They'd write her name and her own account number, legibly, on every roll with a ballpoint pen, and then they'd get in her mom's car and drive to the bank where they'd deposit them in Donna's savings account. I know because I went with them once. I think, though, that her mom slipped extra nickels in that jar, because I don't ever remember anyone in our class drinking—or not drinking, as the case might be—enough milk to cover the cost of medical school. Not at a nickel a carton, not to my mind. Anyway, I figured the reason she wanted to be a doctor was because of her father. Everybody knew the stories. It was cancer. He rotted away where you could see it. At home. The neighbors' kids used to say that they could hear him scream. It seemed to me, even at the time, that something like that could make you want to be a doctor. Donna graduated, went to college, and on to medical school. She followed through. She always knew. I got pregnant and married Peter. What a joke. Later, I thought about it and, actually, it was a good joke for the times: pregnant and marrying a peter. I mean, looking back on it, you kind of have to laugh, don't you?

Donna's older brother Greg, I remember, wanted to be a tennis bum. He liked the word "bum." He could spell it. And he liked to mortify his mother by broadcasting his ambitions. "I'm going to be a tennis *bum*," he would announce to the ladies his mother had invited for lunch, to the rush hour shoppers in Price Right, at the monthly meetings of the Junior Jaycees. He's a CPA in Fresno now, I think. God, he must be over fifty.

It seems odd, doesn't it, that when I was a child I had more of an idea of what I wanted to do, who I wanted to please, than I do now? Adults are supposed to know. They're already supposed to be doing it. At least back when I was a kid I knew I wanted to sound smart; now I don't even care much about that one way or another. I survive, I guess. That's what I do now. Survive. Some days are better than others. I keep busy with it. I don't go to work, at least I don't have a job. Evan likes that part, so did Peter. It's in their genes, I think.

In another lifetime, I used to listen, try to understand, maybe even top, what Peter said when he talked about his work, but then I stopped because it finally came to me how stupid I was. It was obvious. It came to me like a bolt: that wasn't what he wanted from me at all. He never wanted me to ask sensible questions on the properties of radials, and he never wanted me to know tire pressures, to be able to list the ins and outs of warranties, not even the per-hour wages of the gas-pump boys. What he wanted, what he probably wants still, from whoever he's playing house with these days, is to simply seem to be heard when he talked about his work and to look pleased that he had won his argument, made his point, or his sale, whatever it was at the time. He wanted whoever it was to be impressed with his knowledge, just like I wanted, as a child, people to be impressed with my wanting to be a big word, a paleontologist. That's fair. But I could act impressed with him, I found out, without doing all that god-awful tedious memorization that I used to do in my feeble, useless attempts to speak his language. I gained time with that realization.

I have such time for myself even now. Even more time. Much more. Jesus.

Today I don't know what to do with myself. I am absolutely goofy with boredom. I can't stand up; I can't sit down. When I walk, my feet swing at such odd angles that either I kick myself in the ankles or bang into the furniture. I'm getting bruises. Something in my neck is tensing up so that it is becoming difficult to turn my head and my scalp seems to be shrinking on my skull.

I sit out in front and rock in the porch swing like an old lady. Today is cooler. I pull my sweatshirt tight around my shoulders and I focus on the graying fringe above my head. I imagine a croquet party. Victorian? Edwardian? Was that the age? Broad green grass-es, the murmur of lots of civilized voices, chirruping, humming, an occasional good-natured masculine laugh, a titter from behind a tree. I imagine me in a long ecru dress, pipe-throated, the family cameo atop a broad bodice of tiny hand-stitched tucks. My waist small, inviting. A single wayward strand of my otherwise soft and perfect gold-brown hair falls deliciously at the side of my white swan's neck and the breeze makes it come alive. I am at ease, in place. I am lady of this manor. Composed, unruffled, a veritable thesaurus of living grace.

It's cooling off.

I slip my arms into the sweatshirt, gather myself in, focus: I breathe deeply, in as the swing moves forward, out as it moves back, like Margerie Ingersall back in the city told me they did in her self-hypnosis class, breathe in relaxation, she said, breathe out tension, in relaxation, out tension. But the swing and my body do not run on the same clock and in a moment I find myself forcing breath to meet with the movement, shallower, wrong, wrong, and soon I am seeing stars, spots, and little twinkles that tell me this isn't going to work, isn't going to work, isn't going to work at all.

It occurs to me that if I walk, the physical tension will let up as a consequence of the exercise, despite my awkward steps, my feet being driven off without me. I move warily down the porch stairs, which seem soft and cushy beneath my feet. I head down towards the path to the beach. I remember as a child I had one eye that didn't want to work, a "lazy muscle" they called it. They put a patch over the good eye, trying to make the bad one work, to force it into use, to force it to develop. The patch was a coarse adhesive fabric, one of those unnatural skin-tones, and ugly. The first day I had it I walked into a tree that I would have sworn was at least four feet to the left of me. That night the black eye and the puffiness made the patch stand out in relief, like some dull adobe-colored grandmother's sock balled up and stuck to my face. I think it was the third day that I walked in front of the car. The patch came off that night. It's the same feeling now. I can force myself ahead, but my steps are unsure. I don't trust my perceptions, my feet are too loose. That clear space could be a tree; that step up could be a hole down. I know this from experience.

I go back to the swing.

*Anxiety is amorphous, Dore.* Lindhurst again. I remember looking up "amorphous" after that session. I do know what he would say now. *You're bored, Dore. Do you know that?* God, I can hear the tone. He'd go on: *I know you don't think so, but it's true. It's obvious. Look at yourself.* I would look at him instead. *Go ahead, Dore. Say it. Say what you are thinking.* And then he'd wait. He'd probably tap his finger on the fishtank while I murmured something hotly down into my lap. This, of course, would be what he'd expect. Goddamnit.

Sure. I know. He would tell me to write it all down. If I can see it on paper, I can sort it out, like making up a room and furniture to scale in paper pieces and then moving the paper furniture around in the paper room to see if they fit. And so I pretend. What is it that's bothering me? Christ. Who the hell knows? Try again. What things matter? There. Good start. Food. Sex. Let's see. Love. Do I love Evan? I wouldn't know what to write. I miss Evan, I know that much. It's the defining of love that throws me off the course. It seems I began with this question. A hundred thousand years ago. Do I love him? This is no longer a question. Desire. Do I desire him? Yes, well, but do I desire Evan, or do I just want someone?

What is it Evan gives me? Why would it be hard to give him up again? Certainly I can't go on like this. Certainly I will have to give up something? Evan? Sex? Evan supports me. Evan is used to me; there will be no surprises. For either of us. He loves me. His way. My way. One way. Am I bothered? It's something else, something that has less to do with Evan than with myself.

Good! A step! Star on the imaginary paper. Hurrah and mark this point.

Nothing is impossible.

Excitement. I need something stirring. I want out. No, not out. Not like after Lise died, not like after it all fell apart, after it was all made so meaningless. God, how I wanted to get out then. I needed to die. In a way, I managed it. It was so fine, so hellish, the sound, that sound of nothing at all. The deep, noiseless hum of nothing.

*The water, much too warm, bites at my cheeks just below my eyes. I think: if I were to pull my face under and stay there, it would be over.*

*I sit up only slightly, raising my face from the water, but leaving my shoulders, my breasts, immersed. My nipples bob like flowers near the surface.*

*I am listening for the phone to ring. Condolences. The kind of help I neither want nor need. I am not certain that, even if it were to ring, I would be able to hear it over the nearer rush of the running water. But I like the sound. I let it run continually. I have only, periodically, to let some out of the tub to make room for the new. It is not a bother.*

*The phone does not seem to ring. I think: maybe it is ringing and I can't hear it. But it is not ringing. Has not rung. People do not know what to say. I give the plug a kick and step from the tub; the towel is coarse and stiff in my hand. It has dried in the sun and smells of fall leaves and, just faintly, of insect spray. The fabric grates on my skin and gives a sober sort of pleasure. I rub harder and note the ruddiness of my usually too-white skin and I reach for my robe. I think: it wouldn't be too hard to rub down to the bone.*

*I tighten the belt and walk from the room. The light switch snaps and I sit alone in the darkness.*

*On the floor, kneeling. My knees are stiff and half-asleep; my bent elbows ache with the cold, with their own weariness. I have been in that position for what seems like hours. I have vomited and, though I am right there, I have missed the toilet. My hair streams in it, my face and arms are spattered with it, and I am disgusted, exhausted. I am holding my head in my hands, trying not to see, not to smell. I stand, and the telephone rings as I bend over the sink, retching, crying. I will myself not to hear it, and it has stopped by the time I enter the room and turn off the light. I think: this is no way to die.*

*I sleep soundly and the telephone does not ring again all night.*

*Again: my hair floats about my head. I think: seaweed, aura, web. I pretend that I am dead, too—float, eyes open, still, seeing only the ceiling, the beginnings of a small spot of mold at the corner of the tiles. In the same position, I rotate just my eyes, rolling them slightly downward. I see beyond the white flatness of my belly the small triangular patch of coarse hair catch at the water, break its smooth surface. Then I remember and turn my eyes back to the ceiling. Dead people don't look down.*

*I think: so this is what it's like.*

Perhaps what I want is the big scene, drama of DeMille proportions, someone to kill himself for me, the big splash, circus dive, no net. I am not proud of this, but if Evan were to do that, then I could mourn, parade it in public, wear black, weep, exhibit my sorrow for all to see, a blotchy, teary face beneath a veil I would hope people would take the time to peek under. Or he could leave me, abandon me. He could leave me for another woman. Better yet, a man. Evan could leave me for a man, that would be the ticket. But Evan would not. Nothing so easy. Drama is the problem. It's a diversion. Just a fucking diversion.

Christ, I am weary of all this.

But how far can I be from wrong? I have sifted, I have sifted all

I know, I have given myself, no, earned, a star, and I have come up with only this: I have an energy that I cannot name, and it is eating away at me, it is gnawing at my core like a worm borne through to the center of an apple, and my seeds, my few lousy seeds, will spill, rotted, worm-wrought, when I am opened. The worm has no name. It will not do me the favor, the simple thing, of having a name. And it is contaminating all the rest.

I remember the first winter. Snow, freeze, ice on the pavement, enough to break my ass when I tried to walk. I remember my bones being cold; they were cold for six months. Christ, I never believed they'd thaw. But what I remember most is the apple, the single apple, brown and shriveled at the top of the tree. The rest had fallen, probably in the Fall itself, but this single apple hung on and it was still there, mid-winter, frozen to the branch tip like a bird on a wire. It did not fall until the thaw and then, when it hit the ground, it hit like mush, wet dust, brown rot, and then, simply enough, it was washed away with the snow.

## XI

## THE WEDDING

The wedding is *al fresco*. Riva's great-aunt on her mother's side is scurrying around the yard, chattering like a blue jay to anyone who will listen. "They have been *blessed* with a beautiful day," she chirps, meaning she had her doubts about this whole unorthodox outdoor set-up, but now, somehow, it's all worked out OK.

Riva's mother's garden is alive with wet, lush color, a frenzy of pastel profusion, like old ladies' kisses; her father is nowhere to be seen. He did not give her away during the ceremony; some man, some older man in a peach-colored linen suit, whom I have never seen before, took his place. The woman standing next to me whispered, if it is possible to whisper and be strident at the same time, that he is Riva's new stepfather. The tone was scathing. Evidently, Riva's gone through quite a succession of stepfathers. The woman's theory is that when Mom gets bored, she finds a husband in a different part of the country. In increments, she has made her way to these eastern suburbs—just withing reach of Riva. "Running fire," I think was the term the woman used. It is too bad about Riva's father. I always liked him. He used to buy us ice cream on those miserable hot days when we were too uncomfortable to play and we'd hang around and bother him while he was trying to do the yard work. I think he never wanted to do that work anyway, but, in what we hoped was mock exasperation, he'd throw down whatever he had in his hands, a rake or an edger, sometimes a bag of clippings (we'd watch them roll back out and clump back over the grass), and he'd say, "Oh, what the hell." Then he'd go to the garage, drag out his rusty J.C. Higgins black racer, and we'd go, one of us straddling the seat, one of us with our butt in the basket, and Mr. Alstairs standing in between, pedalling like a crazy man in the heat, off to get ice cream. It never failed: he always got a double dip orange sherbet for himself. Her mother never had much to do with us kids.

If I had been asked to pick a wedding and match it to Riva, it would not be this one. This whole affair is light and airy. Riva is less light and airy than anyone I know. She is small, but solid and brooding. And today she is surrounded by flitty women dressed in chiffon, men in light-colored suits, some in shirtsleeves now that the ceremony is over. Almost nobody is wearing a hat and none of this seems to be being taken seriously at all. It is froth, aerated and insubstantial. It is like the champagne.

The minister is a bland man, slight and probably balding—it's hard to tell—and before the ceremony I could not have picked him out of the crowd. (He does not wear any sort of ritual garb, which is too bad, actually, because I have rather come to like a certain amount of ritual.) The only reason I can single him out now is because Riva's mother just had him pegged behind the picket gate. She slipped him some money and I heard her say, "I didn't hear. Did they decide to leave 'obey'?" And now she is back at her circulating, and again the minister has become incorporeal, either that or he has left. It is moot. He looks like all the other male guests. I could mistake him for the groom, even, if the groom were anyone but Geoffrey.

Riva, if she has changed at all in the last twenty years, has only gotten smaller. At thirty-seven she is dry and twiggish. She is dark and her hair is still long and dull. She looks like a Brazil nut, those hard, brown shells with shallow, uniform wrinkles, as though she'd gotten too much sun over too long a period of time. But she has always looked like that. She has eyes like raisins. When she was ten, she looked fifty.

Donna Ames didn't make it to the wedding. I'd always thought that she and Riva should have been best friends, though Riva always told me I was her best friend. I never could understand that. But I guess Riva and I, out of the three of us, were the most alike. It was not a too terribly serious business for us, Riva and me, being kids, not like it was for Donna. We were directionless, for the most part, rudderless. Donna always had her rudder. I guess that was what made her different and left me and Riva to be best friends. It is, evidently, that rudder that has kept Donna from being here at Riva's wedding today. She had made her reservations, it seems, had even called and confirmed her flight, and then some emergency at the hospital, something out of her control, kept her in California. She'd missed her plane. She'd been cutting it awfully close, anyway, between her arrival and the ceremony because it was her day to work morning hours in some clinic or other, and so it was absolutely out of the question, physically impossible, for her to make the wedding. She'd called Riva from the hospital. There was just no way, she said. She was awfully, awfully sorry. It had meant so much for her to be there, for all of us to be together one more time, but they just couldn't make it in time. They. Riva picked up on it right away. She was absolutely certain Donna had said "they." We'd heard nothing at all about any "they," and we also figured that we would have been the ones to hear if anybody were going to. Evidently we were more cut off—left out—than we had even imagined. More than shocked, we were speechless. We'd simply marked Donna up as a spinster doctor. Successful, so to speak. So she got somebody and now she's a "they." We're all "they"s now. Then we got to giggling and we wondered how she'd found time in her frantic schedule to make it to her own wedding. But then decided that maybe she hadn't. Maybe "they" weren't married. Donna had never been much for what she was supposed to do, anyway. After all, it was California. Then Riva was the one to bring up her walking out on Mrs. Schwab that morning in school and how Linda Schwab had been confused forever after. She had never really quite known where her loyalty lay: Linda was a chubby girl, with the most incredibly gargantuan appetite for that awful bread they served in the school cafeteria, the stuff nobody in her right mind ate, one gummy white slice, one soggy pseudo-wheat slice, pasted together with a brittle adhesive of white margarine. For Linda, it had been between defending her mother's honor and gathering up all the uneaten bread in the cafeteria. Honor had won as far as Donna's bread went, but only because Donna had, after that scene in the classroom, made a point of throwing her bread away, untouched, before Linda could get to it. She made a solemn rite out of emptying her tray while Linda watched. She always made certain Linda saw the untouched bread go down the chute.

Some fool has just jumped into the pool.

Riva's mother is going crazy. She had the entire pool filled with white gardenias, floating on the top, of course. It was supposed to look like the marriage bed, I think. And now Richard Grotz has jumped in the deep end with his clothes on. I think Riva's mother believes it's symbolic; all the color has gone out of her face. Everyone else is laughing hysterically. When Grotz crawls out, he looks like the pierrot in "Children of Paradise." Big white petals are stuck to the front of his suit like enormous rounded buttons, and he is droopy and pitiful looking. The man behind me at the punch bowl says his suit is going to shrink.

Geoffrey Olsen is Riva's husband now. He is obviously mad for her and hasn't taken his eyes from her since she first walked out and up the aisle. I don't think he knows the rest of us are here. It's cute. He's going to be surprised when he sees the pictures and finds out there was a party going on. I figure he's fortyish. According to Riva, he's never been married before either. Riva's note that came with the invitation said he was a "broker" in the city. I don't know whether that means he's a stock broker or a real estate broker—or if there are some other kinds of brokers I don't know about. I always thought she'd marry a veterinarian. I don't know why. She says they met in her shop, though what he was doing in a dress shop is beyond guessing.

Geoffrey is an enormous man. Why do huge men always seem to pick the tiny, quiet women? The ones who can't be kissed unless the man doubles over or the woman is literally picked up off the ground? Why do they do that? Because that's what they had to do in the ceremony. Everybody giggled. He just bent over and picked her up at the shoulders like she was nothing, like he was holding a can of beer to his lips. And then he set her down. Ker-plink went the tiny lady's white satin heels on the paving stone. Then they turned and walked back down the aisle together. Like Mutt and Jeff, but I don't usually dwell on these things, I don't think, but how do they manage? I mean, sex? If he mounts her, her tiny pea face will be lost, God, in his navel. She'll suffocate. Is there any way to get around that? If she rides him, can he even know she's there? Flyweight, wouldn't she be frightened of being swatted off, like some insect, tickling? Anyway, how can she straddle that large a man? How can she fit over him, encompass him? If the rest of his size is any gauge at all, I'd say it's impossible. Even if they find—

surely they've found—a way to do it without killing her, he'll rip her up the middle, bruise her brain. How can she accommodate him? I'm dying to know. I'm dying to ask, but I certainly can't ask, not even Riva. She never did have that sort of sense of humor. Ah, and the key here is, I think, that Riva is wearing white (at her mother's insistence, it just has to be), so I'm supposed to believe that at thirty-seven she is still a virgin and that this logistical dilemma has not yet been confronted. Let it ride. It's their marriage. It's those damn little nuts. Those awful, inedible little candied nuts wrapped in net that are for ever and ever handed out at weddings. Some little blonde girl in white stockings was giving them out and I've been standing here rolling those nuts between my fingers, trapped in their little net sack. This one has a thin gold-embossed ribbon tied around its top: "Riva and Geoffrey, August" and the year. So I'm standing here quite literally holding Geoffrey's nuts in my hand, and *how am I not going to think about it?*

I think I am going to keep drinking.

It's damn hot out here. And I am keeping my eye on Evan. He's dancing with Anne Schlimhammer. I swear that's really her name. He is smiling at me over the back of her shoulder, gesturing. His waggling finger is saying "cut in." I turn away and follow the man with the tray of champagne. Surely there is food around here somewhere. I'm starved. Lunch in ten minutes, thank you sir. Champagne in the meantime. Evan doesn't know I know about Anne Schlimhammer. Frankly, right now, I can't recall how I found out, but I did. I could never forget that name. Evan and Anne were quite a "thing" in college. She married a roommate of Evan's friend Richard, not Richard Grotz who jumped in the pool with his clothes on, and he, Allan, somehow, through some tangled maze of friendly relationships, is a friend of the groom's, Geoffrey. So there we are. Evan is dancing with Anne and trying not to let me know that he remembers her. He did look surprised to see her. I don't doubt that he was. But with a name like that, why didn't she take her husband's name?

I'm off to see that the champagne does not go to waste.

And all of a sudden, oh, I am swept off my feet by Uncle Delber. It might be DelberT but, if it is, that isn't what he said. It is a total mystery to me who Uncle Delber is the uncle of. I asked him and I think he told me, but either I've forgotten or it was somebody I didn't know, because it didn't stick. Anyway, he, too, was following the champagne trail. We are dancing a fox trot, while Uncle Delber makes jokes about not stepping on his long fuzzy tail, and, though I have never before danced a fox trot with Uncle Delber or with anyone else for that matter, I am doing quite fine! Periodically, we bounce over to the table at the edge of the patio where we left our glasses. It is magic, mysterious and romantic like in those old medieval French stories. Each time we go over there, our glasses are full and fresh and sparkling! Each time we turn I watch Evan sitting with Anne Schlimhammer, and he is watching me watch him. And now that I have his attention I plan to keep it. One more before lunch, Uncle Delber, and keep your tail from dragging on the floor!

I am dredged up out of the arms of Uncle Delber by Evan.

"You will sit with me, won't you?" He is trying to be funny.

Lunch is too, too incredible. What they've given me with a grand flourish on this classic white plate I could put in my eye. A little half of deviled egg atop a thin strip of some sort of translucent meat, a mushroom slice, a dab of sauce running off the top. It's absolutely phallic. Up and coming, so to speak. The young woman in the green dress across from me is whispering "nouvelle cuisine" to the old man who's sitting next to her. The old man has his hand up to his mouth. He's telling her, "I can't eat *that*!"

Nouvelle cuisine, my foot. Their caterer's gone on strike.

I need more champagne.

Cake, cake. I love the cake part. Riva has it up her nose and in between her breasts. Geoffrey-I wonder if anybody ever calls him Jeff?-has it in his hair and a wad of frosting is dangling from his fly.

I tell Evan I want a piece of cake the size of an elephant. He brings me one that the nouvelle cuisine chef must have cut. It's the size of a mouse turd.

I want more. I'm hungry, I want cake, *goddamnit*! I tell Evan, "This piece of cake is the size of a mouse turd."

I must have told him too loudly, because he's just said we're leaving as soon as Riva and Jeff, I have decided to call him Jeff, do. I want to catch the bouquet. I tell Evan, mistake number two, that I want to catch the bouquet. He points out to me, in case I've forgotten, that I'm already married.

I hadn't forgotten.

He goes on to remind me that that's how we met: a wedding, a friend of a friend. I caught the bouquet.

Some fat girl catches the bouquet. She must be all of fourteen and she has zits. What the hell does she want the bouquet for? But I bite my tongue. I'm learning. She's probably somebody's sister. Or a friend of a friend.

I just stand there, still, comatose, the way Evan likes me, while Great-Aunt Mildred, or whatever the hell her name is, chuckles around, handing everyone little baggies of bird seed. She forgot to do it earlier. Riva and poor old Jeff have to stand there like statues while we pummel them with a storm of thistle, millet, and cracked corn. The seeds hit the car behind them and sound like hail.

"Hail!" I yell, "Viva Riva!" It comes out before I can stop it. But it must have been OK. Now everybody is doing it.

"Hail!" they yell gaily, drunkenly.

"Viva Riva!" I yell again.

And before they drive off, I run to Riva and we throw our arms around each other and we kiss and I tell her to be happy.

"I hope you live happily ever after," I tell her. And we are both crying now.

I really mean that. I do. I do hope she lives happily ever after.

## XII

## ON INFIDELITY

It has been going on for over a month, in the city, it is not love, it is not even lust, but it felt like the right thing to do at the time, he tells me.

"An affair."

The instant the words are out of his mouth I am emptied. The rush leaves me hollow, deadpan; there is none of the all-too-likely shrieking or catapulting of flatware. Rather, I am suddenly aware that Evan, except for his narrower face and less perfect nose, looks almost exactly like Robert Redford.

I cannot get over the likeness.

Nor can I get over the fact that it took me this long to see it. Neither can I believe that this is what I'm actually thinking in the face of what Evan has just told me. I know I should be doing something else. Blaming. Fainting. Throwing. Certainly something else. But I cannot think of what it is I should do.

". . . I can't even blame her," he tells me. He looks down at his hands.

I have to ask: "Is it Anne?" I conjure up their faces from the wedding, their guilelessness. I reconstruct the currents of familiarity that shot between them. I feel their champagne under my own nose.

Evan looks at me blankly. He is wholly taken aback. "Anne who?"

So it isn't Anne.

I am relieved. Somehow if it had been Anne, that would have been worse. I am so relieved that I can afford to push it further, take the offensive. I attack.

"Anne who, my ass!"

Then I am condescending: "Schlimhammer, Evan. Who the

hell else would it be?" I talk to him as though he is retarded, as though he needs my help to explain.

Evan is incredulous. His mouth hangs open and, for the first time, those perfect teeth of his nearly drown in the deep pool of his mouth. "Schlimhammer?" His voice starts low and rises, a bird in flight. He understands his position in this conversation all to well, yet he is amused. "Why on earth Anne Schlimhammer?"

I have nothing else to say.

"Who else?" is all I can come up with.

His eyes light on his hands again. He is studying the creases in his knuckles. They fascinate him. "A woman in the pool," he says, meaning the typing pool on the floor above his office.

He does not bother to tell me her name, not how he set it up, where they went, whether she's married. It isn't the point. He feels guilty about her, too.

"I was punishing you, I think," he tells me. He has the eyes of a young boy. He is repentant. "It's silly, isn't it?" He is looking up at me because, so far, I have refused to sit down.

I nod "yes" and think: No, no of course it is not silly.

"What's her name?" I ask.

I think he doesn't hear me.

"What's her name?" I repeat.

He is shaking his head now. His blonde hair falls into his face; he has to swipe at it more than once to keep it from sticking like straws at his eyes. He needs a haircut. Now he is a waif. He has no intention of telling me her name. I know what he is thinking because I know Evan. He is thinking that in punishing me, he has punished her, this unnamed, invisible woman. He is right. It isn't fair, wasn't fair. It stinks.

"Are you going to continue to see her?"

I hear myself say "see her" rather than "sleep with her," "fuck her," "use her." And I am thinking of another, of Hope, and I am thinking that if Evan does not love this phantom woman, or some other woman, that I am lucky, I am in time. I am thinking that this was inevitable. I wished it. I am thinking of all the other things I have wished for, perhaps, and chosen not to see.

Evan looks up. The first sharpness of a growing impatience shrinks his face, wizens it. "I won't see her again. Of course not," he says. He is disgusted.

I finally sit down. I sit across from him, but immediately I see that this is not what he wants at all. When I raise my hand to touch his, he pulls away—I am too hot, too hot to touch, or too sharp, or too dangerous, or, maybe, and more likely, not dangerous enough. He does not want to be understood. He wants to be beaten for his crime.

"Could you have loved her?" I ask him. Not "do you" or "did you," but "could you have?"

"I don't even know her," he tells me. "Not really. It was the chase." He sighs; he shakes his head and I can see that the room and I have melted away for him. He is talking to himself now. "I was lonely," he says. He is confessing. Legitimizing. Qualifying. "I felt wicked," he says. "It was good."

"And it stopped being good?" My question startles him. I am sincere in wanting to know.

Evan does not answer me.

"Does she love you?" I ask. This is a new possibility. I wonder if he has thought about it.

"I don't know." His voice is flat. "I don't think so. I haven't thought about it."

"Well, has she said so? Does she tell you?" It seems such an elementary question now that I have asked it. His pitifulness, and my own impatience, make my bile swell and burst like a boil. "Well, what the hell were you thinking about then?" I shout at him. "What the fuck did you think you were doing? Plumbing the depths of your goddamn soul?"

The outburst sets Evan back only mildly. He has been waiting for it. He watches me, looking for a clue, a giveaway gesture now, but I am a stone wall. He keeps his hands on the table, and when he cannot decipher me, when he sees that I am through yelling but not giving anything else away, he pulls them in closer to his body. "I'm sorry," he says to his hands. "I'm sorry."

I stand. "Me, too," I tell him. I pull down on my sweatshirt, push up at the sleeves, and turn away from him. "Me fucking too."

*The room is littered with faces I know I'm supposed to recognize. They are the women she worked with, all who know me by name, who know me in context, with my dead mother laid out at the front of the strange room. They are women who, if they met me on the street, would, without a doubt, keep walking. There are these women, and there is one man, a man who visibly shoulders the weight of some enormous, some debilitating burden which he wears like a shawl across the breadth of his back. I cannot imagine who he is, the husband of one of the women, perhaps, a cripple, or a sick man, or just curious. I cannot recall having ever seen him before. But when he sits amidst the women, distinctly alone, when he bows his head but does not cry, does not speak or pray or look my way, the name comes: it is Herb. He is my mother's lover. His name itself is only a spark, but I am certain of it. I do not know why I know it; my mother would never have told me about him, never anything as personal, nothing so seedy for her daughter to know, a daughter too selfish, too crazy, too distant.*

*Yet I know his name.*

*He is a big man, big and broad, with short-clipped gray hair, hair that hugs his big, square skull. He is clean and awkward. His hands, which rest on the back of the bench in front of him, are large and veined, his fingers are tufted with light brown hair like patches of dry weed and I easily imagine those hands moving across the skin of my mother's arms, her back, down her side, and resting at her waist. In my mind, the two of them are dancing, dancing or making love, and they are content. And I am suddenly terribly sorry for the man who is left, this enormous man who carries such a loneliness.*

*He does not speak to me, nor does he sign the book after he has filed past. His head is bowed, he is invisible, and nearly gone.*

*It is impossible for me to let him go like that.*

*I follow him, catch him as he opens the door to an old green Chrysler—and then, for me, a whisper of possibility: have I seen this car before? This man? Are they at all familiar? I touch his arm.*

*When he turns to me he is frightened, older than I had imagined and frightened. He does not know what I will do or what I may say. He has only my mother's words for how I might act. He looks as though he will erode, crumble, and wash away in the California fog before I can stop him, before I can speak. His own eyes are wide, very wide, bugged from his face in expectation, riddled with red, and as I speak they fill like fountain bowls and spill.*

*"Herb," I say softly, "Herb, I am so sorry."*

*It is too much for him, the recognition. His chin falls to his chest and the sound that comes from him seems to emanate from every pore. It is a wail of pain that pours out from the bone, hushed by the flesh. He lowers himself to the edge of the Chrysler's seat, holds on to the wheel for support. He does not look up at me, does not make another sound.*

*I lay my hand on his shoulder. It looks small there, powerless. Then I turn.*

*I walk back to the door of the funeral home where women I do not love are gathered, watching me through the glass doors, watching between the stencilled letters and the streams of condensation, and wondering what I am up to.*

*When I come out again, the Chrysler is gone.*

It is not that I have not had lovers. It is that I have not had what I felt were illicit lovers. I am convinced that they must be different, they must be very different. Sweeter? Hotter? Too many people around me are dipping into that particular pot for it not to be different. I wonder what comes first—the seeking or the opportunity? Or perhaps the simple need for a secret? How bored do you have to be? How alone? Myriad combinations, myriad possibilities. Transmutations up the yang, and still I didn't see any of it. It is too much. First I isolate him, drive him to it, then, when he loses his pleasure in it, I beat him over the head with his failure. Yes, I am angry. At Evan. At myself. There is a tumult of jealousy, of responsibility. And no energy left for spite. But I do wonder: who is going to forgive whom in this one?

I just feel so foolish, being surprised.

It is no secret that I pick through reality, pick and sort as though reality were a mixture of beans and stones. No secret that I have treated Evan like a stone.

No, nobody plays it right all the time, and the names, the names are only important when they are all you have.

Evan and I do not eat dinner, nor do we speak much more. We sit on the sofa, both stunned and silent, and we look out the window until, in the dark, we are watching only our own reflections in the glass. It is in that glass that I can see that I am closest to Evan when we are falling apart.

The evening is longer than most when he is home. He brings me tea; I peel oranges and offer him half of each. And when we rise to go to bed, that other woman does not drop away from us as she should, as I want her to; her presence is as strong and as real as the acrid, sweet smell of the oranges, the oil and pulp that has clung to the undersides of my fingernails, to the flesh of my fingers. We are angry and awkward, and at the sound of Evan's bare feet on the wood floor, at the sound of his retching behind the bathroom door, I swear I can see her, though I do not know what she looks like. And I wonder if she loves him, if she has had time to love him, if she is waiting for him now, or if she is using him, too. And I wonder who else has made her feel that way: used, user. And I think that I am naive and that I have asked for this. And that she took me up on it.

I do not know her name, but she does not leave our bed all night.

## XIII

## BUS

Last night I watched the fog roll over the hill behind our house. It came in just the way it used to in California, moved in heavy-footed and round, a lion's paw of fog over the crest. All those years there, more than thirty years, a lifetime, more than a lifetime for some, and the fog booming over those foothills nearly every night in just that same way, and then I leave that fog and come east, a whole new place, a whole new time, a whole other sort of chance at doing it right. And I drag that old life with me like a dead cat in a sack.

I watched that fog, studied it. The recognition bred memories and stirred up a restlessness about the past and a sadness about the present. It made me think: I am not enjoying solitude. I am suffering isolation.

There is a difference.

I hand the driver my ticket and scan the length of the bus. In the darkness, it is like peering down the throat of Jonah's whale. Occasional reading lights dot the length along the windows; they give me just enough light, just enough so that I can see that the bus is more than half-empty.

I can sit by myself.

In the back, there is a corner, nearly bright from three working lights in a row. The seats there are vacant. While I wait for the driver to ring me in, I wonder what the secret is, what the other passengers know that I do not, why they have abandoned or rejected that particular quadrant of the bus. I decide that either the lights scared them off, made them think they could not drowse there, or fate is on my side. I accept the latter cheerfully, look no one in the eye, and turning slightly sideways, scuttle to the rear, claiming the deserted section for myself. I toss myself into the seat three from the back and squirm out of my jacket. I put it on the window seat beside me. I am settled for the duration. I pull the book I picked up at the station from my pocketbook, and I crack open the spine with satisfaction. It is not a scary book; I have decided on a love story. I have come this far.

The bus is idling and the man who boarded behind me has chosen the very front seat. He is joking with the driver. I am appalled.

The sign above the driver's head states clearly: Do not talk to the driver. It is a sign like Do not feed the monkeys; Do not fold, spindle, or mutilate; Do not pass go, do not collect two hundred dollars.

It never occurred to me choice was involved. My knowledge of myself is reinforced: I am literal of heart.

I sit back and admire the ease with which the man violates the simplest of commands. The driver himself makes sounds that indicate he is pleased with the exchange. Then the gears mesh and the men are silent.

The bus jerks forward and, as quickly as it staggers into motion, it stops again. A dull and persistent thud is coming from the front, a *thwump* like a flat tire. The door swooshes open again. A man, breathless and red-faced, steps up and in, brushing at the edge of his hand where it has gathered dust as a fist banging on the bus door. He nods to the driver who takes his ticket without a word. We are in motion again when this new man slides into the seat one up and across the aisle from me. He sits easily and then, as though he has forgotten something, stands back up; he removes his coat, folds it, and places it on the rack above his seat. He nods in my direction and smiles. His face is ordinary, but his plain gaze lasts just an instant too long. I dip my head and pretend to read my book. Then I forget about him, lost already in the aura of romance that issues like smoke from the first page of my paperback book.

I am already pleased with this voyage out. There is no one on the island who will miss me, no one in the city who knows I'm coming. I will surprise Evan with a call when I arrive. I will be there just in time for lunch, another surprise, an extravagant lunch, and then I'll spend the afternoon wandering my old haunts, getting reacquainted. I will buy coffee beans, thick beef, wine, brie, cheddar, and fruit. The staples. Then I will meet Evan at the apartment and spoil him with dinner, keep him home. I'll bring him flowers. I will stay the night.

Yes, I am already pleased with this junket of mine. Five hours on the bus, five hours and then I will gambol like an adolescent. I will enjoy the astonishment on Evan's face.

I will tell him outright: I missed you.

I am several pages into the love story when the sound begins.

At first, I am concerned that something has gone wrong with the bus and that we will be delayed and the day spoiled, but, as it continues, the source becomes more and more obvious. It is the sound of a rodent in a cage. It is forward and to my left. I pinpoint it.

Superb.

I am going to spend five hours on the bus listening to the man in front of me suck his teeth.

Traffic is botched in two places, both at the joining of roads where one highway gives in to another, so that it is past noon when we arrive at the terminal. Even at this hour the cops are rousting the indigents. The terminal smells of urine and weak coffee, sugar from donuts, and orange juice. There is a man, perhaps forty, lolling on the floor outside a shoe shop. Though it is only September, he is bound up tightly in what must be his winter coat, his only coat, but he wears no shoes or socks. His feet are as gray and as tough as the bark of oaks, and he howls, gibberish, as though he is speaking in tongues. But the cops have gotten to him and there will be no translation today. He will move along or he will be moved.

All the telephones are being used.

I wait in line, slip over to buy a Butterfinger at the magazine stand, slide back in at the end of the line. I'm hungry, but I can't get the wrapper off.

I want it frantically.

I am ready to stomp on it when I decide to go against all I've been taught: I tear at the wrapper with my teeth. Whatever happened to paper wrappers? This is some sort of plastic crap, no doubt carcinogenic—I can't even break into it with my teeth. I would like to resort to an axe, but I settle for the fingernail file I rummage from the bottom of my pocketbook. I puncture the wrapper twice, then again in the middle, and I squeeze the candy out like toothpaste from a tube. I bite in eagerly and dream of chocolate against my tongue.

But a dream is the only way I'll get it. There is something waxy and strange about the chocolate and, after the first crummy mouthful, I squeeze the rest back down into the wrapper, and stuff it in my pocket. I look up to find that a businessman in a charcoal gray suit is stepping away from the last phone and, miraculously, it is my turn. I assume his place.

Evan's line is busy and people are queuing up behind me now. Rather than give up my place, I pretend to talk. An artsy-looking woman in red and black is waiting, looking at her watch and tapping her alligator-shod foot on the tile. She is eyeing me, and I am almost certain that she knows what I'm up to, sure she saw me press the cradle down with the fingers of my free hand; she knows I am talking to no one at all. So I talk louder. I keep one eye on her and decide she looks like Olivia de Haviland. When she turns away, I lift my finger and I punch in the number of Evan's office again. This time it rings, but the secretary's voice is not familiar. I assume that I have missed the passing of the familiar Penny to some deserved administrative job and I am happy for her and sorry that she is gone at the same time. This new woman is nice enough, but mostly she is officious, and then long into the conversation she tells me that Evan is not in his office, that she is certain he has already gone to lunch. They have all already gone to lunch, she says. She has no idea where he is. She is sorry, she says again. I ask her to take a message: Meet me at Riminicci's when you get back.

I do not leave my name.

From the outside, where I stand, the restaurant looks busy, but not so busy as it might be. It is well past prime lunchtime. I decide I cannot live another minute without deviled seafood pasta salad and I fling myself inside the double doors with the brusqueness of a person who has never left the city. I am animated, independent, and only slightly self-conscious. I stand at the maître d's station and wait while he seats the young couple ahead of me. When he returns, he does not say, "My! Mrs. Dover! It has been a long time. We have missed you!" He also does not say, "Dore! Darling! Where have you been all these months? We were concerned." He does not say those things, though I know him to be quite capable of saying them. No, instead, he looks behind me and then directly at me as if to say, "Where is your other?" He says, "One, Madam, for lunch?" And I nod. His question is a reprimand, though you could never nail him on it, as though lunch is necessarily a duet, and it takes some of the city wind out of my countrified sails, but I walk behind him as though it is I who lead.

When I am seated with the first gimlet—gin, not vodka, straight up—I let my eyes wander the room. I do not need the menu. I know what I want. It has been a long, long time since I have been in the city, though not so long since I have been alone in a restaurant. I think that it is not so unusual now, for a woman to be alone. It is only that, here in the city, I am unaccustomed to it. The city is accustomed to it. I wear it a little awkwardly.

When the old, starched waiter takes my order, I watch him walk away. Just past his left shoulder in one of the dark corners, a man gestures familiarly, though not at me. His features are nearly hidden in shadow, but they are ridiculously familiar. The woman with the man is in the glow of the candle. She is petite, redheaded, and more self-conscious than I am. The two of them do not click for me, though I know I should know them. Their table is tucked in the corner behind the screen that separates them from the door to the kitchen. They sit close, but not too close; they talk as though no one else could possibly bear any import at all. They are obviously in love. She is chic if cautious; he is less than well-dressed, but easy and comfortable, an old slipper of a man.

The waiter brings my dish with a bored flourish. Pepper grinder. Salt. Thank you. I stab the first perfect pasta shell, and I know who it is.

The man in the corner with the woman is Finch.

Lord knows who the woman is, but now that I recognize Finch I see that the woman is much like Hope. No matter what her name is, I can see that she is Hope. I can't help but wonder if Finch sees it.

When I am finished, I contemplate Finch and the redhead. They are preparing to leave, and, though they must walk past my table to get out, Finch does not see me. His eyes are on the woman ahead of him. She, however, is aware of my staring and she has the good grace to be embarrassed by it. Unless I am mistaken, she walks more quickly past my table than he does and she waits outside the door for Finch while he retrieves their coats.

I suppose it is premature, but I like Finch's redhead. She is somewhat unsure of herself, tentative, but obsessed with Finch. I like the deference she shows. She does not take him for granted. I wonder how long it will be before we meet her. I vow, though, that I will not question Finch about her, not admit that I have seem them together, not corner him, not pin him down. Not ask how long they have been a "thing." It will be difficult. I will wait for him to tell me. I will.

I drink more wine and wait for Evan, but by three-thirty, he has still not arrived, so I make my move. I leave a message at the front station just in case, and I am off to gather our dinner, tipsy enough to shop for a meal for fourteen.

It is sixteen blocks to his father's apartment. I cannot resist: I walk it. I am imbued with energy from Finch's pleasure and from pasta. It has become my own. I stride like an Amazon, stride and smile, and the breeze that I make as I go pushes my light coat back around me, lifts my sweater at the edge, and lets the tiniest trickle of cold lick my stomach. I wish now that I had worn my jeans, my sneakers, my denim jacket. I was wrong to think that these were city clothes. I like the others better.

The building is unexceptional, like most city buildings, anonymous, his father's pied-à-terre, unusually humble for his sort of man, but I have always liked this apartment. It has none of Matthew Dover's style, none of his bluster. It is delightfully shabby and it makes me think of Alia, Evan's mother, though I am certain she never stepped foot here.

I feel like a spy, a burglar. I can't wait to see what state Evan leaves the apartment in.

I struggle up the three flights of stairs under the weight of two bulging grocery sacks and I pass the old doors in a row, lined up like peas on this pod of a wall. Someone has put a philodendron at the end of the hall. I wonder if it is Evan who has placed it there, but I doubt it. Someone who was tired of the naked hall, the dull beige of the slightly dirty walls, the slightly worn carpet.

The key slides into the lock and the door opens with ease, virtually inviting me in.

The apartment is tidy, but lived-in. Not immaculate, not radical in any way, shape, or form. The paint is buckled on the window sills. The drapes are stodgy and thick. It is, my best word, "mediocre" in all applications. It could be Evan's, it could be anyone's. There are no telltale clues, not a bit of excitement. It is almost a letdown, but it's a letdown I'm willing to live with at present.

I drop the bags onto the kitchen table and pull off my coat, let it fall onto the sofa along with my pocketbook. For no reason I can think of, I walk to the bedroom and look in. The bed is made loosely; the bedclothes fit like a baggy button-down shirt. The door to the bathroom is open and Evan's bathrobe lays across the lid of the toilet. He was in a hurry when he left.

The loud *thwack!* behind me is the bag with the tin of butterscotch toffee falling over. The round can hits the floor and rolls across the small kitchen to crash into the cupboard baseboard. I pick it up, open the can, unwrap and pop a piece into my mouth. I toss the crumpled wrapper in the sink, set the can on the drainboard. The candy is buttery and sweet. I close my eyes for a moment, almost against my will; then I begin to put the groceries away, odds and ends in the cupboards, those things I will use for supper divided between the refrigerator and the counter. I am at ease in this kitchen, though I do miss the expanse and freedom of the kitchen on the island. Here I have to keep my elbows close in at my sides while I scrub the potatoes.

There is no answer at the office. He must be on his way.

I straighten up around me as though it is company coming, as though it is my apartment, my near-clutter. I shuffle things here and there as though I am accomplishing something, but I am only killing time, waiting for Evan.

The potatoes are done. The salad is built and spectacular. It is on hold in the refrigerator. The steaks are aging on the sideboard.

I try the office again. I catch Penny. Penny! I thought you were gone, no *really* gone. . . .

Penny is just back from the gym, out of breath, on her way out the door again, she only came back because she forgot to lock her terminal. They go crazy when you don't lock your terminal, she tells me. I am pleased with the confidence, but, Penny, where on earth is Evan? Did you see him leave? Did he get my message? She doesn't know what I'm talking about. I called? Didn't the girl tell me Evan was gone? The meeting at the southern plant? Good Lord, she says, where is that woman's mind? "Temps," she says harshly, "temps don't give a damn because they don't have to come back." She is disgusted with their ephemeral nature, with this one's carelessness, though she is kind and sympathetic to me. Evan is due back tomorrow evening, she tells me; he'll be in the office the day after. Can she do anything for me? Am I OK? Do I need anything?

No. No, I am fine.

Well, then, if I am sure, she will go on. She's late already.

Yes, yes, do go. I am sorry I held you. I am sorry I held you, but I am awfully glad you are still there. Thanks, Penny. Thanks.

I do not explain.

On the street, the toffee tin protrudes from my pocketbook like a tumor.

The bus is crowded and as humid as an armpit. I follow the morning man's cue, and, before I sit, I take off my coat, roll it in a ball, and stash it in the overhead rack. I sit back in the seat and wriggle within the waistband of my skirt. My squirming disturbs the old man next to me. He snorts like a bull, a wet snort that makes me hope old age is not catching. I am tired, disappointed, my feet hurt, my calves throb, and I'm sweating this out because, for some reason, I have to. I could have stayed at the apartment. I could have surprised Evan tomorrow night. All but the salad and potatoes would have held. The salad, the potatoes, and my enthusiasm. He will wonder where it came from, the strange food in his kitchen, the wilted salad in his refrigerator. The note I left at his office will baffle him, drive him wild. He will never believe it was me, will never think it might have been. I will have to explain to him. It makes the basic premise of life clear: you gotta laugh. You really have to laugh. Now, I would like to just go home, to go home and to sleep, to rest this one out. I eat toffee and throw the papers on the floor.

The man five seats up has fallen asleep. It's amazing how limp they get when they're sleeping. He is falling out into the aisle; his head flops, loose on his neck with all the firm flexibility, all the tensile strength, of a dead fish. You'd think it would hurt. You'd think he'd wake up. He is interesting enough to watch until his coat from the rack overhead dangles its sleeve through the bars and wakes him. He swats at it as though it is an insect, but it is pendulous, persistent, and he wakes up finally with a perturbed snap. He is self-conscious and makes an enormous effort to look alert all the rest of the way to the island. It costs him dearly, his diligence. He holds his back straight as a board. Periodically his head drops forward and he jerks it back up so hard that I can nearly hear it crack.

He was better off asleep.

The sun is still tucked beneath the horizon and seems to have burnished the water from beneath. I am so glad to be home that my sighs are all that I can hear, and with my sighing, my tiredness, and the lighted water, I feel as though the long, disappointing day has not been wasted. I have had my adventure, learned this particular lesson. It is not lost time.

While I drive, I dig the candy bar out from my coat pocket, pick the lint off the top, and enjoy every bite. It will be a good story for Evan. We will both laugh at my impetuousness, my foolishness. We will laugh about the way things work out.

I pull up the drive, stop at the mailbox, and retrieve the few envelopes delivered today. Back in the car I drive slowly up to the house and stop in front of the porch. The wooden columns and platform are nearly the same color as the night amidst these trees. I gather myself up and drag my body and my belongings into the house with the most amazing mixture of relief and weariness. Inside I pour myself a glass of wine and throw myself onto the sofa. Still wrapped in my coat, I sift through the mail. The only thing of interest is an envelope addressed to me, handwritten, a hand that is not at all familiar. The postmark is unclear. I tear it open and go directly to the signature. It is from Geoffrey, Riva's husband. I am surprised enough that I set down my wine and go back to the beginning.

*Dear Dore,*

*I know you must be concerned . . . I want you to know . . .*

What he is telling me isn't possible.

I read through to the end, then read again. I read again and again, barely believing what I'm taking in.

*prognosis . . . good spirits . . . healthy . . .*
*well-being. Our love.*

*Geoffrey*

I am spinning.

Riva did not write because she did not want to worry me. I know Riva. The strength is coming back to her arm now, the prognosis is good. Geoffrey, no doubt, is making her nuts with coddling. Riva has never been much for sinking down. She is tough. She is ready to do what needs to be done. She does it. Geoffrey did not know; obviously, it never occurred to him that she had not told me. It never occurred to him that, perhaps, she did not want me to know or at least not know now, not yet. Riva must have told him otherwise. That is the only answer. No man would assume this much.

It has been a little over a month since the wedding.

Riva has lost a breast.

I lie in bed. My sheets are cold, and I bring my hands up and cup my own breasts, feel their weight, know their value to me, to Evan, recognize the vanity of it, of owning them, like a pair of matched valises or deerskin gloves. I try to imagine the severing, the separation, the not-having, the habits of being there broken by something as crude as a knife. It feels like a loss like all others, an indescribable absence, a sorrow, a not being the same. And though I lie here and cry in Riva's name, holding on to my own breasts, it is not for Riva that I cry at all. I cry for how fast the severing can take place, for how empty it can leave you. Riva lost a breast. I lost a child. I lost even myself for a while. Evan thought he lost a wife. Finch did. And I wonder if the fog has rolled in yet in California. The fog like an emptiness that cannot be tossed away from you at will.

The phone wakes me from a sound sleep.

Evan says he is sorry he is calling so late. The meeting went on and on, he tells me. He sounds tired. Even now he has not gotten back to his room. I can hear his boss in the background yelling, "Hi, Dore!" from his barstool. He is bellowing, "The old man would rather be home. He's a pain in the ass!" Evan is laughing and says, "It is true. I would rather be home. I would rather be there." It is cold where he is, and the meeting was boring. His boss is drunk. How was my day?

I laugh.

I laugh until the tears roll from my eyes because his voice is welcome, because he is with his boss, because his boss shouts to me as though I am one of the guys on this business night out. I tell Evan about Riva. I tell him about the letter from Geoffrey. I am shaken, but not desperately so; my voice is steady. I tell Evan that I guess the world is not set up for my convenience, not mine, not Riva's, not his. I tell him: I guess you gotta laugh.

I tell him about my bus ride, and about the woman in the alligator shoes, about the temp, the messages, the pasta salad, the gimlets, about Finch and his redhead. "She seems an awful lot like Hope," I tell him, believing that Finch has good sense, feeling that he has done the right thing. "Of course she does," Evan says to me. "She would have to." He is understanding, interested, and he is a kind man, I think. Kind. There is no note of blind indignation on his sister's behalf.

I tell him about the Butterfinger. He laughs. And I know we are meant for each other. He understands. About Riva. About candy. He says he is sorry he missed the steaks.

I don't tell him about the toffee.

I tell him I love him, I love him dearly. I tell him: I miss you, and hurry home, Evan. Hurry home.

## XIV

## SOLDIERS

Stick it out.

I suppose we have to.

We made our choices and we haven't fulfilled our obligation to those choices yet, not yet. We've discussed turning around, but decided we can't, not this early. It is early. It only seems like half of forever. Besides, maybe there is never any turning around. Early or late. Maybe there is only change, loss and gain, change. Recognition. And sometimes there may be understanding.

I told Evan: "I refrain from making any comment about sticking it out and having it cut off."

He said: "I don't think we have to worry."

For the last two weekends, lovely, short September weekends, Evan and I have made things right. We are comfortable. Hungry for each other, but not voracious, not mindless. We talk more now, we make plans, and, though they are plans only from one weekend to the next and maybe one more, we are thinking ahead, working together. It is like the merging of waters almost; we seem to lose ourselves, we become a we. Then Evan goes back to the city and I become an I and he, from my end of it, becomes a figment, then only a voice on the phone. All my good intentions drop like winter leaves. I get lonely. I get bored. I get angry. I don't do whatever the hell it is I'm supposed to do while I'm here. It is as though I am on ice until he comes home again.

We have talked about it, whether I should come to the city, whether we should both stay in the apartment, whether or not, as beautiful as it is, as peaceful as it might be, I should be here. Alone. Whether anyone in or out of his right mind should be alone like this. And we decide, yes. Yes, I should be here. We have not given it its full due; three months altogether, two on the absentee plan.

Lindhurst would love this. *Work it out,* he would say, as though I hadn't thought of that, and his eyes would roll around in that fat head of his, *Think about it and work it out. What do you think is right?*

But we are good soldiers, Evan and I. We prove ourselves again as we have proven ourselves over and over. We are keen on authority. We obey the rules, color inside the lines. We will stick it out until something better comes along.

I just hope to hell we can recognize it if it does.

In the afternoons I walk the beach. I am constantly surprised at the changing textures of the sand, at the number of faces the water has, expressions that radiate and spread right up to the beach edge. Sometimes I walk as far as the Point, but not often. Sometimes the other way, down to the old man's shack, never any farther in that direction than that. I try to walk barefoot. The sand is pumice. My feet are beginning not to look like my feet; the skin is soft and brown. They are firm, purposeful feet. I use them to massage Evan's back when he is home, I manipulate him with my toes, with my softened heels. I am proud of these feet. They are sand-walker feet, metamorphosed from the calloused, city-pasty blobs that moldered inside my sneakers when we first arrived.

Yesterday I walked back to the old man's shack. The long length of beach was dotted, only here and there, like clumps of spurious weeds, with small groups of people, one or two single figures holding their own. There was nothing going on. The bag I'd left at the door was gone. I turned around and walked the miles back without thinking of it again.

Today I will walk to the Point. I will watch the fishermen, talk someone out of some perch or scup. I am almost always successful. Sometimes I remember to take money, but almost never will they take it, not for the small ones that I beg. Fishermen are good men, the locals. The tourists would no more give me a fish than their paycheck. Nor would they sell them to me. They are not mean; they are on vacation and every fish counts for retelling. They do not get brownie points for handing fish over to strangers, and no one fishes for dollar bills.

The sand is like silk beneath my feet. My pants are rolled up to below the knee; my shirttails hang out and flop front and back like tongues of sweaty dogs. I am content. I can feel the difference, how light my arms feel, how easily they swing at my sides, how they balance my walk. I wear sunglasses against the sun which insists on smiling in my eyes, and my hair flies around my face in waves like a teenager's. It is a good day, I'm off to a good, if late, start. I overslept, but it was good sleep. I won't begrudge myself that. It is a day for walking. I bring a net bag for the fish.

I walk long by myself, passing the few beachcombers as though they are posts. The air is as sharp as salt in a cut, and it is warm, as warm as August, though it is late September, the end of the season. It is a clean feeling, an abrasive sensation. Fresher than anything else I can name.

When I have walked to where the land curves out, I spot an occasional fisherman, no one, though, that I would approach, until I see the young figure in white rolled pants and chambray shirt up ahead. He wears sunglasses and a straw hat. He moves easily and is not in the least self-conscious despite the fact that he looks as though he has been magically liberated from a page in *GQ*. He is carrying a bucket, and his feet are bare. He is making no effort to keep his clothes clean. The gritty bucket brushes against his pants leg as he walks. The blonde hair above his bare ankles sparks in the sun. If there are fish in that bucket, he's the one.

The fish are the color of old dimes and the bucket is full. He hasn't been fishing at all. He has wangled them from fishermen at the Point's end. He does it all the time.

I talk to him with one hand perched over the rim of my sunglasses to keep the sun out. My weight is shifted to one leg and that leg is firmly planted in the sand.

Then he says to me, "I know you."

It is not what I expected to hear.

He pauses. "Scampi, extra garlic, house wine. Right?" Despite his own dark glasses, I can tell he is looking me right in the eyes. "How are you?"

This close up, I can see the flag of blond hair hanging out beneath the brim of the hat. The forearms are familiar. He is the waiter from the restaurant across from Happlett's! I say nothing, though my silence and open mouth are dead giveaways. He's caught me at it again.

"Startled you again? You startle easily." He is smiling beneath the sunglasses, and he reaches up and takes them off with his free hand. "Lew," he reminds me. His hair falls free from the tops of the frames and his eyes are the color of the shallow water. He holds the bucket up for my perusal. "Hungry?"

"Not startled. Surprised," I say. "Dore." Then, "Yes." I extend my hand, but he laughs pleasantly at me and shrugs his shoulders helplessly, pointing out to me his sunglasses in one hand, the bucket in the other. His offer is natural and friendly. I am eager for the company and the fish. He spares me the "your place or mine."

"The restaurant is closed today. We'll sneak in the back door." He smiles like Evan at his best. "It's a beautiful day for clandestine activity," he adds, giving me a playful, sly look from the corner of his eye. He is holding the bucket up again, enticement.

I tell him, "Sure. You lead," and we turn away from the sun and head across the sand to the road.

When he asks me if my excursion was business or pleasure, I hold up the net bag and tell him I was out to mooch fish. I don't think he believes me.

The restaurant is empty and dark. Lew props the back door open with a heavy wooden mill and the fresh air streams in on the soft breeze from the alley behind. He extracts a bottle of cold white wine from the enormous walk-in refrigerator and we settle at the small table in the corner of the kitchen with two glasses and a basket of breadsticks. I drink the wine gratefully, while he cleans the fish, but I do not touch the breadsticks. I watch him work. The entrails come free with the heads. He is fast, accustomed to the action of the knife, to the feel of the fish.

"Panfish," he tells me, and hefts the biggest fry pan I've ever seen from a hook above the stove, "is an art." He wields the pan like a baton. "Watch this."

The work is fast and hot. He is totally absorbed.

The platter is on the table and the steam rises straight up. There must be three dozen crispy fish piled there. Lew says, "Think there's enough?"

I've already got my fork in one. "I don't know," I tell him seriously. I lift the center meat with the edge tine of my fork and the bones lift out whole. The flesh there is snow white and flakes like layers of paper. The skin crackles. "Sit," I say to him, but he's already down and pushing fish after fish onto his own plate. He drowns his in malt vinegar. "Aquatic creatures," he explains knowingly. "They need the liquid." I take the bottle from him and douse my own.

We concentrate on the fish, our heads down, forks active. The aromas of wine and vinegar blend beneath our noses. We are enveloped.

He gets the last fish, but I was too full anyway.

We walk to the end of the pier where the small café's coffee is strong, oily, and delicious. The dining room is fern-lined, and the lowering sun throws a rosy light on the brass railings. It is still crowded and we have to speak loudly to make ourselves heard. End-of-the-season tourists, a small throng of them wending down the narrow street, add to the din that swims around us.

Lew is all the things the magazines say the perfect companion should be: witty, casual but refined, interested, interesting. He chooses his words carefully though not laboriously. His conversation is easy, and he tells me about summers here, summers all his life. He has been everywhere, but he comes back here. From May through October, it is home. The rest of the year seems unimportant.

"Why don't you stay all year," I ask him, "if this is where you want to be?"

He tells me quite seriously, "It would ruin it." He runs his hand back through his fine hair and smiles. "I miss it when I'm gone. It's good for me. It works better that way."

I pretend I understand, but my curiosity is stronger than I am. "Have you ever spent a winter here since you've grown up?"

"I have come in winter, but I've left again." He laughs.

"The weather?"

"No. It's not the weather."

It is clear that either he does not know the answer or he is reluctant to yell it across the table in this café.

And he will drive me home.

His car is a vintage Volvo in tip-top shape. It is wonderful. From the back it looks like a pig's behind, but it is intense carmine red and the chrome is nearly white with shine. It hums down the highway as though it is hovering above the ground. The inside smells of leather.

"This car," I tell him as he makes the turn onto my road, "is a museum piece."

"It's just a car," he tells me, shrugging. "But it's cute, I like it."

He drops me off at the edge of our meadow and makes no motion at all of wanting to come further. I thank him for the fish and for the company, both were delicious and lent themselves to begging for more, but I do not tell him that. When I step from the car, I do not push the door hard enough and it half-closes. Before I can right it, Lew has pulled it shut from the inside, the car is humming again, and he is waving with one hand and steering with the other while the red Volvo glides backwards, away from my yard.

I do not walk in the tire tracks to the house. I walk in the taller grass adjacent to the worn car path. When I walk past the station wagon, which I've left blocking the porch stairs, I brush at its powdery, dull surface. Dirt and a thin ghost of paint come off on my fingers and I cannot believe I have let this vehicle fall into such dishabille. Instead of being exhausted from my walk, from the exhilaration of finding Lew, of enjoying him, I am stuffed full of energy.

I know it is getting late, but there is no stopping me.

In the house I gather bucket and sponges, soap, rags, and I pile them at the hood of the car. The hose is harder to find, but Evan has coiled it neatly at the side of the house and I drag it back across the field, the nozzle trailing behind me like the head of a snake. In my head I dissect the car, a fender, the bumper, the hood, a side panel, and I attach the hose at the faucet beneath the steps, fill the bucket so that the white foam spills from the top like the head on a beer, and I scrub each section, one at a time, scrubbing hard and rinsing the sponge and scrubbing again, and each time the bucket turns a dirty color like the paint, each time rusty reddish soapy water dribbles down my arm when I raise the sponge. I change the water. I rinse as I go, spraying the fender, the hood, and feeling the spray blow back on me, cold and fine, covering my length, my breadth. I see the light go dim around me, know the sun is setting. I kick off my wet shoes and throw them on the porch, let my naked feet sink into the mud I've created, and I brandish the sponge as though it is more than just a sponge, as though it were a spell in itself, like Moira what's-her-name in *The Red Shoes*.

The sun is down, the porch light is on, and I am rinsing the last quadrant, the final back fender and taillights, when the telephone rings. I am too close to being done, though, too near finishing the project I have begun, and even though I know it is Evan on the phone, I let it ring. It rings and rings, and when I finish the rinsing and that final section of the car is ready to be swabbed down with the rags, the phone is still ringing, and I begin again, move to the head of the car and rinse my way to the back. The telephone stops making its racket when I am to the driver's side door, rinsing what I have already rinsed, and I know that Evan will be concerned that he cannot reach me, and I know he will call again later, worried that I have done . . . what? What could he think I have done? Will he think I have been murdered in my bed? Robbed? Beaten? Will he worry that I am stranded on the side of some highway, out of gas? flat-tired? I choose not to imagine the worst thing that Evan could think of. I am wiping down the car, and the dull red paint is coming off on the rags, rag after rag of grainy red paint, and he cannot imagine where I am.

I will rise early in the morning, before the sun gets too hot, and I will wax the car, polish it and watch more and more paint come off, and watch more and more of what's left of the finish come through. When I am done the car will have regained at least some of its external shine, its original integrity, and I will recognize the change, the alteration more, much more than anyone else, Evan or anyone, will, because I have experienced the process, seen the small, slow change, done the elbow work, and all that is OK. It feels good.

When the phone rings again, I am in the kitchen washing the soap film and grit from my hands. I pick up the phone from the wall, tuck it between my ear and my shoulder, and wipe my hands on the dish towel while I say my hellos.

"I called earlier. You weren't home. Is everything all right?" Evan's voice is calculated and calm.

"I must have been outside," I tell him.

"Dore, it was dark by then. What on earth were you doing outside?" He is not chastising me. He is merely flabbergasted.

"Washing the car."

"Washing the car? In the dark?" I can tell he believes me.

"Washing the car. Probably wiping it down by then. I had the light on. I must not have heard the phone. The car looks good, Evan. I did a good job."

Evan does not really know what to say. I can feel his thoughts casting about for something firm and safe to hold on to.

I go on without him. "I'm going to wax it tomorrow, early, before the sun gets too hot." I am certain he will like this, that I know enough not to wax the car in the hot sun, that I am planning ahead, that I have direction, and that one day's living carries on into the next, continuity, no fragmentation, no mindless obsession, no nameless halting.

"Good, Dore. Good." He is sincerely glad I have moved into the explainable. It would be senseless, useless to try to make his understanding clearer.

And the conversation lapses into the predictable.

When it is time to go to bed, and I am undressed and swaddled in my bedclothes, I cannot go to sleep. My mind races with the things that I should do, the places I will go. I try in my mind to picture the wax can, to remember where I last saw it on the shelves of Evan's shed. I am much too caught up to sleep, much too driven, too wound up, too speedy.

I throw myself onto the floor at the foot of my bed, and I do leg lifts, properly, and I count: one, two, three, then double time, four-five-six, and I stare up and out the window at the pines, the garbled grove against the night sky. I count my leg lifts silently and listen to the owl. His voice is as resonant as a loon's and it carries like stark light on the night air. As it envelops me, lifts me to hover with it somewhere above the ground, I realize that, though I have heard him a thousand times before, I have never really taken the time to listen.

## XV

## THE OLD HOME

This time he knows I am coming.

I am rolling by nine in the morning, and the drive back up the neck of the island is barely the start of it. The car still sports a suspicion of shine from the workout I gave it two weeks ago. Salt and sand and wind are hard on a finish, but it still seems to crow a bit with the attention. I've been feeling the same myself lately, less dusty, more visible. I have been rising earlier, walking more briskly, been more steadfast in my leg lifts. I have not eaten a single spoonful of chocolate-chocolate chip. I can feel the difference in my thighs.

I gas the car up on the mainland and go for the big prize: I am driving to the city to spend two nights with Evan. Thursday afternoon, I will meet Riva for lunch; Friday night, Evan and I will drive back to the island together for the weekend.

I am anxious to see Riva. I will meet her at the store, take her to lunch, see for myself that she is well, that she has survived, more or less intact, the accident of fate that has taken her breast. I need to see her to know. Her voice on the telephone was no different. She was embarrassed because of what she called Geoffrey's "goodwill gaffe" of a letter. She would have told me herself. Soon. She did not want me to worry about what I could not affect one way or the other. "It is one more near miss," she said on the phone. "We have so many near misses. Some we don't even recognize." Of course, she was right.

The grayness of the roads off the island is more than a little overwhelming. It is so easy to forget what it is like on the outside. I stop for lunch though I am just tired of driving, not really hungry. Over the usual weak coffee and a grilled tuna on rye, I am still pondering the things that work on us from the outside, the exterior situations that rob us of control. I think of the crazed cells in Riva's breast, of

Hope's invisible decision to leave Finch. I think about my own life. I am thinking of how we manipulate ourselves in such strange, strong ways. And I can imagine Lindhurst, I can imagine how this whole thing would be if I were wacky enough, or desperate enough, to take it to him:

*"When I went to the East Coast," I would tell him, "it was all so clean."*

*He would push me, of course. "The city?" he would ask. "The city was clean?"*

*"God, no. My life. There was only Riva. The rest didn't know me from Adam."*

*"Or Eve," Lindhurst would say.*

*Jesus Christ. His type of joke.*

*"Right. Or Eve." I would humor the bastard.*

*"What was it they didn't know, Dore, the people on the East Coast?"*

*"About Peter. About Lise. The whole thing."*

*"What about Lise?"*

*Always Lise.*

*"That she was dead. That she had existed. How she died." He would know all this. He is an asshole.*

*"How do you think Lise died, Dore?"*

*"You know damn well how she died." The man is a sadist son-of-a-bitch.*

*"Could it have been an accident?" he would say. "Have you ever thought about the meaning of 'accident'?"*

Lindhurst, in all his vainglorious reality, has said this more than once, his virtually omnipresent "Could it have been an accident?" Now, it's crept into my hypothetical interview. He has left his mark, the shit.

*I would tell him, "I was the agent. I was driving the car."*

*He would lean back in that chair of his and he would clasp those hateful fingers and exhale thoughtfully. "Do me a favor," he would say, has said more than once. "Think about 'accident.' Look it up in a dictionary, Dore. Mull it over until next week. Then let's talk about the implications."*

*He would wait for me to respond, but I wouldn't give him the pleasure. There are some times when Lindhurst asks too much.*

There are people in the windows of the house.

I don't know why this surprises me, except that I just didn't expect it. I pictured the old house empty.

The filmy curtains we left at the top windows have been replaced by heavier, thicker drapes. They are drawn open now, though, bunched gracefully to the corners of the living room, held, I would imagine, with loops of fabric to the side. The people who live behind these windows are not so visible as we were here, and it is clear I will see only what they will allow me to see.

The woman in the red dress who stands at the outside corner of the room where my ficus stood has close-cropped blonde, blonde hair. She is still, and seems to be staring towards the back of the house. Her arms are straight at her sides, and her shoulders are very, very broad for a woman's. A man with dark hair comes and goes in front of the window, he is there and then he is not. He is working at something, but I cannot tell what. The blonde woman pays little attention to him, however. She moves occasionally to accommodate his bulk, but she is constant in her attention to the back of the room.

I feel dissociated from my own house.

But it is not the house that has changed. The physical, squatting animal of the house is the same. Though the bricks do not seep today, they are the same bricks; though the windows do not shine as they did the day we left, they are the same windows. It is the soul of the house that has changed. The ghosts are gone, nothing is familiar. Recognizable, but not familiar. These people have brought their own ghosts and they are invisible. I do not know them.

I throw the car in gear. Evan will be home from work in less than an hour. I want to be there when he comes in.

Evan has caught one of those terrible late summer colds. I am going to get it and I don't even care. I suck playfully on his lip when he kisses me hello; in turn, he pretends to dance me across the apartment floor, snuffling as we go. He stops for a moment, wipes his nose on the back of his hand, and then gallantly dips me in the most eloquent of exaggerated dips, but has to haul me back up quickly and dash into the bedroom for a tissue because his nose is running again. He is the very picture of a miserable human being. He says to me, "My body is betraying me. I had bigger plans than blowing my nose." He is funny with his red, chafed honker of a nose and those swimmingly watery eyes. It is obvious he feels like hell. He is the color of concrete.

I feed him a can of chicken rice soup which he eats eagerly in front of the TV, pushing the rice to the side with his spoon and scooping up as much unadulterated broth as he is able. He is asleep on the sofa before eight o'clock. I wake him and put him to bed.

I pour myself a glass of wine and scan his father's bookshelves. I discover a field guide for birds near the top of a shelf that has not been disturbed or dusted for, perhaps, years. I am certain the book has never been cracked open. I wipe it off and flip through its pages. It is exactly what I want. I turn on the light over the sofa and I find out that the big oily black bird back home, the one with the yellow eyes, was a grackle—a grackle! I was going to be ready for grackles! This one snuck up on me. I discover, too, that I have house sparrows and titmice by the barrelsful. I find that mourning doves have tails shaped like spades. I spend hours on the sofa with the birds and am not in the least unhappy.

Riva's boutique is not the sort of place I would ever think to shop in. It is small, exact, and selective, like Riva herself. Today it is awash with customers. Three salesgirls and Riva herself are bustling, and the voices of this gathering of women are buzzy and constant like the drone of a factory. I see Riva, though, long before I can pick out her dry, low voice from the others. She is wiry and strong, looks almost exactly the same, in fact, and I cannot tell which breast has been taken from her. The only difference I can make out is in Riva's face. The skin around her eyes, I think, seems softer than before, less papery, more supple, and for some strange reason this makes her look, if not wiser, even older.

I stand by the two white loveseats in the center of the floor, waiting for the opportunity to catch Riva's eye. I watch her dash up the mirrored stairway ahead of a well-heeled young woman in a cashmere sweater, but Riva is ahead of me, too, as is nearly always the case. The sound of her familiar voice falls on me from the balcony overhead, "Five minutes, Dore! I made reservations. . ." and the voice is off, taking care of business.

"I am thirty-seven years old," Riva tells me as though it is news, "and I think I'm getting the hang of it."

She is talking about life in general. I tell her overstuffed flounder, "I thought you always had the hang of it," but I am wary. I am beginning to see things differently now, beginning to see more of this life in general, and I am not so certain any more about what I think I know.

Of course, we drink too much wine.

"Geoffrey is a bonus," she tells me. "It was hard getting used to his taking up so much room, but, like I said, I'm figuring it out. It's a sort of trade you make for the company."

This close, I can see that it is the left breast that has been removed. Though her breasts were always very small, up close there is a visible loss. She will be fitted with a prosthetic bra. "But there is so much else to do," she tells me, and, though I know that Riva has never been vain, I wonder, though I do not come right out and ask, why she would wear her loss so openly. She tells me anyway. "I could tape a Kleenex there and get the same effect. It hardly seems worth the bother." She spoons up her mousse mindlessly and tells me that married life suits her. "It is so convenient," she says. I wonder what she is comparing it to.

I am mid-cheesecake and Riva is just dipping into her raspberries when she tells me that she has seen Hope and met the man she lives with. "Michael," Riva says. "Michael, call him Mike," she mimics his voice not altogether pleasantly. "I don't know if I like him."

I am amazed. It never occurred to me he might not be likable. I think of Finch and his redhead, the woman I liked immediately, yet have never met. I thought, if I thought of it at all, that it would be like that. Immediate. Organic. I wash the cheesecake off my teeth with coffee, and I tell her, "It doesn't matter, I guess, whether we do or don't. What's he like?"

Riva describes a man very much like Matthew Dover. "Younger," she says, "but yecch." Her voice tells me that, at this point, she is either much more certain that she doesn't like him or that last glass of wine put her over the edge. "Hope seems very taken with him, in a mature sort of way," she says.

"You think she's made a mistake," I say to her.

She shrugs. "I like Finch," she replies. She looks at me.

"I like Finch, too." I don't tell her about the redhead just now, though undoubtedly I will later. She may have, in fact, already gotten the scoop from Hope, assuming Hope knows. I will try to call Hope tonight. I tell Riva and get one of her looks.

"Don't call her this week," she says. "She's in San Francisco at some convention. "Mike—" she draws the short name out of her throat like taffy—"went with her."

Aha.

I consider telling Riva about Evan's affair with the nameless woman from the typing pool, but I don't. It would ruin the day. And change nothing else. Later. I'll tell her later when the damage is more fully repaired. If it becomes more fully repaired. When distance is my friend.

We flip for the lunch bill. Riva tosses wildly, misses the quarter on its trajectory downward. It strikes the handle of her fork with a clang, bounds to the intertwining roses of the carpeting, and rolls silently, invisibly across the restaurant floor. We split the tab.

Beneath the brown canvas canopy that protects the doorway to Riva's shop, I hug her and she hugs me back. "Give Jeff a kiss for me," I tell her. "And one to Evan," she counters. "Keep me posted," are the last words that are exchanged, and Riva is scooped up by her salesgirls with God-knows-what-dilemmas when she is barely inside the door.

I take a taxi to the apartment and puzzle over the bird guide for the forty-five minutes it takes Evan to get home. I decide that the gulls on the island are primarily herring gulls, and the naming of these ubiquitous birds gives me enough of a giddy sort of pleasure that, when Evan arrives, mildly recuperated from his cold, I allow him to sweep me out the door for a dinner at Riminicci's. We see no one at all that we know and dinner is a pleasant anonymous hour. We eat no dessert and we walk to the movies. From eight to ten we think of nothing but eating buttered popcorn and escaping the bad guys.

Evan surprises me Friday morning by not going to work. He calls in sick from the living room phone, pleading relapse of his nasty cold. I pretend to be sleeping when he comes in with a tray of steaming coffee, fresh bagels, and juice. "Surprise," he says to me.

We eat breakfast in bed. We make love in the shower and dry each other on his father's thick cotton towels. We dress quickly and walk the six blocks to the enormous, outrageously expensive Italian deli.

We shop together for the entire weekend: pasta salad, seafood salad, Greek olives, peppers, provolone, salami, fresh crusty bread, rye, pastrami, prosciutto, ripe melons, crisp apples, chicken cacciatore, meatballs the size of a child's fist, and slices of veal, all in little containers that I will guard with my life the long way back to the island.

The island is cooling off.

We turn up the thermostat and build a small fire. I have not gathered wood from the property for kindling as I thought I would, so it is touch and go for some time, but then, finally, it is go, and we put the city bounty away to the crackle of the fire in the next room. It is the material of honeymoons and we give ourselves to it fully. Before dinner, we make love again, quickly, heatedly. We worry about nothing at all. The only brow that is furrowed this evening is the brow between my thighs, and the only wagging tongue that is evident is the sweet arched tongue that passes like a phantom at that brow. It is the warmth of Evan clamped over me, fitting, hot and tight, that makes me know how I love him, when it is easy, after all this time. We come quickly and violently, together.

We drag ourselves up about nine to eat a much smaller, less hedonistic meal than we had imagined, and we go upstairs early. Because we have turned the heat up so high, because, despite my laziness in the kindling department, the fire has caught so well, upstairs is overwhelmingly warm. I go back down and adjust the heat, check the fire for the last time. When I walk back up the stairs and enter our bedroom, I see that Evan has already fallen asleep.

He is naked, has slipped off to sleep atop the fully made bed, waiting for me. He is the picture of trust, unprotected, unwary. His face is soft in sleep, and his chest rolls upward like a wave with each slow breath; at its crest the thick blonde hair like foam catches the light. I study him: the real flatness begins at his belly and continues down, past his nest of pubic hair, past the now pale and flaccid penis lying off to its own right, past his balls. His thighs are thin and strong, his calves are narrow, and the ridge of shin bone down the center lifts the silky hairs. He is entirely exposed. Yet, for the first time in a long while, there is no vulnerability on either part, none as there would be were he openly giving himself over to me. He is asleep. He has been sick. Men sleep. It is their nature.

## XVI

## CRABS

I do not even have to go looking for him. He comes to me.

I am balanced precariously on the top ladder step, mounting the bird feeder in the October remnant of the oak when the spit-shined Volvo pulls into the driveway. I watch the car prowl animal-like while the driver quickly takes in the yard. He parks the car nose-to-tail to the station wagon and walks around to the steps. He is oblivious. He walks like a man in a hurry. Evidently, I am invisible in my tree.

I have the strategic advantage. I use it.

"Boo!" I have to grab at the branch over my head to keep from falling off the ladder in my enthusiasm.

Lew's surprise settles visibly in his feet. At the sound of my voice they betray him and he nearly takes a tumble from that third step. He is pink to the throat and looking around to see where I've come from.

From my gingerbread bower, I give my best witch cackle. "Scare you, little boy?" My head is still in the branches, but finally he turns my way and spots the ladder under the tree. I watch his gaze follow the rungs up to my legs and I am found.

"You would not believe what I have," he says smiling and walking to the ladder where he holds the base while I am descending, laughing, wiping my sweaty, seedy hands on the seat of my jeans.

"You have . . . a broken leg," I say, stepping onto the brown grass beside him.

I am glad to see him, ready to play. I bombard him with guesses.

"No," he says, dead serious.

"You have . . . chicken pox? . . . Frostbite?"—he is shaking his funny blonde head—". . . sleeping sickness? Grass stains?" I'm getting into the jazz of it, "A load of laundry? Apple cores? Thumb tacks? Big Macs? Income tax? A duck that quacks? Thirty whacks?"

He cuts me off. "Crabs," he says. "I have a bucket of crabs." He is obviously pleased with himself. He shoves his hands into the pockets of his jeans and nods his head so convincingly I almost believe I've contradicted him in some way.

"In that case," I tell him, "I'm glad you've come." I reach up and give him a friendly peck on the cheek. "I've just been waiting around for a man with a bucket of crabs," I say and we move, as though it were planned that way, towards the house.

"Do you know what today is?" he asks me while we clear away the last of the soft, shattered shells from the old table. He picks up his bottle of beer, sucks out the last drop with a "pop!" and raises the mouth of the green bottle to his right eye. He is humming "Popeye the Sailor Man." It is not a clue to the question he has posed; it is pure silliness. He pretends to hoist up his jeans, he juts out his strong smooth chin, and then wraps his face into a crooked smile. I wait for him to break into a salty jig with those tricky feet of his, but they remain planted firmly on my kitchen floor.

I wind the crab discards tightly in newspaper and throw them, with the four empty beer bottles, in the bin beneath the sink. "What is today?" I repeat. "Tuesday," I tell him. "And Tuesday is Red's Tamales Day." It's a recollection that surprises me because it comes out of nowhere.

Lew looks at me as though I have lost my mind.

"Red's Tamales." I say it again for him. He must not have heard me right. "Tuesday is Red's Tamales Day."

"Maybe the crab was bad." He draws his voice out dramatically—it is Dr. Lew's stab at a diagnosis. He circles his finger around at the side of his head. His eyes are wide, oggly-looking. "I zink," he says to me, "zee voman she is ba-na-nas."

Cute. "Bananas" in three words.

"No comprende Red's Tamales?" I ask him.

"Non compos mentis." His smirk is rich. When he was a child, he must have been a real stinker.

I grew up on Red's Tamales. I know what I'm talking about.

"Tuesday is Red's Tamales Day," I say again. "It was an ad campaign. For years. Frozen. You boiled them in paper. Thick squishy cornmeal outside, squishy red tamale stuff in the middle. You could get them at the drive-in movies, too." I look him in the eye so that he will see that I am speaking with conviction. "They were great." I flash him my best TV commercial smile so he will see how good they were.

He counters my move. "Wednesday," he tells me flatly, piously, "is Prince Spaghetti Day."

That stymies me. I've never heard of that. I regroup. "What's today?" I ask.

"My birthday." He is pleased with himself again. He's enjoying this.

I am caught off guard—surprised, I think, by the intimacy of the revelation. The rest has been anticipation and horseplay. This is personal. Suddenly, I feel I've been caught quite empty-handed.

"Well, Happy Birthday!" I say to him.

"I want to celebrate," he says. "Let's go out to dinner."

I am still licking crab juice from my fingers, wiping it off my elbows. "You must have missed it," I tell him, wagging my head. "We just ate."

"Lunch. We ate lunch. It'll take us until dinner to get there."

"Where?" I ask.

"Wherever we decide to go." He is serious.

"Maybe the crab was bad," I tell him, and start to roll my finger around at my temple. Then I stop. "Do you have a fever?" I ask. I move towards him, hand lifted as though I will check his brow myself.

His own hand shoots up to "HALT!" position in response, then comes down. "I think I do," he says, and puts his palm to his forehead. Suddenly he looks very concerned. "I'm hot as a tamale," he says, breaking into a grin. "Let's go."

I must hesitate, because his face clouds slightly and he asks, "Is your dance card already filled?"

"Of course not," I tell him. I grab two more beers from the fridge and hand him one. "I didn't even know I was going to the ball."

We toss around the idea of driving to the mainland for dinner, but we are plainly half-hearted and riddled with indifference—it is no secret that the meal per se is not what we are after. We opt out.

We go to the beach instead.

Our inside arms are wound around each other's waist, we've each got a half-full beer bottle in our outside hand, and we walk tandem-style, exaggerated, left foot out, right foot out, like the Three Stooges, across the dry meadow. We are smooth, as though we have practiced for a long time. When we come to the grove of trees, we have to let go and walk single file. I go first. We move forward like that over the path through the grove.

We come out on a beach that is so deserted that I would bet a half gallon of chocolate-chocolate chip we could run stark naked across the low dunes and be absolutely unobserved. It is too chilly to drop our shoes on the sand, too damn cold even to go barefoot. It is a weekday, past the end of the season, and the wind is up. The salt on the air is strong and dry and it mixes with the bitter taste of beer on our lips.

In the open, the two of us are struck momentarily shy. We stare at the rough water from our separate footings as though there is something promising on the horizon. We tip back the beer bottles and drink—less because we are thirsty than because we need to fill those moments. I take the initiative: I motion to Lew to go left, away from the Point, out in the direction of the old man's shack. I lead the way.

We walk down closer to the edge of the water. Our footprints are swallowed up almost immediately in the dry sand. Lew does not reach for my hand as we make our way down the beach, and, secretly, I am disappointed. I would like to be twenty and in love in this place.

This afternoon, the beach is desert sand, I think, more than sea sand or bay sand. It is sand in enormous quantity, gray-white sand, bristling with intensity, with potential, and with treasure. Today it is a vast, improbable sea of sand, broader and more boundless than any desert I can name. I think: if we never faced the water, what would we use to anchor ourselves, to compass ourselves, to find our way back to where we began? It is so much the same. There is so much of it.

I turn and look back at where we have come from, but it is

impossible not to see or hear the water.

Lew talks to me about the grasses that catch the wind along the periphery. He tells me names: salt wort, dusty miller, sea blite. He points out the tatters of dry weed, the dessicated berries and tufts that take the brunt of the wind. He tells me how the color of the water depends on the light, the tide, the depth, and the activity of the water itself. His voice is muted by the wind.

He tells me that the gulls that bleat overhead are scavengers—voracious, smart, and fast. Then he laughs, more to himself than out loud. He says how one winter he watched grebes in a creek, watched them for days as the ice closed in on them and they did not move. I nod vigorously, glad that I can join in now too, because, yes, I have heard of swans, enormous, stupid swans who were caught in the ice. And we just keep walking. I watch his face, his strong throat, as he talks.

We pass the spot where I ran into the band of teenagers and their midday conflagration, the place I flew to believing that the old man's shack was on fire. Not even a trace of that enormous burning is visible. No debris, no clue, as though the beach has been washed clean.

We continue down to where the old man's shack is plainly visible. We sit among the stout rocks, Lew down on the sand, his back propped against the stone pillow, me perched on top of the largest rock of all, my legs dangling to Lew's left side. The empty beer bottles are anchored upright in the sand. He lets the sand play through his hands; I stare out. The forever shack is unchanged.

"What do you know about the old man?" I ask Lew, pointing my chin out towards the tiny spit.

"I haven't seen him in years," he tells me, surprised.

I am taken aback as though the wind has forced itself down my throat. "You mean you know him?"

"A long time ago," Lew tells me, looking up, and then out at the shack. "When I was a kid. Is he still alive?"

"You really knew him?" I am incredulous. This information brings about the same sensation my trek out to the little house did, when it became real, physical, no longer a figment at all.

It is Lew's turn to be amazed. "Why is that so surprising?"

"I didn't know he was real," I say.

He glances up at me again, though this time it is as though I have said something amusing. “He’s real. Or was, at least.” Lew looks over at me and I believe he is going to tell me a secret. “We used to bring him cigarettes,” he says. “Then he’d let us hang around.” Lew remembers the old man fondly, I can hear it in his voice. It is obvious, too, that he hasn’t thought of him for a long, long time.

“And . . . ?” I want to hear more.

“And what?” Lew shrugs, at a loss for words. “And that was it: we brought him stuff and he let us hang around.” He looks up at me over his shoulder again and smiles as though that’s the end of it. He cannot imagine what sort of information I am mining for.

Son-of-a-gun. The old man is real.

We sit for some time at those rocks, Lew and I, each in our own little bubble of a thought-world, and we are as silent as the sand around us.

Dinner four towns up the island is a classy affair, damask, silver, a lobster Newburg rich as Croesus. And this time around, I am not shy about dessert.

The restaurant clientele is split down the middle: half, dressed to the nines; half, our half, in beach clothes, sandy and windblown. The clatter of crystal and silver is a breezy backdrop and conversation provides a pleasant hum to go with the buzz afforded by Lew’s pick from the wine list. Over brandy, we decide that nothing will do but cappuccino from the tip of the island.

We ride with the windows rolled up, the heater on, and, because of the late season hangers-on, we have to park about a half-mile from the café. It’s a brisk trot along the main street to the brass door, and our full-bellied semi-comas dissipate and are carried off in the process by the stark wind. By the time we sit down, we crave the warmth as much as the company and the cappuccino. We drink more than is reasonable, cappuccino after cappuccino. When our tongues dull to that, we take a vote and switch to Irish coffee. We talk about everything in the world, all that fertile topsoil people scratch when they are new, surface stuff, the easy stuff, the interesting and noncommittal trivia, the vague good-impression-making altruistic philosophies. We drink and drink in the hope that the evening will go on. Finally, when the café population thins and the waiters are slow enough to be bored, and when we can find no reason, no reason at all, to take up space there any longer, we walk slowly back to the car and head home.

Lew seems no worse for the drinking. The only clue he gives is his sweaty palms—one at a time he keeps dragging them across the thighs of his jeans. I, on the other hand, am drunk enough to beat the band, there's little doubt about that, and, when the Volvo thrums up to the front steps and slows to a stop, I am glad and I am sorry, and I am excited, and weary, and thankful. I am virtually struck dumb and my eyes, when I can control them, are cast down in my lap. I do not want to make mistakes. I do not know what is right or what is best, though I do recognize that there could be oceans and oceans of difference between the two.

I do know it is very late, and that the moon is as white as the skin of a red-headed child, and that I would really like to sleep on those thoughts that roll in my head like surf.

I know that I need time and sleep and at the same time I seriously doubt I will ever sleep again.

Lew waits until I get inside. I flick the porch light on and off. He starts up the car, and I watch from the window while he backs up the long path to the road. When his tires move from the unpaved to the paved, he sticks his arm out the window and waves. I can see it dark against the moonlight.

I pour myself a Bailey's to sleep on before I remember that my tongue has probably died. I set the glass on the table by the wingchair, intending to abandon it, but I must be sipping it because it disappears while I name my thoughts: I am confused, delighted, thankful for Lew's passivity, and, amusingly enough, more than a little hurt by it. I had cultured fantasies of passion. I pictured candlelight and lust. I imagined being carried off, overcome, thankfully ravished—all of it out of my control, all of it as innocent as milk. One fairy tale. And another: I am bereft of inhibition in this daydream, barefoot. The sun is warm on my brown arms. The taste of the sea lingers, spreads like a spice across my tongue. My mind is bright with light, slow motion, time-lapse special effects. I meet my lover on the beach at sunset. The colors that envelop us are as opaque and as varied as enamels; there is no evening wind. I take his hand and lead him behind the wheat brown dune grasses, over the pinked sand that would be our privacy. And I am not self-conscious. He is fluid. The light is our cushion. I ask him: Would you like to touch me . . . here?

and here? And he would and he does, and it is a faceless, fingerprint-less moment.

It is hard to reconcile that radical whelp of expectation with the reality of Lew.

He enjoyed today, it is clear.

In another month, less than that, he will be gone, leave the island until next May. We have made plans to have dinner again in two weeks, far, far in the future because for these next fourteen days he will be gone, staying with friends, spreading himself around.

I have to think about what I will do.

On Thursday, Evan calls earlier than usual. He wants to know if I really believe that no two snowflakes are exactly alike and do I prefer the fennel left out of the bouquet garni because he's going to shop for Saturday's ragout on his way home from the city Friday.

"The time has come," he says to me, "for you to make a decision." He is mock-adamant, in the finest of moods. "Fennel or no fennel? Decide," he says.

I can see, even over the phone, the small creases at the corners of his eyes draw together, his smile is that audible. "No fennel," I tell him. I am firm.

"Eight," he says to me. "Dinner will be at eight sharp Saturday night. Will you be ready?"

"I'll be here."

I replace the receiver gently, as though it has skin, sensation, and I pull my hand away from it reluctantly.

There must be something in the air.

I have just made a date with my husband.

With a sharp knife, I poke holes in the crust of a frozen chicken pot pie and stick it in the oven. While it is cooking, I tackle the back porch.

I am determined, at last, to rid myself of the dead houseplants that I stoutheartedly refuse to feel guilty about. I gather up big green garbage bags and dump in dirt and plant alike, setting the pots aside for Evan. The pothos, the philodendrons, the spiders are no problem. The soil has dried out, shrunken. Dirt and foliage tumble from these pots with no reluctance at all. The ficus, however, fights me. The corpse is as tall as I am myself and as stubborn. I tussle with it until it breaks off at the soil line, then I put my foot on the center of it, break it in two, and wrestle with those portions in turn. The whole woody caboodle gets stuffed into the bag. The soil is another matter. I hoist up the unwieldy pot and turn it over the edge of the porch. The enormous clot of dirt, gallons-large and bound together by the efficient glue of ficus roots, falls to the ground below with a single dull thud. I decide to let the next rain break it up for me. I line up the bags and tie-wrap myself into a happy frenzy, then drag the bags of plants and soil all the way out to the small knoll behind the house, and scatter their remains down the hill.

The porch poses a bigger problem. It needs applied sweat. The chrome and glass table is barely recognizable. The glass is mottled tortoiseshell from repeated dews and dustings of dirt. The plating of the chrome on the legs and supports has lifted in spots, is curled back or missing, and is rusting underneath. There is nothing I can do with the table. I will try to talk Evan into getting rid of it this weekend. To appease myself, and in case I fail with Evan, I swipe at it with water and vinegar and dry it with an old towel.

Then I start on the floor. I have no pretensions of being so thorough as the old widow, and for just a moment I wonder how she is faring, that old woman alone. And I wonder, too, what her garden holds this time of year. I am certain that particular ground never lies fallow.

I douse the planks with too much of my sloppy mixture and push at it with the mop. I achieve mud. I switch to the broom and coax the mess out the back door, get the floor as dry as possible, and pray that I have not ruined the wood. The old woman really did do us fine.

When I flick on the porch light to check it again before I go to bed, I see that, though the floor has gotten well-soaked, it appears somewhat cleaner than before I started, and I believe it will survive.
In the meantime, of course, the frozen pot pie has boiled over and the crust has burned because I did not set the timer. I am hungry enough, though, to improvise. With a wad of paper toweling, I hold the tin plate over the garbage and scrape the black crust into the bin. Then I sit at the table and spoon up what is left of the lava-like, pea-dotted stew. I blow on each spoonful carefully before I bring it to my lips. It is good.

Sleep is a long-eared dog curled up at the foot of my bed. I coax and plead, but the bed only grows longer, the foot moves farther away. The dog never blinks and, above his head, images hover like dreams:

Herb, my mother's lover, still howls in his Chrysler; Finch's redhead eternally hurries past my table; Evan makes love to an invisible woman; Hope is in transit; Riva's breast is severed, and severed; Rose is waving from my father's car.

*My mother is bent over the sink, washing her hair.*

*"Mom? Who is Rose?"*

*She lifts her head, grabs a towel and wraps it swiftly around her hair. "Rose? What do you know about Rose?"*

*It has been a long day. My father was drunk. They fought. I can see that I have asked too much.*

*"She's sleeping with your father, that's who Rose is." She is furious with me, for knowing, I guess. Her hands are trembling.*

*"Stay away from her. Do you hear me?" Her voice is as shaky as her hands and it is the first time I really see that she is no longer young, that her hair has gotten thinner, her skin more feathery.*

*I want to ask her how I can stay away from someone I don't know, someone I have never met. I am young enough to worry. What if I meet her on the street and don't know her? How much trouble will I be in?*

*My mother's face tells me I am a traitor. She is wild with a vague anger and her eyes are on fire; they burn as though they would cauterize my own, and, for her sake, make them clean again. "Don't speak to me about Rose," she says.*

It is not until tonight that I understand my mother, realize she was afraid. Finally, I recognize what she knew all along—that Rose was a common fixture in our lives. I can see her with no difficulty at all: it is the company picnic. She wears pants and works in the factory with my father. Her hair is tied up and she shakes hands like a man. She pitches horseshoes like a man, too, and her arms are tauter, stronger than my mother's arms. She beats the men.

She is the only woman there who plays that way, and she plays even harder when she knows I am watching.

I remember this clearly, as well: the choppy sound of contact. When the horseshoe hit the pit, the sand flew up in a fine, dry spray. It got in my eyes.

The dog gives in, and I sleep.

# XVII

# EPIPHANY

Lew's studio is a shock of white. It is wide, clean and open, a huge rectangular box, like a hangar or a barn. It is one room, all white, with a wall of enormous curtainless windows looking out over the water. I know the beach is there, sheer reason dictates that it is so, but it is so ribbon-thin, so narrow, that it is almost impossible to see it at all unless I stand right up to the pane and look downward, my breath hazing the glass. The water is magnificent, though. It spreads out, a wide blue field before my eyes, the white fringes, foamy alyssum.

Compared to the deep hue of the water, the room is stark, gallery-like, and my eyes are flooded with the glare of it. Towards the center of the room, on a pedestal, white, too, is a small statue, darkened with age, bronze, I think, and graceful. It reminds me of a piece my mother had, lost to some relative or other now, a small, heavy statuette salvaged from the quake and fire in San Francisco. It was a monkey, a man and a monkey. The man wore a turban. I imagine this one, too, Lew's, is very old. When I move closer, I can see that it is a woman, a woman draped in something like a toga, long, flowing; she is full-breasted, Rubinesque, and she is crying. The bronze tears hang, petrified, from her cheeks. The sculpture itself hovers atop its pedestal like a small black cloud in the room.

In the far corner is a futon, a thin envelope of mattress folded to look like a couch. Alongside of it, in front of it, are cushions, huge ones to fit the scale of this room, and most are so thick that they are nearly round. A lamp, a chrome globe, pendulous, suspended over the corner by a nearly invisible white cord, balances the space between the floor and the ceiling. This apartment is exact. It has been executed, not furnished. It is a mathematical feat. And he is comfortable here. I cannot make this fit in with my image of him, his worn jeans, his, I thought, natural nonchalance. It is obvious I do not know him as well as I thought. This room is a test. I am failing.

Lew is behind me. I can hear him rattling—metal, glass, the squeak of cork—and then I turn. I am expected to, of course. He is standing, barefoot, at his "kitchen," a portion of the inside wall, outfitted in still more white, a small waist-high refrigerator, a white stove, and cabinets above and alongside. All white. All immaculate. The only color is from the two small prints, shell-like convolutions in blue, that hang above the sink and seem to reflect the water from the windows opposite, those and a knife block, wood, on the counter. The block is crude, uneven, a gift from a young child, I would guess. It does not belong here; it is too fallible. I wonder if he has children, is divorced, is older than he appears. Lew sees me staring. He smiles, but he says nothing but the obvious: "Here, let's sit down."

When he hands me the glass, I cling to the stem as though I am afraid I will fall if I let go. I am stupidly wordless, feeling foolish and half-blind. I am, surely, fifteen or sixteen, and I am waiting for this boy to kiss me. I do not know that he plans to, that he wants to, but the situation is made for it. He is supposed to. But, if this apartment has anything to say, it is that Lew is not an easy read.

The backdrop of Lew's voice is a comfort. It is a hum, the drone of an electric fan at the height of summer. I am counting on the wine to still my nerves. I am shaking, silly; it is all I can do to keep from giggling inanely, for no reason except to fill the gap. I have gone much too long without speaking, and it is awkward. Though I have heard him, I have not been listening. Torn between looking, between taking all this in, this apartment, the bright snow flavor of this room, and acting normal, or at least trying to act some version of normal, I am stymied. I would not recognize normal in this situation if, as my mother would have said, it were to spit up my nose. Normal is being back at the house; normal is frying an egg for lunch; normal is washing my hair whether it needs it or not and waiting for Evan to call home.

The glass weighs nothing in my hand. It is fine, thin; it is etched deeply, beautifully. I am afraid it may break off between my lips. My heart is beating somewhere in the back of my head.

Lew is settled comfortably on the futon, a good three feet from me. His legs are curled beneath him, his bare brown toes are sticking out at the side. He's set his wine glass directly on the polished hardwood floor. I would have, but I was afraid of rings. There is no table here, so I've been holding the glass. The bottle is behind him on the floor. I keep my eye on that.

He is talking, speaking of something familiar, though I couldn't say what. All I can think of is that I am seated awkwardly. I shift, trying to settle in, trying to be inconspicuous in doing so, but I'm getting nowhere. I tell myself that in just a little while I will loosen up, but my back feels like a plumb line. Lew doesn't seem to notice. He is talking, chatting as though I belong here, as though I do not stand out, fluorescent, against this white screen of a room. But I know better. My iron posture on this mound of too-full cushions is ludicrous. My new jeans still too blue, too perfect. I am a studied fool.

Then, without my knowing it, an hour has passed, then two, and somewhere along the line of speeding time I have forgotten my nervousness. I handle my glass with ease. Once started, he spoke so easily, with such eagerness. He was hungry for it, I think. I tell myself the scene has turned around. I have learned much: his degree, his father, wealthy, estranged. My surprise must show, my eye catches the statue, my fingers inquisitively fondle the thin glass.

"No," he says easily. "It's mine." His voice is amused. He means that his father has not financed this apartment, not the statue, not the glasses.

I am embarrassed at getting caught, and say "I'm sorry."

He laughs. "Not to be," he says. "I bought the glasses in the city. Couldn't live without 'em."

"And the statue?" I am forward in my question, and eager.

"Same thing."

"Couldn't live without it?"

"You're getting the hang of it!"

"What else haven't you been able to live without?" Even as I ask it I am surprised at what I am saying.

"The woman," he says. "It's always the woman, isn't it?"

"Sometimes it's the woman," I say. "Sometimes." And I just let it go.

And suddenly he is telling me, "I didn't marry her. I don't

know why. I just knew it wasn't right. And so here I am," he says.

"What happened to her?" How long ago? Shit, I wasn't listening. I am possessive, jealous. I want to laugh at myself, but I am too overcome with the greed of having him here, at the surprise of having him here.

"She married someone else."

I want to ask if she is happy, but, of course, I don't.

Then it's like intermission at the drive-in when I was a kid—we'd get out of the car, stretch our legs, play on the swings, go to the snack bar, pee, and pressure somebody's parents into buying us something to drink so we'd have to pee again, later, before the movie ended. But this is no planned break. It is just that Lew has come to the end, has talked right up to the present. "And so here I am," he says. Then he stands and shakes himself as though he's just risen from a long nap, and I, automatically and on cue, rise with him.

I walk around the room, stare out the windows. The sun is settling, just on the water, at the horizon. It sits there, buoyed, bobbing. The day fades in front of us. It is beautiful, though there are no clouds to reflect the light, no bright edges of pinks, no showering storms of reds and grays.

Behind the closed door of the bathroom I straighten my hair, touch at my face as though to freshen my makeup, though I do not. I am looking, really, to see if it is still me.

When I come back into the room, Lew is lighting a fire. It is the first time I have noticed the fireplace against the wall, Scandinavian, white enameled metal, black screen. Camouflage. Anonymous, it sat there until Lew brought it to life. He has laid the fire expertly. I wonder where the wood is kept. There is fruit, cheese, chunks of meat, a fresh bottle of wine on a tray in front of where we sat. The corkscrew lies askew on the floor, a cork trapped in its springy maw. The light overhead is subtle, raining down from the chrome globe like moonlight.

Lew refills the glasses and we drink. I do not know how many times he has done this today, this afternoon. But we are easy now, old friends. It is as though I have known him all my life, and I pull a cushion over to the fire and settle in.

It is as if he already knows it all, though I have said nothing, or very little, and I think I will not have to tell him a thing to have him understand me, to have him know me.

"Your turn," he says lightly, half-kidding, as he falls easily onto the cushion next to me.

So, he doesn't know, after all.

I begin the trade, self-consciously. I was born. . . I got good grades. . . I hated boys until the time. . . And then it rolls; it is all so easy then, the stories are water, flowing, now spilling.

I tell him all the stories I can think of that will amuse him; they are comfortable like old clothes, like boots broken in and warmed by the fire, like hungry, wet sex, starving, voracious, slippery, and easy. How I tried out for Glee lead and lost to Ida Garcia who couldn't even speak the language; how I went out for girls' after-school soccer because the boy I liked, and who didn't know I was alive, was going to be the first male cheerleader, and how, at the first game of the season, I kicked hard, missed the ball entirely, fell, and broke my leg in two places. I tell him how, still in high school, I tried to seduce my English teacher. I tell him the funny parts, the laughable lines I have been rehearsing for years, just edged with enough of the marginally painful to keep his interest, to make him feel that, after his own tales, he is not being cheated, I am not holding back, that I, too, am sharing whatever it is I may have to share. I tell him about my mother's death, how it was the last straw in a series of straws, really, how I left Evan, how I went to California.

*I am standing outside the tin door. I have to pee. The man inside is jerking off. I can hear him grunting, straining; "Good, oh, good," he moans, haltingly, too loudly, his elbow rhythmically banging the wall from the inside.*

*He's in there jerking off and I have to pee. The bastard.*

*He comes out still zipping his fly. He is fat and pockmarked. His face is florid. When he smiles his hello, his pardon as he squeezes by me, I can see the saliva stretch between his teeth. I nod and push my way into the cubicle.*

*Back in my seat, I stare out the window. The clouds look like popcorn now. It seems as though, just moments ago, they were thick layers of white, like batting that I could not see through.*

*The landscape changes each time I look down. Rivers and lakes, a few mountains, nothing like the Rockies, of course, until we get to the Rockies themselves, but imitations of mountains, shrunken ones, like the mâché fakes around electric train sets, and then those large flat-looking brown and red areas, divided up, geometrically blocked out, even, colored plots.*

*The flight attendant and I are getting friendly. When she makes the rounds with the liquor cart this time, she stops and asks again, Have I changed my mind? Would I like something to drink? I want to tell her that my mother has died and that a man was just jacking off in the bathroom, but instead I accept a drink. "Yes," I say. "Finally, yes." She hands me the plastic glass and I sip, slowly. It wasn't what I wanted after all. I gaze back out the window.*

*"I'm going to my mother's funeral. She's dead."*

*I have it all planned out, how I'm going to say it if someone asks me. No one has asked, however. In fact, no one has spoken to me at all except the bathroom man and the crew.*

*I look around the plane. There are a lot of empty seats. Don't people go to California anymore? Why? This bothers me. What do they know, those people who are not here? What do they know that no one told me? Have they had some sort of vision? Some foreknowledge of an accident? Prescience? Am I going to die too? A crash? Why aren't they here in their seats where they belong? Where the hell are they? What the fuck. . . .*

And we are laughing, Lew and I, laughing till the tears are streaming down our cheeks. "What the fuck. . . ." I repeat, and we fall over on the cushions.

He touches my arm, "My God, Dore," he says, and he is still laughing.

But stupid. Stupid!

Those tears were a mistake, those tears wrung out of those stories were wrong, wrong, I can feel it. They have loosed something, tapped something; they have formed an alliance with the wine, a liquid alliance, and I can feel something inside give, feel it shift, like the mantel did beneath my arm in the house on that first day. Nothing has tumbled, nothing broken, not yet, but there is a difference now. I know it. Something has come undone. Despite the laughter itself, I will have to be more careful of the tears.

But it is too late. The film is in reverse, rewinding, and I trust him with too much and still it is too easy, and I find I am telling him about Peter, Peter and Lise, and my life then. I say, "God, the first one," and I am talking about our marriage, Peter's and mine. "The first one," I say, "should have been against the law. I was pregnant; we did what we were supposed to do." I can hear it go on, tape loop, faster and faster, as though it isn't even me speaking anymore. It is mechanical. Or it is someone else. "All those years, boredom, anger. Then suddenly the reason for it all, the cause of it all disappeared. Poof! As if it were never there at all. As if she had been a dream, a shared dream. Then there was all that history, all that unhappiness and bitterness, and no reason for it any longer, no reason at all. It was as if the beginning had been wiped out, erased after the fact, leaving just the effects, so that it all meant nothing. Then there was the guilt . . ."

*And then she is gone.*

It takes my breath away. It is so natural to lean over, to take his fingers in mine, tighter. I can see that he doesn't know what to say, that he seems to see what is coming. I feel sorry for him, but I've got to tell him now; he has asked and I've got to know what it is I will say.

*Someone screams and it is louder than the crunch of the metal. My God . . .*

*And I think, Jesus, I am caught, no license, not allowed, oh, Jesus I am caught. And then the silence. And then I feel the blood, and I reach to the seat beside me and she is gone, the baby is gone, and I look for her, I look on the floor in the front by the pedals, on the passenger side, I look behind the seats, on the backseat, where is she, Jesus, the baby, where did I put the baby, Christ, where is she . . . ?*

*And when they wrap the blanket around me, when they make me lie down, I don't want to tell them, can't tell them that I don't know what I have done with her, don't know where she is . . . And I look back, back towards the car, and all that is there is a crumpled mass the color of the car, and glass, and glass, and blood, my blood . . .*

I try to tell him the hopelessness of the feeling, the sensation of deep, deep bewilderment. And guilt. I tell him more about the guilt than I knew myself before, and the doubts. I tell him about those. I want to explain to him how, when she was born, after she was born, I would look at her and see something totally separate, something strange and foreign, not a part of me at all, certainly not a part of me. I tell him instead how at intervals, I would be overcome with emotion, with caring, and that I would pick her up and hold her, rock her close to my breast, and draw the warmth, draw the touch I missed so much, draw it from her, from that tiny, foreign other person. I was so sure she would love me. I tell him how Peter, after the services, fell silent. How in less than a week he was gone, how the papers simply came in the mail, and how it didn't matter, how it didn't matter any more at all.

Lew stops sipping his wine. He is still and his eyes are turned away. He isn't really here. He doesn't want to hear this, he doesn't want to know. It doesn't matter, damn him. It doesn't matter. I will tell him anyway.

"I was driving and I was angry, angry at Peter and angry because of the crying and at my life and at my choices and she was crying and pulling and whining and it was all so much, all so much and then that car came so fast, from out of nowhere it came and he wasn't looking, he didn't see us, and she was crying and I slammed on the brake, hard, so that I hit my head on the windshield, mashed my chest against the wheel. I was so startled, so hurting, but the first thing I remember is the silence, the silence, no crying, and the silence was so wonderful and so peaceful and the silence let me rest, let me lean forward and lay my head against the wheel and rest. But when the man came to my door, when he came and opened the door and said, 'Lady, Lady . . .' and I said, 'I'm OK,' and I looked at him and he was sick and green and I said again 'I'm OK,' and he said, 'Lady, the little girl . . .' and then I remembered the baby, my baby, and the silence, the crying had stopped, and why wasn't she crying, and where was she, Jesus holy shit where was the baby . . ."

*"Dr. Lindhurst, I don't want to do this."*

*"It's OK, Dore. Let's work it out. We'll work it out together. What happened, Dore? Tell me."*

*"She was gone."*

*"Explain it to me, Dore. Gone where?"*

*"Dead."*

*"How did she die? Tell me."*

*"Broke her neck."*

*"How, Dore? How did she break her neck?"*

*"She flew out of the car. The impact broke her neck."*

*"Did you see her, Dore?"*

*"No, I told you."*

*"What did you tell me, Dore? Tell me again."*

*"I told you. She flew out of the car onto the sidewalk. It broke her neck."*

*"Dore, how did she look?"*

*"She looked dead. You could see it right away, she was dead. Her neck was all wrong, her head was wrong. You could see it. She didn't breathe."*

*"And how did you feel about it, Dore? What did you feel when you saw her?"*

*"I don't know."*

*"Dore, think about it. I want you to think about it. How did you feel when you saw her?"*

*"She looked like a broken doll. Like someone broke the head off a doll."*

*"Dore, you're telling me how she looked. I want to know how you felt. Think, Dore. How did you feel when she looked like a broken doll, how did you feel? That was your daughter, Dore. That was Lise. You must have felt something."*

*"Something. Nothing. I don't know. I just don't know."*

And I rock back and forth on the pillows.

I tell Lew about the breakdown, the first one, about the beginning. I tell him: "When they found me I was still in the tub. They said I wouldn't help myself out of the water, that I just stared at the ceiling, that I had to be carried to the ambulance. I don't remember, myself, so they could be right. It wasn't until later, in the hospital, that I began to think about it and even then much of it, evidently, escaped me. I think I just couldn't take any more, no more weight, no more thoughts, no more movement, because I wasn't unconscious. There was some sort of choice involved, I can see that now. It was easier not to move, to be fed and washed and dressed; it was almost peaceful, like the silence, at first, after the accident. No one expected anything from me. They had to take the responsibility for me; they had to do the things somebody had to do. It was out of my hands then, you see, out of my hands."

From the window we can see the outlook. The island is beautiful, the air is clear and cold, very cold, and the lights play against the water as though they have lives of their own.

I do not go home. I spend the night there, on those cushions, and I sleep, sleep like the dead.

In the morning, when I wake, Lew is gone. The wine has been cleared; the meat and cheese and fruit from the night before, untouched, are gone.

There is a note taped to the bathroom mirror. It says: "The knife block is mine. Eighth grade."

## XVIII

## THANKSGIVING

The jays will imitate the hawks.

The old man from the shack told me this. In the dream, his back was to the water, and his hair shone whiter than the gull feathers that punctuated the beach at his feet. His hands were as brown and as hard as rust. He said to me, "Listen." He could hear it, he said—the asthmatic wheeze, slurred and bigger than the bird itself. *Key-urr-r-r-r.* A sound like grief. "Listen," he said to me. "Listen."

At first I couldn't make it out, only, now and again, hear snatches of what I thought might be it. Then, the more I heard it, the easier it was to identify. It was perfectly obvious: the smaller birds were mimicking the larger, more powerful ones—their own chertlings rearranged, manipulated to reproduce the breathy squeals of the hawks.

In the dream, I discovered this: if you were paying attention, the jays' hoarse orchestration was a blatant ruse. If you weren't keeping your eyes open, well, then it was a different story altogether.

"Hawk," said the old man. "Red-tail. Broad body, thick-set, thick and muscular." He nodded at the sun, at the point from which the hawks wheeled and surveyed us. "Buteos. Red-tails. Like Japanese kites if you watch them long enough, circles like rings around the sun."

And then the jays.

Over the phone, Evan says that he thinks we should have a baby.

"It's not too late," he says. He throws this out to me, not as a sop, but casually, pragmatically, as though he might be suggesting that we patch the roof or, because it is November already, put up the storm windows.

There is the dim buzzing of flies inside my head.

"Dore, just think about it."

Then he tells me that he will see me in two nights, that we will mull it over together, that we will have time for a long serious talk before our company arrives and, before I can think, the line is dead in my hand.

Oh my God, Evan. You're out of your fucking mind. I can list for you, Evan, all the reasons I do not want a child.

First, I have had my child. This is not news, Evan. I have had her and she is gone no matter how much I would like to believe it is not true. It is my choice not to try again. My conscious, rational, well thought-out choice. Second, I am thirty-seven years old, thirty-seven. Not seventeen, not twenty-seven, not even thirty. I am too old, if not chronologically, then some thing beyond the physical, some other old. I could no more suckle a child than suckle your dead mother, or my own. No more give my breast or my life to a child than nurse a litter of Happlett's kittens. I am dry.

Do you know what you are asking, Evan?

But I forget: men are given so much sway when it comes to romanticizing someone else's pain. Not only the physical. Put it in the context of our dead fathers, Evan—men are groomed to spread their seed as thin as their advice. They believe it is magic. Their self-deception is my own, as well. It is nothing to be angry about, but it is something to know. But that particular brand of pain is ephemeral, anyway. It is the other one, the one that resembles expectation. Watch out for that one. Try to fuck away that kind of pain, Evan. Shall I share it with you? Do you really want to know? I will give the pain to you secondhand, if that is what you want. Here it is. Take it, Evan. Live it. Breathe it. It is the closest you will come. It is the closest you will come while you are with me.

*Lindhurst says to write it down on the paper. "Bring it in. I want to see what you come up with."*

*I write: The lesson learned is that nothing exists simply, nothing as it seems. It is the hardest lesson, that no thing is static. No person will live forever, no situation is assured. My mind is a bridge of little cubbyholes, black and white, white and black, a checkerboard of comprehension. Then you tell me neither black nor white exists. I can't afford the luxury of believing that. I admit to no gray areas. None. Things that change are out of reach, or they never existed. They slip between your fingers, between your eyes. Sharp as knives, cutting invisible. I acknowledge them, but I know they are not real. That answer is the only answer that will never be any different.*

*I wonder about this: Statisticians prove varying points with the same data, each one able to substantiate his own private explanation. Physicists agree on what? Gravity? Atoms? What? And Geologists? Granite upheaval? Magma at the earth's core? On what, then, do these supposedly knowledgeable people disagree? I know they disagree. On infinity? On God? On whether life itself is measurable like a quart of milk or a bushel of corn? Is that what it is? That is what it feels like. I don't know where I got the idea.*

In another session, I bring this on a scrap of paper: *The hardest part was giving away her clothes.*

In another: *We did not say goodbye.*

Now, we are a married couple of a certain age and we are childless. If it is a matter of family and lineage, then Hope's Anna is welcome to the silver, to the china. It will not fall into the hands of strangers.

Evan looks forward to a child the way another man might look forward to a tool, or a piece of hardware, literally a coupling, a joining piece. His intent is not a cruel one; he has not examined it from this pragmatic angle. But there it is nevertheless. What Evan wants to have again is baby squirrels, that sharp focal point in the third position, a repository for energies that might crop up at night, energies that sex won't wash away. He said to me he would like to have a child, but he would settle for politics or ecology if I promised to be consumed by it, too.

Frankly, Evan does not need a hobby. He has me.

It is the old recognizable unit: Hope drives the dusty wagon, shores her front wheels against the front porch steps. As the five bodies bail out of the car, I check to see that they still have all their arms and legs, that they are all whole and cheerful. And they do and they are. Thanksgiving is an understatement.

Michael, Hope tells me in front of Finch, is in Germany. "Another convenient business trip." She smiles.

"Convenient for everyone?" I ask her, handing over the ice bucket.

"For the time being, yes," she tells me. "For now, convenient for all." She drops three ice cubes in noisy succession into a tall glass and hands it to Finch, who seems to be focusing on some invisible blemish on the kitchen wall.

Hope turns the topic to Finch's missing friend. I would like to tell him that his redhead would be welcome here too, but it looks to be too soon for that. Hope says, "Mad's a lovely woman. She's good to the kids, and, well, just look at Finch." I scan her voice for evidence of reproach, but there is none, only a modicum of hesitance and a great deal of respect. Her enthusiasm is real. We find out, then, that this new woman, too, is a part of all of these lives. Robin and Anna voice their consensus. "She's neat!" Anna says, and means it. Robin's "Nee-ee-eet" is close behind. Doug waits for an opening and then says, "Nice lady." He looks at his father while he speaks and there is something new in his eyes. From other lips his words might have been an evasion, or a lie, but it is no insignificant compliment coming from Doug. Finch offers no explanation of how this redhead of his is passing this Thanksgiving holiday; he is ill at ease, I think, with the wide-open ground of the subject. The poor man does not even know that Evan and I were aware of her existence before this exchange. Nevertheless, this new addition seems an amenable and familiar phenomenon to all. I find out now that the young ones call her Red, but that her name is Madeleine, and that Anna breaks up hysterically when Robin gets confused and calls her Red Mad.

Robin is growing out of his baby self. He is voicier and more demanding, now, and, in the tradition of all children, has moved out of his pudgy stage and come into his lanky period. His corduroy overalls and striped shirt define the route of his growth. The pant legs are too short; the shirt is too large. Hope calls him her "Mommy's boy," but she, herself, is a prized plum at this point and their appreciation is mutual. This is the newest aspect of their familiarity and it smacks more of a new delight than the intensity of disintegration.

Doug has, since last July, made the transition between boy and man. He may have grown taller—it is hard to tell—but there is a new air about him. He is now wholly, unconsciously, one of the men. His manhood, if I am not mistaken, has recently been validated in the usual way, and his newfound assurance is more relief than cockiness, I think. He is openly drinking beer and he has given up chastising and instructing his parents. From what he tells me, there is a Monica—the Monica of the validation, I assume—who matters now.

Hope still gathers her brood around her and curries them, chides them. They are still a family. The ever-loose Finch, however, is thinner, firmer, and a little jumpy. He looks healthier, though, harder, in a sense. He has joined a health club and works out now, "to a small degree," he tells Evan and me when we ravish him with appreciation. "Nothing big," he says, and shrugs it off. "Overboard on this old frame could kill me," and he gives us that old lovable Finch-look from behind his new eyes.

If any of them are horribly unhappy, it does not show. Tension. Appreciation. Not unhappiness. At least not here, not now.

Anna is the one who seems to have, momentarily, lost her surefootedness. She is at the fulcrum of change. She is nearly thirteen.

Right after the welcomes and the first round of hugs, pleasantries, the promise of eggs, and the quick rundown on Madeleine, Anna disappears. I see her go, but her mother doesn't notice. When she does, she will search and find like one of those heat-seeking missiles and then she will, in private of course, reprimand the child sharply for her unmannered, antisocial ways. Or she would have.

Maybe that is no longer what she will do.

When Anna escapes the shelter and chaos of the house, she has a set of earphones clamped over her ears, and she walks out towards the back of the house. There is more than music going on in her head. Her hands are free and her narrow fingers keep time to her private music, tapping their rhythm on her outside pocket. Her head is down and she strides across the dead grass as though she is in search of something important. Her lightweight jacket touts a row of buckles like instruments of torture, no reasonable coat at all for the island at this time of year, but, as though the world is recreated for the child, adequate for today's spring backwards into humidity and something near warmth.

She will find answers. She is one of the magic-breakers, one of those who will always demand to see behind the curtain, demand to know the technique behind the illusion. She will be stronger for that skill. I can see it taking shape in her. I admire it. Her sort of wisdom is akin to the great wisdom we used to attribute to our elders, or to men, but she is in that half-land now, not child, not adult, neither magician nor master of herself.

When Hope sees she is gone, mother-noises tumble from her mouth. I tell her that Anna is outside playing, that I saw her searching for the cross-backed peepers on the trees. I tell Hope that it is a quest that could keep her occupied for half of forever, that she is safe and she is warm enough and that the child is getting exercise and isn't that great? I poke a finger at the inside of my ever-so-slightly-firmer thigh—a reminder—to make my point. We both laugh. Peepers are virtually impossible to find, I tell her, and I am surprised to hear myself say it and know it is true. I have learned a lot about the natures of the animals in these last months. I promise Hope I will go gather Anna in myself when dinner is ready, and she allows me that responsibility.

She says to me, "Have you taken a look at that girl, lately?"

I nod.

If Anna is a lucky child, she is easily alone out there. The tree frogs will keep her company. She will never hear them with that tape playing and her ears closed off by that headset, but it doesn't matter. Like herself, the peepers seem to have come back suddenly to this place and will do whatever it is their nature to do whether anyone pays attention or not. At thirteen, or nearly so, no one needs frogs.

I wouldn't want to be that age again.

We are seven bottomless pits at the table, and still I have prepared too much food.

After dinner, we gather like locusts in front of the television. Our seven pairs of overfed eyes focus on a man in a well-fitted blue sports jacket who goes on and on about a storm he insists is headed our way. He is no master oracle, however. There is not one of us here who has not already felt it in the air, but we give him our attention anyway, and, as though we are an audience made up entirely of young children, he holds up a series of drawings on cards. They represent, he says, the "Preventative Steps" we all should take before the event of a power failure. He drops each crudely illustrated card face down to reveal the next:

1) fill the bathtub with water
2) store more water in pots and pitchers for cooking and drink ing
3) turn up the controls on the refrigerator and the freezer
4) make sure there are fresh batteries in the house

and

5) set out candles, matches, and flashlights where they can be found easily in the dark.

He is a man of my own persuasion, with his lists. It is evident that he is certain it will bear down on us long and hard.

He repeats the list a second time, and this time the little symbols from his cards appear magically beside the instructions which are now printed across the television screen. These ghostlier images are superimposed on his own and they roll upward over him as he reads down the list. He stresses that the storm will hit no later than tomorrow night, but he covers himself by pointing out that atmospheric conditions can and, frequently, do change. He is careful to allow for change.

Ours, however, is a gathering of glad and easy hearts. No one here shows any indication of taking his warning seriously. Evan and I will have to sit it out, because that is the nature of our being here, but, by the time the storm hits, if the permutations of weather do not affect its timing or existence, Hope and Finch and the kids will be out of its range. They will have achieved their separate destinations, and their lives will be unaffected by this particular tumult. They will go on in their same or new directions.

It is as though the man on TV—with all his effort—has predicted that night will fall.

Last night I avoided Evan by delivering myself up to turkey. Preparation. Getting ready. I am good at this. I poured a small libation on the kitchen floor and sang, "Thaw turkey, thaw. Siss-boom-bah." I dropped a dishtowel on the spill and danced over it, through it, and around the kitchen floor and, while I did, I alternated between watching Evan's face and avoiding it. I juggled radish roses, celery sticks, and slews of apples. Eggs. I scrubbed and scraped potatoes and set them to rest in lemon water. I lined up bowls and platters and flatware on the old white table until I thought it would collapse beneath their weight. I folded napkins and folded them again. I rattled every paper bag, clattered every utensil I could get my hands on. I suppose I was cruel, him waiting, wanting to talk, but I was not trying to drive him away for good. I was trying to put him off for the time being. I had not chosen the words yet. I filled the space with noise so he didn't have room. And I was successful.

When we finally went upstairs to bed, Evan took the bathroom first. By the time I came out, he was asleep. He lay there covered to the neck and the outline of his body showed like wood, rigid beneath the blanket. His arm was thrown across his face as though he were protecting himself from unseen punches.

I crawled between the sheets and got as close as I could without waking him. I wanted to feel the coolness of his skin on my back. And it was there—despite the heavy blanket and his frustration, his skin was cool against my own.

I drowsed, trying to imagine Evan's eyes in a time that was easier on us both. I pressed closer to his back, took the chance of waking him, and I could remember clearly that his eyes were the golded-green of shaded water. I could see those eyes clearly, as plainly as if they had been open before me. His eyes are dryer lately, harder; they have been compressed by the weight of the distance between us that comes and goes like a migratory thing. The eyes cannot tell lies as easily as the mouth.

Then, I could not remember the color of Lise's eyes.

My own heart wanted to stop from shame. I knew the color, I knew they were the strong remarkable blue of lapis, of my father's sky eyes, but I could not see them. I used to see them everywhere, and this new blindness took me by surprise.

I tested myself, ran through my mental list:

Hope's eyes are hazel.
Lew's green.
Finch's eyes are gray and cloudy.
Riva's are flat, deep brown.

I could see all those eyes.

Then I thought: what color were Peter's eyes? And I could not remember. Could not recall his eyes at all.

Then I slept.

Evan, no doubt, believes that he opened a new door for me and that I have rudely slammed it shut in his face. But it is not true. It seems, this time, that Evan has closed a door. A door that had swollen and stuck with time, a door stuck open in an old abandoned house.

Is it really possible that I considered saying "yes" just for that tiny moment it took my heart to lurch? I felt it, deep in my chest like a bullet or a bomb. Holy God, I did, for a moment, think of saying "yes."

Hope is teasing Evan about his new beard. She is taking pictures of him with the Polaroid and lining them up on the coffee table. She says he looks like two men glued together at the nose — the top half, she laughs, is the brother she has known for thirty-five years; the bottom is some ruffian stranger who has cultivated auburn silk-worms at his throat as pets. She puts her finger across the bottom of the best of the pictures. "See?" she says. "Look up there." Then she moves her finger up. "Now look," she says, "down here." She insists that the bottom half looks like a wild man from the deep woods. And it is partially so. Evan's new beard is the color of madrone. When he smiles, now, those teeth of his stand out like the eyes of night creatures caught in the headlights of a car. They flash and seem to stand alone in that dark bush.

I liked the beard until I got angry, but, then, even the way he lifted his fork to his lips made me mad.

I swallowed it, though.

I could not name the anger, could not say what he had done to make me so furious, and something in the back of my brain told me it was not Evan at all. I made the list inside my eyelids:

1) I am not angry with Lew for leaving the island.
2) I even truly believe that, at this point, I am not angry at Lise for dying or at Peter for being such a prick.
3) I am not angry at this house. I love this house; it has done all it can to soothe me.
4) I am angry at my husband.

and then

5) But it is an unjust anger.

We have done what we were supposed to do. I am certain that even Evan sees, now, that he bought the role of savior that I offered him too cheaply, too easily. We did not read the fine print, did not demand to see the warranty.

Who the goddamned hell led us to believe that the man would be the protector?

He is no protector; he is barely even a guide. Evan was not quick enough to save me from my own passivity. He joined me in it. He is in most senses no stronger than I am. Not even very different. He must be equally as disappointed in the outcome of our blind trust.

As if a penis could be a magic wand that grants protection.

Protection is a lie, too.

There was no protection from Lise's death, no protection from that loss. Peter could not have done it. My father could not have done that had he lived. No one could have done it. No more than Lew could protect me from my past, my marriage, or myself. He couldn't even protect me from my fantasies. And Evan cannot protect me from his soft, pseudo-protecting ways. All these people on the outside, they offer figments, mirages and wishes, wishes of good will, but wishes nonetheless.

Christ, no wonder we get crazy.

We do not control, at all, what we think we do. It is an overwhelming realization, the potential of that surprising bend in the road. You get to thinking that it's your vision that's distorted, but you're wrong there, too. It's the goddamn bend in the road. The whole thing is like walking through a world made up of funhouse mirrors.

Had Evan been my protector, he would have been able to tell me about the potential.

At this point, it does not matter that he did not know. It doesn't even matter that it doesn't make sense. It is not his fault, and I'll have to remember that.

But I need to be mad at someone and it will not be easy.

The children have spread out as though they have been flung centrifugally from the center of the house. Robin has discovered sleep upstairs in the brass bed. Anna has scuttled back outdoors. Doug is beating Evan at checkers in front of the fire. And Finch's eyes are closed and his long new body is draped over the sofa from one upholstered arm, across the entire length, to the other.

Hope and I are left to talk.

We move ourselves to the kitchen and settle at the table with coffee and pie we don't really want. I can't help but think about the last time we were together, how I wanted her to reveal her secret of happiness to me. I wanted her to give me, in a few words, the distilled truth of that happiness, her pearl, my treasure. Today, I know it was no pearl, no treasure at all, but beads of hard work and recognition as red as rose petals and as sore as open wounds. I study Hope's face, and she is changed. Not for the worse, not for better. Just changed. I ask her, "How is the job?" And I find that I really, really want to know.

Out the kitchen window, the birds gather at the second feeder I have hung. I have read that they are not likely to do this as a storm builds, but perhaps I misunderstood. There are still so many things I don't understand, and so many things that are exceptions to the so-called rules. Sorting them out is either a long-term or impossible thing. But I have been good about learning the birds. I know who these are: crazy chickadees, acrobatic nuthatches, and titmice, unmarked, subtle grays, and as mild as herb tea. Some stammer after the insects that are left in the bark; some eat the seed I leave them. They bargain for foot room. The jays have been more cagey than the others. They raid squirrel storehouses. They have stashed acorns in the ground, some of which they can locate, some of which they will never find again and which will become the wayward seedlings I pull next year.

Beside the gemmy blue jay, these littler birds are all grays and browns and blacks. It is like watching an old movie. These birds are the same color as everything else around us this time of year.

The departure of Finch and his crew takes place during one of a sequence of cloudbursts. In a flurry of open umbrellas and bags of foiled leftovers, the kids are scooted into the car along with all their essential paraphernalia. Kisses are quick and perfunctory, though not insincere, and there is a lot of yelling and waving from the front of the house to the car and back. Hope and Finch linger a moment on the porch with us, wordlessly. We seem to be studying the rain, but I think we are all wondering if it will ever be like this again. No, we are not wondering. We are acknowledging that it will not.

I kiss Hope and then Finch. I want to tell them, "Michael is welcome here; Madeleine is welcome here. I love you," but the time is not right. Evan squeezes his sister, who yowls like a stepped-on cat and ducks from his beard as he goes to kiss her on the cheek. He slaps Finch on the back, and then stands there knowing it is not enough. The two men share a single hug that encompasses us all.

Evan and I sit quietly after they are gone. I think we would talk about it, about Hope and Finch, about what has turned around, but this silence, for a change, is the kind that is full of confirmation and the beginning of a more placid understanding. We have learned enough to let that be enough.

It is late when we go upstairs, hand-in-hand and eager for sleep, but sleep, like so many other things, is elusive.

I am draped sideways in the chair that is like a mouth, head tucked, body folded, bent in the middle like an elbow; my legs hang over the lacquered seawood arm, dangling like exposed roots. It is late, darker in here than I would ever imagine it could be with the stars and moon as present as they are; only the fire, burnt low in the grate on the other side of the bed, gives shadows, forms that come and go, appear and then disappear again as I sit and rock with just the merest sound, laminated rocker against hardwood floor.

It is late and I haven't got a sleepy bone in my body, though Evan is wrapped tightly in sleep on the high brass bed in front of me, his rhythmical, light snore a wet part of the night sounds around me. This day, for Evan, has been longer than most, more difficult. He has been weary since early on. It would be wrong not to let him sleep.

Yet there it is, sex building like an itch.

I can slide my leg out, slip it between the thick blue terrycloth edges of my robe, break open the cache with that single move, labia, like the pink-blushed lip of a shell.

Just the thought tips the balance, and the want of it washes through me like hot, wet sex itself.

I glance at Evan. He sleeps soundly; I won't wake him. He won't know that he has been left out, I won't tell him, though he must know that I can do this, scratch this particular itch without him. He must know it, yet, in all likelihood, he does not think about it.

But the means is there, right there in my own hand; intuitive as hell, my fingers know their way, and, like a too-young lover, they are unabashedly eager though I am quite practiced now, now that these months here without Evan have passed.

The first touch is good. My fingers probe, explore like sensitive antennae. The chair rolls forward like a wave on its smooth, splayed rockers as I reach, back again as I find. Equilibrium is all.

The first touch is good, yes, but the entering is better, and the wetness of it triggers an unbelievable thirst, a thirst as immense as a craving for salt.

I drop my head back, and the chair finds its balance, more stable, upright, but that dull, starless ceiling suspended overhead is not what I want. In response, my eyes close like the eyes of a doll, but it is no good. And like the same doll thrown upright again, my eyes fly open and I bring my head back down, forward on my neck; my fingers smooth flesh that is moist, like the inside of a cheek. Yet, I am not watching my fingers, but seeking out Evan, facing me on the bed, naked in the heat of this room, the covers thrown back like an enormous petal curled behind him. It is Evan's sleeping form that I focus on, his curved arm, bent knees, genitals at rest, nestled like a rosebud at the very center of him. He sleeps like a child himself tonight, but I could swear, as he shifts and brings his arm up to rest on his side, that he is responding, that he is aroused under my gaze, if only slightly now, and, with this warmth of speculation, my own need swells; urgency becomes a din behind my eyes that drowns out the rest of the night.

And my fingers do my pleasure, close to the bone, deeper, sink in and gorge on it while my hips rise like a tide, careful not to overturn the chair, not to make noise, not to wake Evan, and the wetness surrounds, the swollen flesh envelops, pulls down, nearly swallows in the heat, a lickerishness that bites its own parched lips.

And it builds. . . .

It builds and I throw myself up to it, arch like a strong fish, near now, and the chair below me trembles, and it builds, and I am carried by it, fingers, palm, elbow working, and I am stiff with it, taut, strung like a wire between the poles of myself, and when I come I buck, slam against my own strength, deeper and harder, exactly there, exactly right, and my eyes squeezed so tight that the pressure is nearly more than I can bear. . . .

And it is over, a wave, and then over again.

When I bring my fingers back, draw them out across the mouth of the cache, they slide out, out and over, strike like a nerve that small nub that beats like my heart.

And when I can breathe and I roll back down like liquid, fold back down into the curve of my sweet, grotesque chair, Evan's eyes are on me, moist, open, suspended calmly above his strange new beard, eyes greener in this dark than the grass in the moonlight.

His invitation is mostly silent, thoroughly explicit, as he smooths the sheet in front of him. The sound of his hand on the linen is like a wash of breeze through new green leaves, and his smile and his welcome are wider than the dark itself. And he will wait; Evan will wait silently until I move, until I am able to move. He will wait for me and then, when I am willing to stand, I will go at my own speed to him and the night will close around us, will absorb us, and, when we have done, I'll gaze out the window and I'll choose a star and then I will certainly sleep, sleep like a water-smoothed stone, like agate in a stream.

## XIX

## COMBER

The boat's name is *Aggie's Beacon.* She's local.

She is lying on her side in the beach slag, crouched in a sort of sideways limbo-squat, as though she still believes she has a chance of righting herself, as though she, or someone else, could still save her.

There is no one on the beach now, other than myself, but dozens of people must have been here since the rain. Ribbons of footprints, like long strands of enormous seed pearls, elongated and uneven, are laid out in all directions, deep into this half-frozen sand which the tide will not touch for some time. They run across the beach and in tight circles around the *Aggie's* footing where the sandy debris of gurdy, line, and fractured outrigger spill from her like spume. On the shattered scope, light plays like a gray ghost, and the stony corpse of the aborted diesel engine, loosed and heaved through the side of her split and battered belly, lies amidst miles of kelp, everywhere, weed wound like rope and stretched like chains, drying now, one day, two days, beached like this.

She is a working boat, a one- or two-man troller, maybe forty feet. Private. No fleet boat. She is too old, too small. Wooden boats like the *Aggie* are relics, now. They are fragile, hard to work, and the hours required in upkeep surpass those on the job. Either someone loved her desperately, or she is all he could afford. And as if the desolation of shipwreck is not enough, she has already been vandalized: FUCK YOU scraped into the hull through thick coats of dulled iron-red paint, through barnacles and slime, to the old raw wood beneath.

I stand there until I think I will settle into the sand with her and take her shape.

Slowly I become aware of activity around me. Everywhere

birds scavenge detritus. The wild nature of all the motion, in fact, makes me wonder whether the choppy water behind the *Aggie* and me isn't more a product of wing beating and daredevil diving than the wind. The brash, uncouth calls of the feeding birds cut through even this machete-like blow which has rocked me on my feet for miles. In less than a hundred feet of shore, more than a hundred glassy-white gulls feast on clams thrown up by the storm. They are wildly smart and drunk on the bounty, flying high with the closed shells and dropping them on rocks, on wreckage to break them open, then diving to retrieve the meats. Offshore, what looks to be thirty or forty sleek gannets circle high and then dive like stones thrown at an angle, wings broad-open until the last second. And there are birds I do not know, cannot name, who scour the edges of the water, others who wrench tiny scuttling crabs and invisible mites or entrails from the dead bodies of their brothers on the sand.

In all this area I have called my own, my walking territory for all these months, there is no thing familiar but the division between water and land, and even that is blurred. Everywhere are spread the artifacts of storm. Long belts of rockweed and bladder wrack loop themselves around bits of driftwood scattered like arms and legs, and washed-up jellies, ejaculations from the water's body, litter the acres of sand. And there are the bodies of birds. Some have washed in, others have been dashed against the ground, some few literally driven into the sand or covered by the wash of heavy minerals sucked up from the bottom and carried forward in thin winding sheets to the beach. The sand itself, beneath all this havoc, is mixed liberally with fish scales, giving it a dressed-up, party iridescence that seems, beneath the *Aggie* and the grounded birds, both indecent and unkind.

It is only three in the afternoon and the Point light is like lead. I walked long and slowly along the edges before I found the *Aggie*. Even if I were to head back now, it would be near dark or past by the time I reached our house. Evan will grow concerned, and, when I am not home by shortly after dark, he will become frantic.

Yet the *Aggie* needs mourning.

I squat in the sand by her tangled lines and I keep my head down. I think of what she was, what she has come through, how she has torn loose from her mooring and has failed to keep herself aright. I imagine her lobtailing like a great fish in her going down, and how, once she sank, the wind and the tide must have worked together to bring her to this spot. And I wonder if I have ever eaten fish from her lines. I grieve for the *Aggie* as though she were my own, my livelihood, because, it is obvious, even to me, that there is nothing to be salvaged from her, that she is far beyond any sort of saving.

I look up to see a solitary figure moving down the beach towards us. His is the walk of a man who is ill at ease walking on solid ground, but he makes slow progress beneath the weight of what he brings with him, something unwieldy and darker, even, than the heavy clothing he is bound up in. And he is grimacing, less under the burden of what he carries in his hands than at my presence by the *Aggie*. I watch him steadily and am surprised at how quickly he makes his way.

He stands in front of me, bearing his cumbersome chainsaw as though he would like to use it on me. His face is hard with wind, though it is not an old face, and it is obvious he is in a fury over the ruin of the *Aggie*. He juts his black-stubbled chin at her and looks at me from under his oily watchcap with eyes that have no room at all for my kind, a kind he has defined early on and privately. "You find anything you want?" he asks. His voice is low and ballasted with disgust.

"Is she yours?" I ask him as I stand and brush the caked sand from my behind. I am surprised to see that he is a small man, no taller than I am.

"Is now," he says shortly as though he would brush me away like a sandfly if he could.

"Did you work her? Did you fish her?" He must hear the wretchedness in my voice, because the cruel lines in his face diminish somewhat and I believe the fact that he looks as though he will answer is proof that he is sorry he thought I would loot her.

"Off and on. 'S my father's boat," he tells me. "I'd crew him time to time when my own work was slow."

"Did she pull her mooring?" I ask him, knowing the answer.

"No."

Where he meant to jerk me up short with his crack about stealing from his boat, already picked clean by ruin and looters, he failed. His answer now, though, this strong and contrary "No," makes my heart stagger. I have difficulty finding the words to form my next question, but he gives me neither time nor opportunity to speak.

"Damn fool fished her late," he tells me. Finally, he rests the heavy saw near the toe of his boot. "Sixty-five years old." He shakes his head; his thick features and the sweat that coats them are worn with the same air of indifference. I can see that his is an anger mixed with both loss and pride. "Goddamn him," he says sadly, angrily, then rights himself. "Leaves the old woman alone, my mother, but she'll live without 'im. The husbands of her friends are down there too."

If I could, I would touch him. "I'm sorry," I tell him, and pull my jacket tighter around me. The light is beginning to go quickly now, and the wind has an edge like broken glass.

He points to the desecration on the *Aggie's* hull. "This is no good," he says flatly. "I can't leave her with that."

I nod and begin to turn away. This, I think, is a private service, and, for me, it is a long and dark walk home.

"Got far to go?" he asks in a wholly different voice, but, again, does not wait for a response. "This'll take me fifteen minutes. I've got the truck. I'll drive you."

From this man with the dark clothes and manner, it is more like a plea than an offer. I doubt that he will cut me with his chainsaw and leave me at the side of some road. He does not want to be alone after the *Aggie*. And, frankly, after what he has told me, I am afraid of what I might stumble over on a beach lighted only by a hazy moon.

I nod my thanks to him, and I smile. My gratitude is real. "I'll wait over there," I tell him, and I walk up the beach, perhaps fifty yards, in the direction from which he came.

The start-up is a shock, abrasive and terrifying, like a cry in utter darkness, but the roar of its operation is dragged out, drawn to a lamentation in the wind.

Time, in these circumstances, is slicker than he imagined, and it takes much longer than fifteen minutes to erase the sentiments of the vandal.

I wait for this fisherman's son with my back to *Aggie's Beacon* and I try very hard to understand a kind of life that would make an old man fish late in the face of a storm.

*I am a child; I do not know how old. My father is staying with us at the motel and I believe with all my heart that he is magic, that he can do anything, make anything happen. At this point in my life, I am still certain that all men are like this, certain in the way that I never question, never consider the possibility of questioning, of its not being so. It is merely a fact like air, or the ocean. The three of us, my father, who has come from his house in the desert, and me and my mother, are spending this week together in the swimming-pool blue motel just over the small trestle bridge from the boardwalk and beach.*

*My father and I are walking on the boardwalk. I am wearing a white sunsuit, tiny sailboats sprinkled over the fabric, the kind of sunsuit with the stringish ties at the shoulders and elastic at the waist, and I am holding my father's hand. I have to crank my neck up at a steep angle when I speak to him or I can't see his eyes. He has remarkable eyes, milky blue, as blue as the patches of sky that slip between the fat white clouds overhead.*

*I ask him why is it called a boardwalk when it is really cement, not boards at all. While he is thinking about my question, he looks ahead of him as though he sees up there the image of what he is about to tell me. Then he breathes out deeply, and says that when he was a young man the boardwalk was made of boards, that it was raised up, just like it is now, off the sand by tall, strong vertical beams that were anchored in the earth beneath the sand, and that, from underneath, he could, from one day to the next, see where the sand had shifted around the bases of the uprights. He says that it rolled smoothly, fluidly, like the waves themselves, from base to base. But he also says he never really saw it move, not really. He just saw that it was different from one hour to the next, or different from the day before. He laughs and swings my hand in his and says that he has not been beneath the boardwalk in a thousand years, but that he used to, all those years ago, wander around down there scouting for coins that had dropped between the planks; only once, he says, did a coin, a nickel, fall through while he was standing there, and it landed on the sand at his feet with a dull, shallow thud. The odds of that, he says, were one in a million. "One in a million," he repeats, shaking his head. He tells me that the coolness in the shade beneath the boards sometimes wrapped around him like a cold, wet sheet and that slits of sky like blue straws showed through over his head when people weren't standing right on top of him. He tells me that at one time, there were lots of lumber mills in town, that he used to work them himself when he was young, when he still made the girls' heads turn. It was a real lumber town back then, he says, smiling again. He says that the first wooden boardwalk washed out to sea during a violent storm, that the struts and platform crumpled and fell like an old man who'd lost his footing, that the Casino went, that all the old booths and games, the dance hall and the arcade, broke up and went out with the waves. Then it was all rebuilt. His own father had worked the crews, he says, and he will take me to the new Casino at the far end of this boardwalk, evidently the third in a series of reconstructions, where there are old photographs of the wreckage. The destruction and the loss, he says, were devastating, but it made jobs.*

*With this information, the cement below my feet takes on a new significance. I cannot keep from looking down, not even while we walk. I can hardly get over the fact that grownups would be idiots enough to make something this gargantuan out of wood, something a million times bigger than a house, this high up off the sand, with all these people walking on it, with the weight of all these stalls and rides. I am convinced that it was an intolerably dumb thing to do, and what else could they expect but to be washed out to sea? I tell my father this, but, while I do, I am struck by the possibility of another storm, another wave, a wave that would come and take all this away again, drag it out to sea without even a struggle while we are standing here. I can imagine the carousel horses bobbing in the ocean waves, their petrified manes, their dead eyes and stark carnival paint peeking from the green ocean like Easter eggs from our April lawn. I can see us out there with them, but they are out of reach and our bobbing is syncopated and helpless. There is no chance that we can catch one and save ourselves.*

*In the distance, nearer the middle of the boardwalk, the roller coaster rises up; it arches and coils like a serpent. My father and I walk closer. The two of us have ridden this roller coaster every day, some days more than once. I have closed my eyes, thrown up my hands, and screamed the most piercing scream I could summon up while my father's arm encircled my shoulders tightly, tighter when I screamed, a safety feature infinitely more reassuring than the thick metal bar that locked down over our laps. But the crisscross white structure and the brightly enameled, dashing, diving cars have taken on a new face today and the smell in the air of hot dogs, up to now enticing, is overwhelming, greasy, rancid. My father seems not to notice. His memories have stirred him and he is anxious now to ride and feel the wind. He hurries off to the ticket booth while I dawdle near the gate.*

*I do not want to ride.*

*I am afraid.*

*When my father returns with the two yellow tickets, he holds one out to me. I do not take it. Instead I stare at the ground, at the white plastic thongs on my feet, at the gray treacherous concrete, sticky from a million spilled sodas, from tens of thousands of smashed wayward kernels of Kandy Korn. My father seems to have no idea why, after all this time, I am suddenly hesitant, and I cannot tell him. "You know," he says looking down at me, "I'll never let anything hurt you." His voice is as soft as fur. I believe him; I do. But I waggle my head "no" and continue staring at the ground. I cannot ride the roller coaster; I can't tell him that I have figured it out, that I know now the reason the people are screaming, that the reason that they yell out like that is because the serpent has shown them the wave from the highest arch of his back. It is coming, the wave. I did not see it before because I had my eyes closed. But it is the wave that will knock down this boardwalk and carry us all far out into the ocean. And there will be nothing to come back to.*

*My father squats down on his heels; he reaches up and takes both my hands, but still I cannot make myself look at him. With this last reluctance on my part, he gives up, shrugs. He stands and sticks the yellow tickets in his pocket. "Maybe tomorrow, then," he says, but I know he is disappointed in me.*

*My father is drinking beer from a can and he wipes his mouth on the back of his hand. I am clutching a watery soda, more melted ice than Orange Nehi, in a waxy paper cup that has begun to cave in where my fingers wrap around it. The cup is sweating and the cold water, dragging with it bits of flaky wax, runs down my wrist and arm; it stops dead at the crook of my elbow. From there it drops off, or, if I am quick enough and lower my arm back down a bit, it rolls back along my forearm to my hand again. I can dictate its speed by the slant of my arm. I have control if I am prudent. This is a good game, to see if I can keep the water from dripping on the cement and leaving those dark shadow-colored drops on the pavement. I repeatedly lift and drop, lift and drop with so much confidence, so much enthusiasm, that I spill much of what is left of the soda. It is a distraction, more fun, I decide, than the CoinToss where I just spent five minutes, and two dollars and fifty cents of my father's dimes, in a throwing frenzy, trying to get just one in the green glass vase that stood near the center of the table, trying to win it so my father could give it to my mother for a present when we return to our room where she is sleeping off a torrent of vomiting from last night's shellfish dinner.*

*My father is walking faster now. I am sure that he is walking like that because he is upset with me, but I do not want to think about that. I am nearly running to keep up, and trying to play my cup and soda game at the same time. With what is to be my one last effort, a nearly spastic maneuver, I jerk the cup upward and soda slops over onto the chest of my sunsuit, leaving the sailboats awash in Kool-Aid-like stains; the soda dribbles down my front, my legs, off my arms, and hits the pavement so that it looks as though I'm leaving a ragged trail of pee on the cement behind me as I run after my father on the boardwalk.*

*The woman in the booth tells fortunes beneath a banner that says, "Your Future Foretold." She is talking to a tall blonde girl in short shorts who is standing on one foot and swinging her purse behind her like a bola. The woman finally says, "Please sit down." The girl stops swinging and looks up at the boy who accompanies her; then she lifts and drops her shoulders as if to shake off some bug or to resettle a strap. She lowers herself into the folding chair across from the woman. The boy steps behind the girl where he can see.*

*The old woman does not look like a fortuneteller. She has no special look at all, no gypsy or circus air. She looks, in fact, like someone's aunt or grandmother. Her short hair is colored a yellow-green. Her stockings bag at her ankles where they poke out, crossed, from beneath the table. You might meet her on any street, anywhere, with a paper shopping bag on her arm from J.C. Penney's or Sears. I do not understand why someone's aunt would want to tell fortunes on the boardwalk.*

*I watch, and am repulsed by, the loose, snakey skin of her upper arm which swings as she spreads out some cards for the girl. They are not real cards, not cards with normal numbers and suits like spades or hearts. These look more like the pictures in the Sunday funnies, people with long yellow hair, some with swords. My father has cards like these. He told my fortune once when he visited us: I am going to be rich and beautiful, I will be lucky in love. I believe him.*

*We step closer.*

*My father is watching. He tips his beer can back and drains the last drop. He wipes his mouth. Then he just stands there holding the empty can. He is watching while the woman finishes spreading the cards for the girl.*

*The girl is older than I am by maybe six years, seven years. The boy she came with now has his hands on her shoulders, and he is looking blankly at the cards the old woman has set out. I get this sick kink in my stomach like a charley horse. It is nothing new, but it makes me want to puke. I have been plagued with these pains ever since summer began. I was pretty sure I had cancer and that I would die, but my mother explained it to me: it is jealousy. I will have it until I get a boy of my own. Then I will get a different sort of hurt, she told me. This particular boy is very handsome, tall with dark, cropped hair, bare arms, a tattoo. He seems to like to touch this girl; he can't keep his hands off the bare skin at her shoulders. I can't take my eyes off his hands. They are incredibly clean hands, and the fingers are long and flat; the tendons at the back ripple like a chill on the skin. The boy with the hands and the girl with the shoulders are both watching the cards, both looking empty. My father is watching them.*

*I want to leave. I do not understand the attraction at all and my not understanding makes me think there is something wrong with me. I get impatient. I hate the sick feeling. It occurs to me that it could be the shellfish, that it could have waited this long to make me sick. I'll be sick like my mother, I think. I want to leave; I want to die at the motel, not here, not where the boy with the long flat fingers can see me. But my father is intent on standing there.*

*When he doesn't respond to my pout, I pull heavily on his arm. I scowl, groan, shuffle in place, and wrap my arm across my stomach as though, any moment, I'm going to barf. He isn't paying attention. He is ignoring me on purpose. I drop his hand angrily and stomp over to the painted garbage can that overlooks the beach and all those colored umbrella tops that stand out like gumdrops on the gray sand; I slam the collapsed paper cup from my soda into the clown's mouth with a vengeance, then clomp noisily back to my father, flip-flops slapping the cement, clapping my heels, making a noise like giant lips smacking. My father does not seem to have even noticed I've been gone. He is watching. The girl is giggling now; the boy is laughing too, his lean, hard fingers sort of rubbing at her shoulders, pushing her long straw hair out of the way. I reach up to take my father's hand, hoping that he will go now, even if it is only to move down the boardwalk, to go to another booth. But my father doesn't move. He just shifts his weight to his other leg and lifts his beer can with a jerk and squeezes it so that it makes a metallic popping sound when it smashes in at the side. Then he drops his arm back down again and just lets it dangle there.*

*When they walk away, my father hands me his caved-in, empty beer can, and he steps over to the chair that must still be warm from the girl's bare legs. The old woman looks at my father peculiarly, as though she does not know why he is still there or why he is sitting down. I believe she knows him, but neither of them speaks. I am less antsy, less painfully aware of the wrenching in my stomach now that the blonde girl and her young man are gone.*

*My father and the woman say nothing as she scoops the girl's cards up and bangs them on the table to get them back into a neat pack. She pushes the cards towards my father. He is looking at her face; he does not look down at the cards. "The coins," he says. For a moment I am confused. At first I think he is asking for the money the boy left. I do not understand, but the woman makes no sound at all; she reaches under the table and pulls up several mottled discs, coins like brass moons. She drops them in front of my father. He nods.*

*My father sweeps the coins to the side of the table with the edge of his hand and then shuffles the cards in front of him. He pushes them back towards the woman. She nods and he cuts. She lays out the cards.*

*The woman touches the card nearest her and I can see that she is going to speak. My father stops her hand with his own as if her hand controls her tongue.*

*"First," he says, "tell me why you lied to the girl about the card." It is not the voice he uses when he speaks to me. The woman shakes her head. My father waits.*

*"They didn't need to know," she says heavily, shrugging her*

*shoulders, lifting them as though they are weighted and being pulled from above. Her voice is quiet, though, as soft as though someone is sleeping near at hand. "What good would come of it?" she asks my father. "Look at the cards. . . ." She is pointing with her chin to my father's cards on the table. "You know it is all the same," she says. "Look at the cards. Problem. . . . Opportunity. . . . It is all the same."*

*My father waits a moment, then bobs his head. "Yes," he says. "Yes." For a second he seems to be gathering strength as though, maybe, he is winding an invisible clockspring that keeps him from running out. Then the look is gone. "Go on, then," he says. He releases her hand and jerks his head towards the cards. I can see that he is upset.*

*The woman touches each card in turn and speaks. Periodically, she looks up into my father's face.*

*I am dancing on the hot pavement now; I've taken off my flip-flops and I let them dangle from one hand like fruit from a limb. I have one eye on my father and the other on a cotton candy stand three stalls down from the woman, but my father is listening, watching.*

*When she is done, he picks up the coins and tosses them back onto the table to the side of the cards. They totter and fall. The woman opens her mouth to speak.*

*"Lie," my father tells her.*

*The woman is silent.*

*Then, "No, don't," he says.*

*The old woman says nothing.*

*My father eyes the coins for a moment and then rises from the chair. He dips into his pocket and comes up with a ball of dollar bills. The yellow tickets from the unridden roller coaster tumble from his pocket, bent, onto the table when he pulls his money out. He snaps the bills to make them flat and drops them, still crumpled-looking, right on top of the tickets. She scoops up the money in the same way she did the girl's cards earlier, patting the edges even. My father does not pick up the tickets.*

*When we are walking again, I want to ask my father what was going on with the coins. Then I reconsider. "Do you know that lady?" I ask.*

*My father looks down at the top of my head. The pause is almost imperceptible. "Your mother," he says, "is waiting for us at the motel."*

*The walk across the trestle bridge is the longest I take that week. By the next summer my father is gone for good, magic and all.*

*Sometimes, after that, I dream that we, my father and I, are beneath the boardwalk while the sand is shifting. Because he is magic in my dream, we can see it move. He is right: it rolls like the small humps of wave that eat at the beach sand. We are passing the time beneath the boardwalk because we are waiting, waiting for that nickel to fall through the boards, the one that will drop at our feet while we stand there.*

It is an old truck, the color of mustard. He reaches over the tailgate and, with both hands, lowers the chainsaw into the bed.

"I'll finish 'er tomorrow," he says as he shoves the door shut loudly at my side. His masque face is unchanged since cutting into the *Aggie*, no remorse, no relief. It is the face he lives behind.

He walks around to the driver's side and pulls himself in.

"Finish her?" I ask.

"Cutting her up," he says, and looks at me to see why I don't know what he's talking about. He starts up the truck and lets it idle.

"I'm sorry," I say again. "I guess I didn't understand." I assumed he intended to cut out only the vandalized section of hull. I assumed he was done.

"Can't just leave her there," he explains to me, surprised at my denseness. "Can't do that." He looks over to see if I'm with him yet, and he throws the truck into gear. It bucks wildly beneath us when it kicks in, but, when its tires move from the unpaved lot to the macadam road, the old truck takes its orders in stride, naturally, smoothly.

"She's a different animal on the road proper," he says to me.

## XX

## SOMEPLACE LIKE THIS

"This is what you really want?"
"Yes."

Today, they tell me, is the shortest day of the year. Tonight will be the longest night. These are facts by definition, because I have accepted the word of others for their veracity. Give me strength, I believe them, and have planned accordingly. For today, at least, I can say where I will be and when.

Our reopening of the time that I was gone was like finding the lost half, the second half, of a roundtrip ticket. "I think," I told him last night, "I think I never really got back." I watched him while I spoke; he seemed to be listening with his eyes. "I'm back now," I said, as though it were a joke that we shared.

He said, "I've missed you."

There are no roads to this place, but I have found it, and it is mine. I have walked along it for miles; for a hundred years, I have allowed the grasses to brush at me and the sand to wear down the hardness of my heels. I have not stood still; I have earned the right to be here.

I can see, now, that getting someplace like this is a Siamese twin, a connected double of never getting anywhere specific at all. It sounds like a negative outlook, but it is not. It is merely a spatial perspective, and, if not exactly spatial, then at least realistic. It is a sort of back-to-back proposition.

We have all heard it before, but I, for one, did not see the application until now. The idea is inscribed on the surface of my eyes: *You can't get there.*

It explains a lot.

I can only account for it the same way we've heard it: there are an infinite number of steps between where you are and where you want to be; each time you reach the halfway mark between here and there, another half of the remaining half is left to traverse. Infinite halves. And, despite the fact you, yourself, are moving ahead, time dictates that you do move ahead despite an obvious propensity for the inert—every single thing around you is breaking up and moving, too. And still it is not that easy, because all those other things that are moving are doing so each in a different degree from the others. You would go mad before you could keep track of or keep up with them all. The fascination is in this, however: you would be obliged to move on even if you were content to stand still. You would be forced to adapt so that you could live in that place.

It is called survival.

"Which is worse," I asked Evan, "the remembering or the trying to forget?"

It is all the same idea.

I'd made up my mind long before the fisherman's son pushed the door shut and we'd started, in that cold half-dark, along the highway towards the house. While we were still on the main road, I told him what I would do. I told him that my biggest concern was not Evan. Evan, I knew, was ready. My biggest worry revolved around the birds. Winter is no time to stop feeding the birds, I said. And, without any trace of hesitation, almost as though he had been waiting for the opportunity, the fisherman's son said he would see to it that his nephew, a kid with a car, would keep the feeder full for me throughout the winter months. It would be no problem to arrange that. No problem at all. The house, he said, is not that far; the roads are kept clear. The moment he said it, I knew it was done. He said, "We are even, then. I'm glad." His eyes never left the road. We drove, probably, half a mile before he spoke again. "Medina," he said, and extended his hand to me, sideways, cordially. It was as though in passing on a favor he had earned the right to pass on his name as well.

"Dore," I said, and gave his hand a good squeeze, then let mine rise easily to indicate the upcoming turn. "Left at the next road."

His eyes followed my gesture, and he signaled. The balance we had achieved showed itself in the easy silence that filled the cab until we reached the driveway. "Here," I told him then, and he turned in.

When the headlights went off, the dark swallowed us. The porch light, not yet replaced, had been a casualty of the storm. In that eerie, unstable black, we might have as easily been nowhere at all as in the cab of Medina's truck. No light shone but the yellow fog that lowered from the windows of the house; Evan's fire from inside threw a strange and undulating light onto the porch uprights which made them look golden and serpentine, alive with fire. Evan must have been waiting at the door, because, at the sound of the truck in the driveway, he'd stepped outside into the cold without his coat and shivered anxiously in the thrown light from the fire. Then, in the sudden and wavering dark, Medina jumped from the stilled truck to shake Evan's hand, and, when the pleasantries were complete, he turned to me, all business.

We exchanged phone numbers. Each, as the other recited, soberly inscribed the number on a scrap of paper from Medina's glovebox. I told him I was sorry about the *Aggie*, and about his father. He bowed his head slightly in a single, nearly nonexistent acknowledgment, and then climbed back into his truck. We said a loud goodbye over the sound of his engine, and I thanked him again for the ride.

He backed out of the drive slowly, as though he needed to retrace, exactly, the tracks he'd made coming in. And as though he would not intrude on our privacy there on the porch, he did not turn on his headlights until he reached the road.

We talked long into that night in front of Evan's fire, and, when the morning came, we rebuilt the fire and we talked more.

We covered territory I thought we had lost sight of, different and the same, all the verboten gaps, the black holes of my life, of our lives together: Lise, Lindhurst, my mother and my not coming home, what went wrong out there and here. The many broken steps we've tripped ourselves up on. We reached far back into the dark corners, for so long left deliberately untended, out of our ignorance, out of our false optimism, out of the blind fear of what we would find. We had nearly sealed those rooms of my other life so tightly and so crudely that they had become obvious and airtight, and they had thrown shadows with edges as sharp as scalpels, shadows so dark that Evan could not be seen in their shade. We turned on the lights in those rooms, examined the furnishings, and found, once begun, we were still free to leave, that we were not trapped there, that we could go. I learned again that what we called that life, all those years, was no other life at all, but this continuum of a life that I am still in the process of living.

I am not such a child that I believe the rest will all be this easy. But it is this chancy examination of the past which may have saved us from going backwards so far that we could not ever find the present again.

We have done the right thing—while we are still in a position to help ourselves, and while we are still in this together.

We will not make the trip in one day. We will spend the night somewhere in between.

We are going back to the city and we will live in the apartment until we find a place that is the kind of home we both want. We don't know what that is yet. We are going to explore the possibilities.

I do, however, know what I do not want. I do not want to live alone, isolated on this island. I do not want to have to make long distance calls to speak with my husband. I do not want to sit here and spend time as if it were pennies; I do not want to toss those pennies down some wishing well so deep that no one will scoop them out, ever. I want to be closer to Riva, nearer Hope, and Finch. I want to go to a movie, to eat linguine with clams at Riminicci's without having to wait six hours to get there. I want to worry about my thighs, almost every day, in the company of people I know.

We are returning things to their rightful places, Evan and I. This house will be a summerhouse again. We will come next year to open it up; we will make repairs as we go along, make alterations as we desire, if we desire. I no longer have a fear of knocking out walls. We will see what we need, what needs we wish to accommodate. And I expect the birds will greet us, too, when we come, the ever-present jays, the wound-up sparrows, and, probably before August, the sleek, hoarse grackles; if we are lucky, others will find us, birds I cannot identify yet, cannot name, and I will grow to expect them, too, at their own times, in their own manners.

There is little we have carried here that we will take to the city. The books we are reading, a few clothes, the food that will spoil. Not much. There is nothing here we cannot live without, nothing essential that will not follow us without our bidding it to do so.

"I love you," Evan says as he turns the key in the front door and pulls the door shut behind him.

I am silent, thinking about what that means, thinking about how long I have been thinking about what that means. There is no truth to what I feared in the beginning, that I do not love. The faces of love confused me; they are so different from what I expected, and they are so many. I did not recognize them.

"I love you," Evan says again as he takes the few steps one at a time, and looks back at me over his shoulder. He has to speak loudly to be heard over the cacophonous jays who have begun bickering at the feeder again. He turns full around. "Dore, are you listening? Did you hear me? I love you."

Evan, with his strange new beard, with his familiar broad smile, his perfect teeth, is waiting for me at the edge of our winter-browned meadow, and no one waits forever. No one ever lasts that long.

I come down the stairs quickly and plant my feet on the ground next to his, and, taking his hand, I say, "Me, too. I love you, too." I practically have to scream to be heard over the noise of the jays who are much too present now, and we laugh, and I reach up to kiss that strong bone that forms his lower jaw. "Let's go," I say.

We pass over the road that takes us off the island, and despite the fact the trees themselves seem lifeless and gray, small hard buds have already risen on the branches of the maples. It is a sort of code. The nubs, if you are paying attention, are easily visible in this final bareness of the season. Everything, in fact, is clearer this time of year. It is as though the green smoke a tree wears for leaves lifts, and the supporting structure becomes visible, stark, and obvious. In winter, there is less detail, less effusion, to confuse the basic shape of things. I keep my face turned towards those trees.

"There will be ten thousand shades of green in the spring," Evan says to me, when he sees me brooding over the landscape.

At last we cross the bridge.

We are long off the island before I realize that, for the first time since our arrival, I did not peer through that clearing near home, did not check on the old man's shack out there as we passed. I did not even think to wonder whether it had stood the storm.

In my mind that place is surrounded by shallow water and the sand there teems with invisible life.

I did not even look to say goodbye.